THE CHRONICLES OF RIDDICK™

By Alan Dean Foster
Published by Ballantine Books

THE BLACK HOLE
CACHALOT
DARK STAR
THE METROGNOME AND OTHER STORIES
MIDWORLD
NOR CRYSTAL TEARS
SENTENCED TO PRISM
SPLINTER OF THE MIND'S EYE
STAR TREK® LOGS ONE–TEN
VOYAGE TO THE CITY OF THE DEAD
. . . WHO NEEDS ENEMIES?
WITH FRIENDS LIKE THESE . . .
MAD AMOS
THE HOWLING STONES
PARALLELITIES
STAR WARS®: THE APPROACHING STORM
IMPOSSIBLE PLACES
DROWNING WORLD
THE CHRONICLES OF RIDDICK

The Icerigger Trilogy:
ICERIGGER
MISSION TO MOULOKIN
THE DELUGE DRIVERS

The Adventures of Flinx of the Commonwealth:
FOR LOVE OF MOTHER-NOT
THE TAR-AIYN-KRANG
ORPHAN STAR
THE END OF THE MATTER
BLOODHYPE
FLINX IN FLUX
MID-FLINX
REUNION
FLINX'S FOLLY

The Damned:
BOOK ONE: A CALL TO ARMS
BOOK TWO: THE FALSE MIRROR
BOOK THREE: THE SPOILS OF WAR

The Founding of the Commonwealth:
PHYLOGENESIS
DIRGE
DIUTURNITY'S DAWN

THE CHRONICLES OF

RIDDICK™

Alan Dean Foster

Based on a motion picture screenplay written by David Twohy

BALLANTINE BOOKS • NEW YORK

A Del Rey® Book
Published by The Random House Publishing Group

www.delreydigital.com

ISBN 0-345-46839-2

Manufactured in the United States of America

First Edition: May 2004

OPM 10 9 8 7 6 5 4 3 2 1

THE CHRONICLES OF RIDDICK™

I

No matter how long or how hard they strive, no matter how extensive their education as a species, no matter what they experience of the small heavens and larger hells they create for themselves, it seems that humans are destined to see their technological accomplishments always exceed their ability to understand themselves.

Certainly there was no understanding, no meeting of the minds, on the world called Aquila Major. There was only the devastation of one mind-set by another. Proof of it took the form of a statue fashioned of advanced, reinforced preformata resin. It was an imposing piece of work, for all that it had been reproduced by its originators on many other worlds. Too many other worlds, according to some. Not nearly enough, according to those who had put it in place, its massive footing firmly rammed into the resistant soil of Aquila Major.

It was a Conquest Icon of the Necromongers. Over five hundred meters tall, it gaped openmouthed at the utter desolation and wreckage that spread outward from its base. Whether it was seen as wailing in despair at its surroundings or moaning in triumph depended on whether one was a surviving citizen of that world's once-splendid capital city, now reduced to waste and ruin, or a member of that peculiar space-dwelling group who called themselves followers of the faith known as Necroism.

They had been preparing for such moments for a very long time. They had burst out of the great darkness to impose themselves on the civilized worlds with a forcefulness and cool brutality that was as stunning in its single-mindedness as it was in its efficiency. Aquila Major was not the first of their conquests, nor would it be the last. As long as there were worlds to be freed, as long as humans lived who dwelled in ignorance of their true destiny, the Necromongers would continue with their work.

Unlike so much of the humankind who had spread explosively throughout the galaxy, the Necromongers were driven by genuine purpose beyond the need to merely exist. They believed fervently in their work, and went about it with a determination and competence that was breathtaking to behold. In the majority of cases, literally breathtaking. Furthermore, there was no meanness in them, no suggestion of brutality for its own sake or of sadism. Like all true believers since the beginning of time, they saw only good arising out of the destruction they inflicted. Everything they did was for the benefit of the destroyed, they knew. Nor was their great work devoid of irony.

For it was the dead who triumphed by passing on, while only the most dedicated forced themselves to carry on the work by continuing to live—until due time.

The Lord Marshal knew this better than anyone. While longing for his own time of passing to arrive, he continued to consecrate his continuing existence on the present plane of existence by seeing to it that as many as possible of his unaware, improperly informed fellow humans preceded him onward toward bliss. During the preceding days, many had done so here on Aquila Major. A great many.

Clad in battle armor that was intended as much to instill fear and intimidate any who cast eyes upon it as it was to protect its wearer, he stood scowling thoughtfully at the scene of desolation and redemption that flamed below him. The fires were beginning to die out. While the capital had been taken, opposition to the balm and comfort his people brought remained strong in other cities and in isolated pockets across the planet. There was still much work to be done on Aquila Major.

As to its final outcome, the Lord Marshal had no doubt. Some worlds resisted the bringing of the message more obstinately than others. A few proved sensible and buckled under at the mere sight of the Necromongers' ships. Such worlds were much more to the Lord Marshal's taste. While they were to be admired for having reached a newer, higher state of being, dead resistance fighters were no use to the great cause. The deceased were to be envied, but could not be recruited.

Nevertheless, by craft or cajoling, by force or by bribery, the faith was advanced. Aquila Major was only the latest, not the last. No time was to be wasted here. As soon as the last pockets of resistance had been eliminated, the armada would move to the next, carrying enlightenment and revelation to the disbelieving. How he longed for his own moment of finality, for his turn to be done with this sordid, unnatural temporal plane!

But he could not simply embrace that of which he knew so much. Having striven to rise to the exalted position of lord marshal, it did not behoove him to surrender it voluntarily. By the edicts of his kind he was compelled to master all that it offered, by offering his talents to the cause. This he would continue to do. That he would not be the one to finish the work he knew well, as had the various lord marshals who had preceded him. That he would be joining them eventually he also knew.

But first, there was much work to be done.

Vaako stood nearby. A fine commander, as dedicated as one could ask for and a superb solo fighter in his own right. While his attention was focused on the Lord Marshal, that of the saintly Purifier, who stood nearby, was directed at the destruction below. Neither man spoke. There was no need. They had done what needed to be done, and saw no reason to comment on it.

Nor did the Lord Marshal have anything to say. The fire and smoke, the ruined buildings and flaming vegetation beneath them were more eloquent than anything those beholding it could have voiced. There were times when it was best to say nothing, he knew. Time enough for discussion later, when the last of Aquila Major's resistance had been eliminated.

Turning, he moved up the steps on which he stood. His commanders and the chief spiritual adviser of their people followed. Once they were within the Basilica, the massive portal, through which they had briefly emerged to view in person the horrendous yet beautiful vista below, closed tightly behind them, sealing them in the ship that was their home and their purpose.

Rumbling to itself, the immense Basilica vessel that had been hovering over the once-striking and now thrice-struck capital city lifted skyward. Slowly at first, but with a gathering speed and momentum that were as formidable as the purpose for which it had been built.

There are habitable worlds, and there are uninhabitable worlds. There are also worlds that can be rendered marginally habitable, but never should be. Foremost among the latter was a hellish, geologically schizoid, melted and re-formed planetary body of unremarkable size and appearance whose astronomical designation no one bothered to repeat because it had long since been supplanted in the vernacular by the name that had been given to it by its inhabitants. Or rather, its inmates.

Crematoria.

On most worlds, the time just before sunrise is a period of calm and preparation. Of quiet introspection and looking-forward. A time to awaken and gather oneself in readiness for a bright, new day. On Crematoria, pre-sunrise was a time to be denied, avoided, shunned. This was one world where dawn killed.

The two prison guards lugging their burden along the rough path that wound its tortured way through the scarred, twisted lava field knew that. They moved with the urgency of men assigned to an unpleasant duty that they had tried, and failed, to avoid. The fact that their load consisted of one of their own engendered no special feelings of additional sympathy on their part, even though they knew it could just as easily have been one of them. The fact that the dead man was a former colleague and friend did not make his demised corpus any less heavy.

Relieved at having reached their destination, they finally halted near a shallow depression that had been machine gouged from reluctant rock. The small hollow was not empty. It was filled with ash, from which protruded a few angular objects. On closer inspection, one became recognizable as a human femur, another as part of a skull. The rest were well on their way to being reduced to the powder that was slowly engulfing them. No artificial agency had been employed to reduce these remnants of what had once been human beings to their constituent chemical components. None was needed.

They only had to wait for sunrise.

From the container they had been carrying, the two men extracted the body of a third and dumped him unceremoniously onto the pile, sending up a small cloud of dust. The body was not intact. It was marred by deep bruises and multiple lacerations. One glance was enough to tell that these wounds had not been incurred in a fall or some other accident. The unfortunate had been involved in a fight that, as clear as the sharp-edged horizon, he had lost. Among the few effects that still adorned his corpse was a visual ident that read "V. Pavlov." Some wag back in the prison had ventured to say that the guard had died like a dog. No one had laughed.

The anxious pair who had been charged with conveying the former V. Pavlov to his final resting place looked around uneasily, plainly in a hurry to get away from where they were. There was no thought of digging a grave. It would be a wasted exercise. None would arrive to bear witness over it or view it. Anything they might erect over such an excavation would quickly go the way of the body itself. Crematoria would see to that.

"Should we, uh, say something? I mean, I knew Vladimir pretty well. He wasn't a bad guy." On Crematoria, this might be considered a high compliment: one that could be applied equally to guard or prisoner.

His companion was gazing nervously eastward. The dull maroon glow that had been seeping over the ragged, distant mountains was beginning to pale toward crimson. Very soon now it would fade to pink, then yellow, and then to white. When it turned white, anything organic would do well to be as far underground as possible.

"Sure. Recite a whole sermon, if you want." He

indicated the motionless body of their former colleague. "I'm sure Vlad won't interrupt you. Take all the time you want. I'll wait for you—inside." A curt nod indicated the coming dawn.

His friend was already starting to backpedal, physically as well as spiritually. "Maybe I'll say something later. I knew Vladimir. He wouldn't want us to be late for breakfast."

The other man had already started for the nearby access tunnel. "Shit, if it was you or me, he'd already have gotten the hell out of here."

It was as appropriate a description of their situation as it was of their surroundings.

Down Below was business as usual—which is to say, messy, loud, crude, and unpleasant. Used to their surroundings, the three guards muscling the transfer box did not comment on it, did not bemoan their fate. They were being paid good money to endure a routine of daily crap, money that was piling up in distant credit accounts even as they toiled to move the box. They often let their thoughts drift toward such accounts. It helped them to get through each day. Sometimes such thoughts were all that helped them to get through each day.

No noise came from within the box. No trouble. That suited them just fine. Occasionally, one would bend slightly to peer at one of the air vents that riddled the container. Its contents did not look back. Just as well. There were rules. As a guard on Crematoria, you bent the rules at considerable risk to your comparatively elevated status. Bend them far enough and you might find yourself on the other side of the social divide. That would be more than uncomfortable: it would be fatal. So the guard kept his thoughts to himself and concentrated on the work at hand.

As they passed one of the kennels, something with eyes bright with murder moved closer to the bars of its cage and began to howl. Its neighbors joined in. No human throat was capable of producing such sounds, though human ears could hear them. One of the guards snapped a curse in the direction of the center cage. Shining eyes swiveled to focus on him. The guard met the luminous, unearthly stare for a brief moment before looking away. He was not concerned. The cages were strong, and the howling things within, insofar as they could be controlled, were allies.

His tone spiced with agitation, the man in the lead looked back at the box. "Oughta know better by now. You act like an animal, gonna slot you up like one. Rules. Shoulda worked it different."

While carrying out his duty, the speaker's nearest companion was also experiencing a moment of unusual thoughtfulness. "Poor fuckin' Pavlov. Never had a chance, one-on-one like that."

The first speaker was less than sympathetic. "He shoulda watched himself. Always relyin' on his size, underestimatin' the opposition. Never, never do that. Size don't mean nothin' if you ain't got the moves." Glancing back, he directed his words to the inhabitant of the box. "You know all about that, don't you, Big Foe? You get what you give 'round here. But *when* you get it—aw, that's the thing. *When.*" It was not a direct threat, but the ugly implication in his voice could not be ignored. However the inhabitant of the box felt about it, the observation was greeted only with more silence.

Still muttering to himself, the other guard in front continued to remember his overconfident dead colleague. "This one's always been trouble. I knew it from the first. I *smelled* it."

Behind him, another guard thought to comment, to make a joke. In the end, he kept his thoughts to himself. Pavlov had always gone looking for trouble. Finally, he'd found it. While helping to move the transfer box, the guard was careful to keep his distance from it.

They reached their destination: an empty kennel. Around them, the howling of the unseen things with the shining eyes intensified. Intent on their work, the guards ignored the inhuman baying. Moving the box was one thing. Safely transferring its single occupant from box to kennel was something else.

Setting the box down in front of the open kennel slot, three of the men positioned themselves at intervals around the container while their remaining two companions warily moved to open it. Safeties were slid simultaneously off box and weapons. Operating together, the pair at the front of the box worked the seals until the doors clicked open. Almost immediately, they stepped back. Fast.

The occupants of the kennels howled louder. Fingers tensed on triggers. Eyes focused with unblinking intensity on the minimally acceptable space between open kennel and open box.

Nothing happened.

Maulsticks came out and were jammed through the box's air vents. Muttered invective filled the air. Delaying the inevitable meant that less insufferable duties were also being delayed. Already in a bad mood, the recalcitrance of the box's occupant was making the guards' mood worse.

It was not improved when the box's inhabitant managed to grab the end of one maulstick, turn it around, and jab its owner in the hand. The guard howled at the pain, a feeble parody of the hellish growling that filled the chamber, and grabbed his injured hand. Blood appeared that was not the prisoner's.

Disgusted, the man in charge of the delivery quintet moved forward. So did a companion. Maulstick still slung at his belt, grim faced, the latter was raising the muzzle of his riot gun.

He did not need to use it. Which was just as well, since he didn't have time to bring it to bear on its presumed target. That individual streaked from the interior of the box into the waiting kennel, a blur that would have been difficult even for the most alert marksman to draw a bead on.

Monitored by automatics, the kennel door slammed shut. Lockseals slipped into place. They were old and well used, but they functioned efficiently enough. Transfer completed, the guards let out sighs of relief. The delivery had gone off more or less as planned. The idiot who'd been jabbed by his own maulstick had only gotten what he'd deserved for his carelessness. A hand that would sting for a few days was a cheap enough lesson.

Relaxed now, ignoring both the safely secured prisoner and the howling of her inhuman kennel-mates, they moved to vacate the area. Behind them, their delivery pressed against the narrow space between the restraining bars. She was, in her own way, pretty. Just like a finely crafted stiletto. One would want to sleep very, very carefully with either. Maybe she was seventeen. She certainly was not sweet. At the sight of a human abandoned in their company, however unreachable it might be, the things that inhabited the surrounding cages redoubled their alien howling. Eyes glistened, damp with unfulfillable expectation. The girl reacted.

"Can we SHUT UP THE GODDAMN NOISE?"

Delivered with the force and sharpness of an ascending razor, the unexpected demand was fulfilled—for about two seconds. Then the howling resumed, wilder and more crazed than ever. Within the narrow cage, the girl sat down on the hard, smooth floor, a surface as unyielding and uncomfortable as that of Crematoria itself. Putting her hands over her ears, she closed her eyes and began to rock back and forth, slowly, reciting something silently to herself even though there was no one else to overhear.

"Big Foe," indeed.

The snow came in waves, like breaking foam absent the surf. It swirled around the disgruntled mercenary like wet sand. On high alert, his thoughts occupied elsewhere, he hardly noticed the squall. He was wary but not afraid. While the storm cut his personal visibility down to next to nothing, his instruments cut through the white-out as if the day had dawned clear and sunny.

He *was* cold, however. Despite his high-tech arctic gear, the wind and damp found ways through to his skin, burrowing beneath layers of clothing to sting like ants. His hands were steady, however. It would not have mattered had they been shaking, because the gun he carried was designed not for accuracy but for spread. It would stop anything that materialized in front of it within a 140-degree range of spray. Telltales on its top and side indicated that it was powered up and ready to kill.

It was a good thing all his instruments were working. Never bright, the light of this world's sun shaded all the way over into the ultraviolet, much as its fauna tended to the ultra violent. Right now there wasn't much to see by, or to see. For the latter he was grateful. With one exception. Despite his advanced gear and a wealth of personal experience in the trade, Codd's quarry continued to elude him. That it continued to do so was beginning to grate. His was a business in which personal as well as professional pride was taken in delivering the goods. This was one delivery that was particularly overdue.

Something stained the low snowdrift in front of him. Moving closer, he flashed his organalyzer at it. Blood. But whose? Or in the case of this particular planet, what's?

His communicator sputtered something unintelligible. Preoccupied with the stain, he moved closer and waited for the organalzyer to deliver a more detailed verdict. The discoloration in the snow was dark purple, but in the light of this world's sun, that was no sure indicator of origin. A second time, the communicator in his ear buzzed for attention. He tapped it with one finger, as if by so doing he could simultaneously clear the static and deliver a smack to the caller at the other end. Dammit, he was *busy*.

"Hang on, hang on. I'm on something here."

The screen on the organalyzer cleared, uninformative statistics and DNA details giving way to a schematic extracted from a series of exploration scans. The result was a diagram of something big, alien, and white as the snow sifting steadily down around him ought to be. It was bipedal and equipped with serious dentition. One did not have to be an experienced xenobiologist to deduce that the latter were designed for something more than masticating vegetables.

There was also a name—provisional, as was usually the case with examples of alien life-forms that were rarely encountered, aggressive, and disagreeably homicidal: *Urzo giganticus*.

Unwilling to go away and let him concentrate, the voice in his ear finally cleared enough to demand, "Whatcha got, Codd?"

"Sit on it a minute, willya, Doc-T?" Holding his weapon a little tighter, Codd checked to make double sure there was a high-explosive shell in the launching chamber before moving past the stain. Beyond, in a slightly protected hollow, he found something more impressive than blood. A footprint, clean and made too recently to have been filled in by following snow. Its appearance was formidable.

"Christ, all we need . . . Like this job hasn't already been trouble enough." Remembering the querying voice in his ear, he raised his voice above the wind as he spoke toward the communicator's pickup. "Hey, Johns, you know that big extinct thing? The one Preliminary kept talking about? Well, it ain't. Watch your spine, and I don't mean when it's held up in front of you. Between this and our other problem—"

He broke off. Was that a shape, moving within the storm? Quickly, he checked his scanner. Nothing. Shit, a man could get twitchy out here. Even someone as experienced as him. He took a step forward. Good thing he knew how to—

His scanner wailed at the same instant he did. Before the feeble lavender light of this world's sun went out permanently, he had a brief glimpse of something behind him. It was massive, and white, and perfectly horrible. Its mouth flashed lethal ivory.

The communicator's earpiece crackled in the snow. There was no one to hear or respond to the increasingly fretful queries it emitted, even though it was still attached to an ear. Unfortunately, the ear was no longer attached to anything except the earpiece.

II

Johns spat snowflakes out of his mouth, took a sip from his hotflow, and adjusted his communicator. It didn't matter how much he fiddled with the controls. Codd had gone cold, a deafening silence most likely caused by something other than the enchanting local climate.

"Say again? Codd, say again. Talk to me, buddy."

The communicator was nonresponsive. Or rather, it crackled and hissed, popped and hummed. It was the absent Codd who had nothing to say.

Equipment trouble, Johns told himself. He kept telling himself that as he plowed on through the snow, in the hope that sheer force of repetition would render hope into reality.

Snow gave way to ice. The fall was a shattered jumble of nearly transparent blocks and boulders, the water from which it had formed as pure as the women Johns could only dream of. Turning slightly, he followed the icefall eastward, searching patiently for an easier way over or through the new barrier.

Snow continued to swirl around him. He fought to keep focused on the task at hand as his thoughts drifted toward memories of warm surroundings and solid food instead of the nutrient soup the hotflow provided.

The face behind the ice startled him badly. Though blurred, there was no mistaking it for a trick of the purplish light. Almost as of their own volition, his hands raised the rifle and his finger contracted on the trigger. The double shot blew a jagged hole in the icefall in the vicinity of the unexpected visage, sending stinging fragments of ice in all directions.

When the frozen equivalent of the dust had settled, he squinted into the cavity his weapon had so violently excavated. A few lingering shards broke free and fell from the roof, clinking against the uneven floor. He ignored them as he activated a light and eased tentatively forward. The gap in front of him was bigger than anything his weapon, destructive as it was, could have created. He'd blown a hole into a larger void.

At first glance he couldn't tell if the hollow was natural or had been melted by artificial means. Regardless of origin, it had clearly been turned into temporary living quarters. Better, he told himself, to think of it as a lair. He had a bad moment when his light revealed an *Urzo giganticus*. The air he'd sucked in went out of him in tandem with the tension when he saw that the monster was not moving. Nor would it move again. For one thing, it was missing its feet. For another, it had been neatly and efficiently quartered before being hung from the roof of the ice cave by its massive right arm.

Urzo blood dripped softly into a collection pail. Neither the pail nor the smartly butchered condition of the massive corpse suggested that the bloody work had been carried out with scientific research in mind. Additional artifacts scattered around the cave hinted that someone hereabouts had exerted knowledgeable efforts with the aim of personal survival.

A slight movement made him turn sharply and raise the rifle, but this time he didn't shoot. As he shifted the light, its beam touched on a second strung-up figure. He recognized it immediately: Codd. John's sphincter tightened. It was Codd's face he had glimpsed through the ice, Codd's face that had caused him to fire. He knew this because the hole in his partner was about the right size to have been made by one of his own explosive shells, notwithstanding that its shattering effect had been somewhat muted by the ice barrier.

He had fired an instant too soon.

But while he might be blamable for Codd's death, he was not responsible for the mercenary's position—bound and secured with his own cuffs. And Codd was not quite dead. Not yet. Not that a wound such as he had suffered due to the too-quick trigger finger of his own partner was in any way repairable.

Johns leaned forward. As he was wondering what to say, or if he should say anything—Codd's lips moved slightly. Johns slipped closer. Should he try to apologize? In his and Codd's business, there was little time or inclination for apologies. Hell, everybody made mistakes. Though the dying mercenary's voice was little more than a whisper, Johns thought he could just make out what the other man was saying.

"Behind you . . ."

Behind . . . Johns whipped around. In perfect condition and as fast as he was, the blur that slashed at his head still grazed him. Ice, wind, and bad light conspired to impair his vision, leading him to fire blindly, repeatedly. Already unbalanced on the slight slope inside the cave, the powerful recoil sent his twisting form stumbling backward. Landing on his butt, he continued to fire in the general direction of whatever had taken the big swipe at him. Obedient to Newton, each shot sent him sliding a little farther backward.

Toward the precipice that fronted the cave.

He nearly went over. Nearly. Reflexes born of necessity saw him throw out one arm. It slid off the rock it clutched, but his strong fingers locked into a crack just wide enough to offer a grip. His other hand clung to the rifle. Carefully, very carefully, he eased off the weapon's trigger. Given the downslope on which he now found himself, one more shot would break his grip on the rock and send him over the edge.

It was all right. He was okay. All he had to do was work his way upward, using his knees and his hand, until he was safely back up on the more level portion of the ice. It was then that a pair of feet stepped into his view. They were white, thick with fur, and not human. Automatically his eyes followed them upward.

What he saw surprised him, insofar as he was still capable of being surprised.

The feet no longer belonged to their original owner. He remembered the condition of the quartered, dripping alien corpse he had seen in the cave. Its feet had been removed. At the time, he had been left to wonder at the reason. Now it was self-evident.

They had been turned into boots for a thick hulk of a man whose hair, while not white, had grown out to the point where it was now a suitable match for that of any urzo. Johns could sense, if not see, the musculature rippling beneath the apparition's cobbled-together cold-weather attire. The man's eyes were hidden behind reflective goggles that were at once minimal in size and of clearly advanced design. Johns didn't recognize the style. They did not look like any of the extensive variety of snow goggles with which he was familiar. It was even possible they were intended to serve some purpose other than protecting the wearer from snow blindness.

Ambling unconcernedly forward, as if Johns no longer held the powerful rifle, the man crouched down to stare at the mercenary. His posture, as much as his indifferent attitude, suggested either lingering brain damage, supreme stupidity, or ultimate confidence. Johns did not have to debate long over which was the most likely. He found that he could see his own snow-scarred, wind-battered face reflected back at him in those shiny lenses that were as inscrutable as their owner.

The man brought one hand forward. Johns flinched slightly. Opening his fingers, the man revealed the contents of his hand. It was a human ear, raw and bleeding at the base.

"Yours?" the man murmured quietly. Though deceptively soft, his voice pierced cleanly through the wind.

There was a pause. Then Johns clamped a hand to one side of his head. His gloved fingers came away bloody. Biting cold and surging adrenaline had combined to numb him to a point where he hadn't felt the appendage being torn away. Unfortunately, in the shocked realization of the moment, he'd grabbed for his missing ear with the hand that had been anchoring him to the protruding rock. Grip lost, he scrambled briefly for a second handhold. The smooth ice was not compliant. He went over the edge of the deep drop silent except for his gun, from which he managed to coax a few final shots before hitting the ground far below. The multiple rounds were as thunderous as they were wild.

Rising, the hirsute stranger in the deviant footwear walked fearlessly to the edge of the precipice and peered over. Thanks to the swirling snow, there was not much to see. His expression unchanging, he backed away from the brink and turned. Though he did not reveal it through expression or emotion, he was surprised at what he encountered.

The double barrels of a particularly nasty weapon were aimed directly at his midsection. They suited the individual who held them. Toombs's name had always been good for a running gag among his colleagues in the business. None of them had ever used it to his face, of course. At least, none could be found alive who had done so.

Whereas his partners, Codd and Johns, had been quiet and businesslike, Toombs liked to talk. He possessed a certain vicious charm that constituted something of an attractant to the ladies and allowed him to get into places and away with things that defeated less animated types like Codd and Johns. He was not feeling particularly charming right now. But he was far too experienced to let the anger boiling within him assume control. Having a good idea who he was facing, he kept his distance and his cool. But neither could keep him from talking.

Using the muzzles of the gun, he gestured slightly in the direction of the ragged, windswept cliff that had recently been depopulated by one. "Two of my best boys. Both gone. You got no idea how careful I brought 'em both along. Had real bright futures in the trade." Self-control or no, his voice rose perceptibly. "And now cuzza you, CUZZA YOU, you subhuman piece of shit, they won't be around to split the reward, will they?" He jabbed the double barrels forward threateningly. "*Will they?*"

He began to laugh. More nasty whoop than chuckle, it was anything but appealing. Not everyone cackled when they laughed, nor made it sound like the final gasps of a dying man. Toombs chortled like a dyspeptic vulture.

In contrast, the man with the reflective goggles was as silent as the snow on which he stood, as unmoving as the rock that had been grasped so desperately, and briefly, by the now deceased Johns. Still crowing over his triumph, Toombs began to circle his trapped quarry—careful to keep his distance. He was in control, and fully intended to keep it that way.

"Let's see," he muttered, affecting a momentary uncertainty that was as false as its purpose was transparent. "Do I need to regale you with the contents of a hardcopy as to why I'm here? I don't think so. Escapee from Koravan Penal Facility. Escapee from the double-maximum security joint on Ribald Ess. Escapee from Tangiers Three Penal Colony. Officially on the outs for the last fifty-eight standard months." Feeling it with his foot, he kicked a rock aside without so much as glancing down in its direction. Unblinking, hard, his gaze remained locked on his silent quarry.

"Is there more? Oh, you know there's more!" He sniggered. "Wanted on five worlds in three systems for . . ." Feigning thoughtfulness, he tapped his lower lip with one forefinger. "Lessee—how many murders? Can I use all nine of my toes to run the tally?" He was fairly dancing now with repressed excitement. "Oh, yeah, baby, I bagged the man in motion, the killin' villain himself! Too bad about Codd and Johns. Shame they won't be around to split the reward. I'll just hafta handle their thirds for them. Life's a bitch, but Death, she can give it up when she wants to. Guess I must live right. Guess I must live." Now he did giggle, a sound more unsettling than his regular laugh.

Finger light on the trigger, he cradled his weapon in one hand. Short and nasty, it had two thick-bodied, large-caliber barrels over and under, butt and trigger snapping out from the lower half. A shot from either barrel would blow a man in half. Let loose with both barrels and—well, there wouldn't be enough left on which to file a claim for payment. Removing a pair of cuffs from his utility belt, he dangled them like an enticement to a dance.

"C'mon. Party time's over. Time to say bye-bye to this shit ball. Fulfill the drill."

Toombs tossed the cuffs at his quarry. They bounced off the man's chest and fell into the snow. The quarry glanced down at them, then back up at the mercenary, still not saying a word. He might act the mute, but Toombs knew he was not.

The mercenary could have grimaced, snapped something like "Put 'em on now, I'm not fucking around!" Instead, he took aim and let loose with both barrels of his weapon. The breeze from the explosive shells passed close enough to the quarry's skull to riffle his tangle of hair. They were more eloquent than anything Toombs himself could have said.

Bending, the quarry picked up the cuffs and worked them around to his back. Cuffing oneself wasn't an easy task, even for a renegade contortionist, but though the big man took his time, he made it look easy.

Edging around behind him, twin gun muzzles never wavering, Toombs checked the cuffs. While doing so, he also kept a watchful eye on the prey's urzo-shod feet. Explosive power sufficient to destroy a small aircraft hovered centimeters from the quarry's spine. With practiced fingers, the mercenary checked and rechecked the bonds. No funny business there, at least. The cuffs were locked and secure.

Even more emboldened than before, Toombs moved closer until he was practically inside the other man's protective suit. Licking his lips, he made his voice as low and intimidating as possible.

"An' just for the file. Just so you shouldn't forget it. The guy all up on your neck right now? It's Toombs. The name of your new shot-caller is Toombs. Easy to remember. It's what you're gonna end up in."

This time the quarry did react but not in the way Toombs expected. He was too big, too wide, to do what he did. The impossibility of it did not fully register on Toombs until later. All he knew was that one minute his quarry was standing in front of him, and the next, he had sprung into the air and backward somersaulted over the stunned mercenary. In the process, he simultaneously dislocated his shoulders and his wrists. One freed hand came around in an arc to smack the weapon out of Toombs's hands. The other caught it before it had flipped halfway to the ground.

A grand total of perhaps two seconds had elapsed. Before, Toombs had been standing behind his bound prisoner, weapon in hand. After, he found himself with their respective positions exactly reversed. Though it had happened, the bewildered mercenary was unsure of how it had been accomplished.

The reality of the transformed situation beggared analysis. All he knew was that instead of holding the gun on his quarry, it was the quarry who was now pressing the double barrels against the bottom of

Toombs's jaw. A single shot would messily remove that important bit of skeletal structure, along with half the mercenary's head. He stood very still.

"Your life or your ship," the quarry murmured matter-of-factly into Toombs's ear. "You decide, shot-caller. And just for the file? My name's Riddick. Richard B. But you can call me anything you want." The barrels pressed harder against the underside of the mercenary's jaw. "You probably will. I don't care. Ship locator. Now. Or I can sort it out for myself."

Toombs's hands began to move, quickly and carefully. All manner of hardware began hitting the snow as he emptied his utility belt, pockets both visible and hidden, side pouches. None of them distracted Riddick; none of them fooled him. Seeing how the snowflakes and the shit were blowing, a resigned Toombs finally dropped the locator. At the same time, he did conjure a few choice new names for his former quarry—but despite the big man's seeming indifference, the mercenary was careful to keep them to himself.

He had plenty of time to give loud voice to them later, when he was strung up inside the ice cave alongside the dead and defeated *Urzo giganticus*. Radically different physiognomies notwithstanding, both man and monster looked equally unhappy.

As he ran, Riddick seemed to float along above the snow, when in reality he was plowing purposely and powerfully through it. At times diverse, right now his thoughts were purely linear. Casual contemplation of multiple subjects was all very well and good—when one was sitting in a warm room with belly full and the only weapons in the vicinity your own. Survival precedes cogitation.

Pausing between drifts that marched across the landscape like fossilized waves and a distant line of rocks, he checked the ship locator. The line he had been following indicated he was very close to something now. He could only hope that it was not a decoy, set by a perverse mind to deliver a last dose of despair to anyone sharp and fast enough to acquire the device from its original owner. Riddick was only slightly concerned. Toombs was good, but the big man didn't think he was *that* good. Proof of the latter evaluation lay in the mercenary's present condition—hung out to dry. Or rather, freeze.

Flipping the ship locator closed to protect its vital innards from the weather, he let his thumb slide over the red contact near its base. In a moment he would know whether Toombs would have the last, cackling laugh. The indications were that what he was searching for lay near at hand. How near, or if at all, he would know in a moment. He nudged the control.

So close in front of him that he took a reflexive step backward, snow began to fall *upward*.

It was a better ship than he expected that rose out of the drift, sloughing off gravel and ice crystals as it slowly ascended before him. A Flattery C-19 undercutter—low-slung, handsome, contemporary construction manufactured on a world noted for skilled engineering. Adaptable and tough, it was exactly the kind of versatile transport a pack of mercenaries would utilize, if they could afford it. In addition to traversing interstellar space and a variety of atmospheres, it could also burrow or swim. Doubtless it had cost Toombs and team a pretty credit or two. Now it belonged to someone else: him. That's the way the comet crumbles, he thought to himself as he pulled out the locator and ran a subsidiary check. Unless the information he sought was being masked, the ship was empty; devoid of life-forms. No reason to mask the interior, he decided as he started toward it. Not with the maskers among the recently departed.

It didn't matter. He always preferred to rely on his own judgment and instinct, turning to machines only when necessary or when left with no choice. The locator said the ship was empty. He entered through the obeisant port as warily as if the compact craft were crammed to its outer shell with a contingent of waiting, heavily armed representatives of the law.

It was exactly as empty as the locator insisted it was.

Settling himself into the command chair, he methodically coaxed quiescent instrumentation to life. Though no professional pilot, he knew what to do to survive. One of these talents involved piloting small spacecraft. Though some of the indicator markings were new or unfamiliar, the controls were basic enough.

At his command, protective internal screens whisked aside. The main distorter drive powered up. With the ship alert and awaiting instructions, he paused to delve into its internal supplementary databases. Another talent. He almost, but not quite, smiled as his own record appeared, glowing softly with the details of his personal history. Alone, as usual, he read silently to himself from the section catalogued under "LEADS."

". . . Now known to have survived emergency reentry and subsequent vessel crash on double-star system M-344/G. Likely killer of Class-I mercenary William J. Johns. Possible sighting on Lupus III. Reported seen on . . . Reported seen on . . ." There was quite a lot of the latter. This time he did smile. To have been everywhere he had been reported seen, there would have to be twelve of him.

An unsealed can of protein rope sat on the deck between his seat and the co-pilot's chair. Popping the lid, he pulled out a length, bit off a mouthful, and chewed as he scrolled through the readout. It didn't take long to find the one labeled "PAYDAY."

The list of worlds where he was wanted exceeded those where he had reportedly been sighted. Unlike those, this second list was not fanciful. A lot of people in a lot of places wanted him incarcerated for a variety of reasons. The justification didn't matter to mercenaries. Only the potential payoff was important. Each individual prison or facility had been handicapped by Toombs and his team. Different slams would pay different fees for delivery of the desired quarry. The rates ranged from three hundred thousand K up to seven-fifty. One glaring exception made Riddick take notice.

One point five million. Universal denomination or specific currency of choice. Hard cash.

Spitting out a piece of the protein rope that had been processed from part of an animal that would better have remained anonymous, he opened the file associated with the oversized cash offer. The place on the screen before him that was normally reserved for an image of the bidder was empty. The accompanying banner bleated PRIVATE PARTY. That was nothing new. Even slam directors and their administrators liked their anonymity. In contrast, the originating source was a bit of a surprise.

PLANET: HELLION PRIME. REGION: NEW MECCA.

"So even holy men have their price," he murmured to the screen. It did not reply. The lack of a response did not trouble him. He was tired and in no mood to talk to anyone. Not even a machine.

The compact ship boosted effortlessly from the surface of a world Riddick would just as soon forget as quickly as possible. Once clear of atmosphere and a sufficient number of AUs out, he entered the coordinates for Helion Prime and prepared for the long haul. There was no reason for him to remain awake and every reason to enter cryosleep. Without artificial aids, humans didn't last long under the stresses of supralight travel. When a ship went into That Other Place, any long-term passengers needed to be properly prepped.

Soon-to-be-unnecessary lights dimmed. The special malleable substance of which the vessel's outer skin was fashioned warped slightly, actually altering its molecular structure. Cryosleep tubing latched onto its single occupant like so many benign snakes, adjusting his internal chemistry, taking over functions, preparing him to cope with the stresses of extended deepspace travel. His eyelids fluttered, closed.

It was good to sleep. He had not been able to do so comfortably and without concern for a long time. Safe in the cocoon of the pilot's chair, nurtured and looked after by the ship's life support systems, he could at last relax. Meanwhile, the small but sturdy vessel went about its business.

As part of the latter, notation of inhabited systems within a certain range automatically appeared on a monitor even though no organic eyes were active to observe them. When one identified a passing system as Furya, the unconscious man in the pilot's chair stirred slightly.

"They say most of your brain shuts down in cryosleep. All but the animal side."

With an effort, he dragged his eyes open. A glance showed that he was as alone as before. Screens and telltales working silently did not supply the information he expected to see there. Something was wrong. Or if not wrong, at least not right. *He had heard a voice.* He did not mistake such things.

There was a reflection in one screen. A suggestion of movement. Nothing on the ship ought to be moving. At a touch, the pilot's chair spun around.

A lesser individual might have screamed at what he saw. Or started babbling uncontrollably. Riddick did neither. Just sat there, tubes and connectors still leeched to his body, staring, studying, trying to make sense of the sight before him. He was having a hard time doing so.

He was, after all, no longer alone.

Though slender and attractive, the woman conveyed an inner hardness that was more sensed than seen. He felt he ought to know her even though he had never seen her before. The impossibility of her presence registered strongly. It was negated by the fact that he knew he was not insane. Dreaming perhaps, but not insane.

Behind her, the ship was gone. It had been replaced by a world of trees that were utterly alien yet somehow oddly familiar. Small skittering things darted furtively through the undergrowth while lightning-fast fliers zipped between the peculiar branches. The ground was littered with objects whose purpose and shape had changed little in thousands of years: gravestones. He had no time to study wildlife or monuments: the woman was talking to him.

"I am Shirah. Think of this as a dream, if you need to."

His mind fought violently against what he was seeing even as his senses accepted it. As he struggled, more and more of the ship vanished, to be replaced by additional forest and more gravestones. There were a lot of the latter. Too many. Where ship met specter, perception blurred.

"But some know better. Some know it isn't a dream. Some of us know the true crime that happened here, on Furya." Drifting dreamily, one hand indicated the nearest of the gravestones. "We'll never have them back. But we can have this world again. Someday."

Riddick's brain had been tuned to coping with the unlikely, the unreasonable, the unacceptable. It refused to dismiss the information his eyes and ears insisted on conveying.

"Once you remember, you will never forget." Placing one hand over her chest, the woman waited until it began to glow softly. Riddick thought he could catch glimpses of the bones of her fingers. Approaching, she reached toward him, fingers extended . . .

Something jolted him awake. Hadn't he been awake? A dream. He'd never had a dream where the other occupant had told him to think of the experience as a dream. What he knew to be true conflicted with what he knew ought to be true. Priding himself on his ability to resolve seeming contradictions and unable to do so this time, he grew tense.

A glance at the ship's instrumentation solved the problem for him. He was closing on his destination. Now was not the time to ponder the source of implausible visions.

Clearing its electronic throat, the ship's communicator snapped him forcefully back from nebulous realms inhabited by memories of distant dreams and fading visitations.

The voice that barked at him via the communicator was an odd mix of emphatic and anxious. "Repeating . . . all spaceports and all landing facilities of Helion Prime, including those designated for emergency service, are closed to flights that have not originated from this locale. Unauthorized craft are prohibited from landing. Infractors will be fired upon. These regulations are in force until officially countermanded by the government of Helion Prime. Repeating . . ."

Something went *bang* and the merc ship bounced violently. As it had not yet entered atmosphere, this was more than disconcerting. Whatever had struck Riddick's craft had blown a chunk of communications gear right off the front. Hopefully, that was all that had been blown off. Nothing was yelling for his attention, and a rapid scan of monitoring instrumentation showed that hull integrity was still intact. Swiftly, his fingers began to dance over the manual controls.

There was only one ship on him. It was a wicked-looking little one-pilot job, its external elegance more reflective of the advanced state of Helion technology than any demand of design. A second bump jolted Riddick, but instead of a proximity charge this one was caused by the merc craft's swift dive into atmosphere. He was going down too steep and too fast. Even as the hull's external temperature began to rise sharply, the ship's dispersion field proceeded to compensate by dissipating the intense heat.

At such speeds, only advanced computational navigation systems allowed the Helion fighter to materialize right alongside the merc ship. He could see the pilot, grim-faced, motioning for him to descend. Riddick nodded compliance and moved to adjust his position. Ever so slightly was all that was needed.

Before the other pilot, or his inboard predictive gear, could react, the merc craft slipped underneath and into it. Debris flew from both craft. Riddick had timed the contact perfectly. Too much, and even at suborbital velocity both ships would have disintegrated. Too little, and he would simply have flashed past his attacker to emerge on the opposite side. But just enough, and one vessel or the other was likely to be severely disabled.

As Riddick had intended, it was the other.

The Helion fighter spiraled away, damaged and possibly out of control. Whether it would manage a successful touchdown or not now depended on the skill of its pilot and not the calculations of its instrumentation. Watching it disappear into the distance, Riddick shook his head slowly.

"Never mess with a guy with a loaner."

He checked the monitors. The merc ship had sustained some damage from the deliberate collision. The longer it flew, the more likely that the damage would become severe, then fatal. That didn't trouble him. Right now, all he wanted to do was get down in one piece. Whether the ship did so in sufficient shape to rise again or not concerned him considerably less. While maintaining the too-steep descent, he punched in some evasive maneuvers just in case the now departed pilot happened to have colleagues in the area and in the air.

The ocean was green. Riddick had seen oceans of liquid methane as different in hue as they were brilliant. Green suited him. He'd always had an affinity for water. As he fought to slow the heavily vibrating ship, blue-green waves gave way to those colored yellow and white and beige: sand dunes, rangy and extensive.

It wasn't the gentlest of touchdowns, but the hull

held as he slammed right into the thickest dune he could find. Blackness covered the viewport. External visuals began to go dark. Forward motion ceased. Following prescribed and preprogammed merc procedure, concealware took over. A battery of small powered devices adjusted the ship's hull. To an onlooker, of which there presently happened to be none, it would have appeared as if the vessel was shimmying itself into the sand. When relevant instrumentation deemed the procedure complete, all was dark within. Outside, nothing appeared to have changed. It would have taken more than a sharp eye to determine that the shallow rut that now ran the length of the sand dune's crest had been caused by anything other than the wind. Riddick let out a deep breath and slipped out of the pilot's harness. He had arrived.

Somewhere else. Again.

III

The immense dome that dominated the skyline of Helion Prime's capital city was impressive, but it was dwarfed by the beacons, the temples of light, that dominated the sprawling metropolis. Shafting skyward, they bespoke the nature and power of Helion's achievements in culture as well as in technology. Famous in this part of the galaxy, at least, they were an unmissable expression of all that was Helion. On its neat, clean streets, citizens went about their business with the air of those who believed themselves just slightly superior. In its skies, transport craft of every imaginable size and description hurried along their predetermined paths. Helion Prime was a crossroads.

The makeup of its citizenry attested to that. The city was home to every variation in stature, shade, and sensibility of contemporary humanity. It was reflected in the city's art, in its commerce, in its entertainment venues.

It was also amply evident in its politics, which at the moment were undergoing an upheaval that found them uneasily balanced somewhere between the fractious and outright hand-to-hand combat. Uncommon to Helion government, yelling and shouting filled the outer chambers and anterooms of the capitol dome.

Pulling on a cloak, one man fled the cacophony. His expression showed him to be as disgusted as he was depressed. Curious beyond restraint, an aide intercepted the fugitive as he strode from the dome. With a nod of his head, he indicated the barely controlled chaos that presently filled the interior.

"Delegate Imam, I have worked for this government for twenty years. Never have I heard or seen such signs of serious dissention. What's happening in there?"

The delegate paused, glanced back. "When all is said and done? Much will be said—and nothing will be done."

Cloak swirling around him, he swept away. Behind him, the aide stared back toward the towering doors that opened into the dome. Like the majority of his Helion brethren, he was keen on order and predictability. The shouting and arguing within did not bode well for a continuation of such things. It was just as well he was not privy to the debate raging inside. More than a few of the comments and observations being made would have unsettled him a good deal more than he already was.

The defense minister was adamant. She was also louder than most of her fellow officials. Even in an age of advanced technology, a strong voice still had its uses.

"Shut down the beacons!" she roared. "We need

to save the energy, save all resources for *this* world! We cannot continue to export at a time of such uncertainty, when planetary defense should be everyone's first priority."

Steramad disagreed, as he usually did. "We can't be slaves to fear. What kind of message would that send to the people? Helion Prime is expected to set an example for the lesser nearby worlds. A specific threat must be identified before radical action is approved. We cannot react in panic to every rumor that—"

The respected clerical delegate ar-Aajem cut him off. "Rumor? Is it rumor that we have lost communication with *another* world?" He gestured emphatically to his colleagues. "One such incident suggests communications failure. Multiple ones suggest something far more sinister. You all know to what I refer."

Someone shouted, "We should try and make contact, negotiate with them."

"Them?" another delegate countered. "Who's even seen 'them'? Who even knows what they want? If 'they' even exist. There could be other explanations, as Steramad says."

A second cleric rose to speak. "Seven worlds, at least seven worlds have gone silent! That is all the explanation I and my department require. Can one be blind to the deafness of one's neighbors? What more proof do we need?" He waved in the direction of the defense minister. "We must prepare, and quickly."

"Twelve worlds!" The new voice teetered on the edge of panic. "My sources say *twelve* have gone silent!"

Steramad's strongest ally in session was Teyfuddin. Raising his voice, that worthy attempted to counter the rising feeling of hopelessness. "But not one in this system. Planets are not countries. We share no direct border with those worlds that seem to be experiencing these problems. With those in our system we share a sun, and they continue to communicate with Prime as efficiently as always." He regarded the sea of anxious faces.

"I share your concerns. Such increasing silence from beyond Helion is troubling. But civilization has known many troubles, and still survives. History tells us that not all troubles visit all worlds. Nobody here today knows where this mysterious silence will descend next. Or even if! I see cause for vigilance, yes, but not for panic."

The defense minister did not sit down. She was growing increasingly frustrated at the turn the discussion was taking. This was a time for action, not for talk! She *had* to convince them.

"Again I say it. Shut down the beacons. Draw in our outer defenses. We only make ourselves more of a target the longer we—"

This time it was her turn to be interrupted. Steramad refused to be stampeded into a decision he felt was not only unnecessary but also counter to Helion philosophy.

"If we show fear—if we shut down the beacons and cower in the dark—our sister worlds will wither and starve. It falls to us to set the example, to be strong for all. For their children, as well as ours, we must stand our ground. We are Helion Prime! And we will do what we have always done: generate energy and then share it with all."

Shouts greeted his declaration—some supportive, some questioning. Politician and defense minister, supporters and detractors, glared at one another across the chamber as the debate raged around them. Both had the best interests of their home world at heart. Neither had any idea of the nature of what was coming for them.

Cloak fluttering around him, a preoccupied Imam hurried along a street in New Mecca, one of the capital's most famous districts. Full of atmosphere, it had been updated with modern technology that had been largely concealed behind walls and under streets to preserve the character of the area. Lost in thought, he barely noticed that the great beacons that were the hallmark of Prime were coming on line, surpassing the setting sun with their brilliance.

Rounding a corner, he came upon an information kiosk. Like scales on a snake, screens riddled the cylinder, broadcasting dozens of different news channels simultaneously. Clustered around it, concerned citizens occasionally adjusted the individual volume on the pickups they wore as they discussed what they were seeing and hearing.

"So tall it touches the clouds," one man was saying. "And there is nothing around this thing, this 'colossus.' Nothing is left. They say it's their calling card."

The man standing next to him was dubious. "How

is it possible? To accomplish so much, so quickly, and so completely? When no one even sees them coming?"

The concerns of his fellow citizens were no less troubling to Imam. As a delegate, it was his responsibility to assuage such worries. Yet how could he do so? He needed facts, hard truths. But when these showed up, a vast silence weighed in. It was more than disturbing. It was frightening. Despite what he had said earlier that evening, and had been saying for days, he had to admit that deep down, he too was frightened. It was not the implied threat of utter and complete destruction that scared him. It was not knowing anything, anything at all, about the possible source.

He was about to move on when something on one of the screens caught his eye. The briefest of updates from a minor broadcast, it showed close-up vid of a single pilot making an illegal entry into Helion Prime atmosphere. A customs craft engaged in forcing the visitor down had been damaged in the attempt. Before backup could arrive on the scene, the interloper had vanished. As no trace of the intruding ship had been found on land despite an extensive follow-up search, speculation was that the intruder too had been damaged by collision and had plunged into the sea. As to the identity of the illegal, there was as yet no firm determination. Authorities were working through records to try and identify the craft and possibly its pilot. Before being forced to break away, the pilot of the customs interceptor had obtained images of the intruder that had been effectively enhanced.

Moving closer to the screen, Imam intently studied the picture of the single human. People in the crowd, disturbed and agitated, jostled around him as each sought a different vantage point.

"'Coming'?" one of them was saying forebodingly. "They may already be here."

Imam could have taken a personal or public transport, but when possible he preferred to walk. It allowed him time to think, away from yammering politicians and self-righteous clerics. It also allowed him to hear the talk on the street, and to participate in it as well. A surprising number of citizens had no idea what the majority of their delegates in government looked like, and were more than willing to unburden themselves to a sympathetic, attentive stranger of their opinions on everything from energy costs to public morals.

Wending his way through side streets, occasionally pausing to chat with those he met, it took Imam longer than he planned to get home. While Helion Prime's streets were reasonably safe, no society was perfect. These rumors and whispers that currently fogged the streets were exactly the kind inclined to fuel antisocial behavior. Better even for a known and respected delegate to be home before dark.

As he came within sight of his destination, the nearest wall glowed to life, bathing the approach to his home in soft white illumination. The automated reaction to his presence calmed him almost as much as the light itself. Out there, beyond the reach of

Helion's sun, something inimical and unknown might be stalking, but here, for now, all was as it should be.

Reading and responding to his biometrics, the doorway opened to admit him. Once inside, he had begun to relax when a sound informed him that he had been wrong: all was *not* as it should be. That he recognized the sound did not trouble him a tenth as much as the fact that he recognized the voice that spoke to him over the steady scrape, scrape of blade against synthetic stone.

"It was the worst place I could find. The worst place where I could survive by myself, without the burden of having to lug around special gear. See, I wanted to be free, but I also wanted to be ignored."

Imam turned toward the voice. He knew that if its owner had wanted him dead, he would already be lying on the floor, a test-drive for decomposing bacteria. Or perhaps, he thought fearfully, his visitor was only taking his time.

There were any number of depilatory sprays on the market, as well as a plethora of advanced hair-removal gadgets. Disdaining them all, honoring self-sufficiency or possibly some unknown tradition, the big man leaning over the small hallway fountain was using the blade he held to shave his head in a manner that was as time-honored as it was currently unfashionable. As he spoke, he concentrated on what he was doing. Imam might have been in the room, or it might have been empty. The delegate knew one thing for certain. If he tried to flee before his visitor had finished whatever it was he had entered to say and do, he would not make it as far as the nearest doorway.

"Where?" he heard himself asking.

"Some frozen heap," Riddick was murmuring as he worked. The blade slid smoothly over his increasingly bare skull; long, thick locks dropping like dead mambas into the small basin. "No real name, no real sun. Just scientific designations. No need for real names for a place nobody would want to go. Chose it just to get away from all the brightness. All the—temptation. Glare from snow and ice, but funny light. Thought it would put certain people off. Did, for a while. Just hoping to exist in the shadows of nowhere." Straightening, he studied his handiwork in the mirror, almost as if he could see in the darkness that enveloped the anteroom. Except that, as Imam knew, there was no "almost" about it.

Riddick turned to the silent Imam. "But someone wouldn't let me do it. Somebody couldn't leave bad enough alone. Suppose I shouldn't have been surprised. People have always been a disappointment to me."

In the poor light, eye contact was made. Imam said nothing. There was no point, until commentary was required, and he particularly did not want to do or say anything that might upset his uninvited guest. From experience, he knew that it might not take very much to do so. Without thinking he cast a glance upstairs. As soon as he did, he was sorry he had done it.

It didn't matter. His visitor knew anyway. "She's in the shower."

Blade in hand, Riddick walked slowly toward Imam. "I told *one* person where I might go. Trusted *one* man when I left this place. After what we had been through together, I thought I could do that much. Was I wrong? Did I make a mistake?"

Imam swallowed hard and gathered himself. He did not want to stammer. Normally, that was not a potentially fatal condition. But in the presence of this man, there was simply no predicting what might constitute such. He needed to sound more confident than he felt.

"Honest and true, I say to you that there is no simple answer."

At about the exact instant the last syllable was formed by his lips, the blade was resting on his neck. He never saw it move. One moment it was dangling from the big man's hand; the next, the razor edge was resting against the delegate's throat.

"Did I make," Riddick repeated with deceptive softness, "a mistake."

Despite Imam's determination, there was a noticeable quaver in his voice as he replied, "I give you my word, Riddick. As a delegate to the government of Helion Prime—" The big man made a small noise that some listeners, had there been any, might have construed as unflattering. "—and as a friend, that whatever has been said was meant to give us a chance, a *fighting* chance. Were it not for the events of the past few months, events without precedent in the entire history not only of Helion Prime but of this entire sector, things might—"

He broke off as a third presence established itself in the room. Riddick noticed it, too. The attention of both had shifted to the stairway mezzanine, where a slim, bright-eyed young girl was watching both of them keenly. While Riddick's gaze shifted, the blade did not.

The girl was nothing if not perceptive. "Riddick?" she whispered, clearly in awe. Emerging from such a young throat, and such an innocent one, somehow made it sound less intimidating. She was not afraid. Her wide eyes suggested wonder, not fear.

The emotions of the woman who stepped up behind her, still wet from the shower, were considerably more confused. "Riddick," she said, echoing the girl. Her tone was neither so innocent nor so indifferent. Her head was cocooned in a setting wrap. When she removed it, her hair would be set in the style she had chosen prior to entering the shower. Riddick guessed her to be somewhere in her mid-thirties, the girl five or maybe a little older.

He had never met either of them, but they clearly knew him well enough to recognize him, even in the shadowy light. If they knew him by sight, it followed that they also knew his reputation. It did not appear to bother the girl. But the look in the woman's eyes . . .

Making a decision for reasons only he could fathom, Riddick drew the knife away from Imam's throat. Advancing, he examined the woman. She did not back away, but neither did she feel comfortable under the stare. It hinted at all sorts of experiences, all manner of knowledge. It made her feel undressed without knowing why.

Having turned his back on the delegate without so much as a care, Riddick now glanced at him. "A wife."

Imam nodded. "Lajjun. We were married not long after . . ." His voice trailed away. He didn't need to explain to Riddick. Riddick had been there for all the "after."

Riddick looked at the woman, down to the girl, then at the woman again. "You know," he said finally, "it's been a long time since 'beautiful' entered my brain. I'd pretty much forgotten what it meant, what it could apply to. It's been even longer since I was able to apply it human beings. How long has it been, Imam?"

"Five. Five years."

It became very quiet in the room. Imam thought he could hear his own heart beating. To her credit, Lajjun held her poise. She would not back down for anyone, he knew. It was one of the reasons he had fallen in love with her, one of the reasons he had married her. But he would not have thought any the less of her if she had backed away, or fled upstairs, or started screaming. There was an exception to every rule, and right now that exception was standing in the room directly in front of her.

She moved to shepherd the girl out of the antechamber. As she did, Riddick took a step forward. Imam tensed, but their visitor only gestured inoffensively at the child. "And a daughter. Named?"

Imam licked his lips. Now more than ever, it was important to do and say the right thing. Other lives than his were at stake. He had traveled with this man, had suffered tragedy beside him, but he did not know him. He doubted anyone did.

A wise man once observed that in attempting to

determine whether a bomb was a dud or not, it was best not to try and find out by hammering on the detonator.

"If you have issue with me," he finally responded, "let it be with me alone. You have no quarrel with anyone else in this house."

"Named?" Riddick repeated softly, his tone unchanged.

Stubbornness would gain nothing here, Imam knew. His visitor was a master of patience. "Ziza. Her name is Ziza."

At the sound of her name the girl cocked her head slightly and met the big man's gaze without flinching, armored with the bravery of innocence. "Did you really kill the monsters? The ones that were gonna hurt my father? On the dark planet, where the sun went away and the nightmares came to life?"

Instead of replying, Riddick shot a look at the man he had come to see. Without saying a word, his expression clearly conveyed his query: *She knows about that?*

Imam shrugged slightly. "Such are our bedtime stories. You know children. They want to know everything, especially about their parents. Ziza is very mature for her age."

Like magic, the blade in Riddick's hand vanished from sight. Imam did not quite breathe a sigh of relief. He knew the knife could reappear just as quickly.

It was as if a signal had been given to Lajjun to leave and take the girl with her. She complied, despite Ziza's desire to remain. The child was fascinated by their visitor. She was not the first to be so.

"Who did you tell?" Riddick asked resignedly. "Who do I now gotta put on a slab just to get this rancid payday offa my head? You should've kept your mouth shut, Imam."

"Events conspire." His host had relaxed a little since his wife and child had been allowed to leave the room. "You wouldn't find them. Even if you looked."

The big man almost, but not quite, grinned. "Why would I look? When you can bring them right to me?"

"It is not so easy as you think."

The shadow of a smile vanished immediately. "Don't talk to me about what isn't easy. My whole life has been about surviving what isn't easy." He gestured slightly with his right hand. It remained empty. "If communications still function on this overlit ball of dirt, it's time to use them."

IV

They waited together on the small veranda of the upper floor: two men who had been through a difficult time together, surviving when all around them had perished. It was all they had in common, but it was enough for the moment, Imam knew. How long the bond would hold he did not know. Long enough, he hoped. Long enough to give him time to at least explain himself.

For now, though, they passed the time in contemplation of the night sky. The glow of the great beacons made it impossible to see more than a star or two. Still, by focusing on a chosen corner of sky, it was possible to observe a small section of the universe in all its nocturnal splendor. Growing up, and for most of his life, Imam had regarded it with a mixture of wonder and anticipation. Now it had become home to something dreadful. Perhaps the end of everything he had known. Much depended, perhaps, on the man standing nearby. Knowing what he did of his guest, it seemed a terrible risk to settle so much hope on so unpredictable an individual.

A comet was crossing the sky, high in the east. Some things, at least, would not be affected by what was rumored to be out there. The thought helped to calm him.

"Nero died, the Roman empire lapsed into civil war, a new Caesar came to power, and Old Earth was forever changed. All under the watchful eye of a comet. Throughout human history, comets have been considered auguries of violent change." He gazed out over the rooftops of the old residential quarter.

"Just one more omen in a season of omens—all of them bad." Turning away from the nocturnal vista, he regarded his visitor. "Do you know what's been happening in the civilized galaxy?"

Riddick's expression twisted slightly. "Sorry. I've kinda been out of touch. When trying to stay alive and find enough to eat becomes a full-time occupation, you tend to give the news a pass."

Imam nodded, not needing to know the details. "Coalsack is gone. Dead and silent. The Aquilian system, gone quiet too. Helion Prime shares its bounty with several less naturally endowed worlds nearby. If we fall, they fall. And after that . . ."

He stopped talking. Riddick was at a table, playing with a knife. As Imam looked on, his guest passed the blade through a pair of decorative metal candlesticks, severing them cleanly. His expression said unambiguously, "Nice edge."

Imam risked the sound of impatience. "Have you

heard anything I've said? Or are you always focused on—business."

Riddick put the knife up. "Yeah, I heard you. Said it's all circlin' the drain. Whole galaxy. Civilization local, nearby, distant."

"That's right."

His guest shrugged. Imam might as well have been describing the loss of a garden to weeds. "Had to end sometime."

The three clerics drew their robes tighter around them. A wind was rising, whistling through the streets of the upper-class residential quarter. Picking up dust and pollen, the breeze carried it along, flinging it in the faces of those who were too slow to turn away. No casual conversation passed between the men. Though they were confident in their purpose, they were not sure of the outcome of their visit. These days, it was hard to be sure of anything. But a respected member of their own had bid them come, and they had complied. Willingly, if not happily.

Reaching the house, one of them whispered toward the pickup set beside the entrance. Ancient bells, beloved antiques, jangled in response. It was a sound from humanity's past, cheerful and reassuring. Characteristic also, they knew, of the owner of the house. An unusual man, who had been through things they could only imagine. It was another reason they had come.

The door was opened by a woman in the full flower of her maturity. There was no need to speak.

She recognized each of them and, more important, so had the door's security system. In response to her gesture, the shrouded trio headed for the stairs. Behind them, Lajjun moved to close the door. Something outside made her hesitate. Staring into the darkness, she saw nothing. Just the wind and what it carried. The door closed with a reassuring electronic snap.

As the three clerics emerged onto the upper-floor veranda, Imam turned to greet them with a gesture. Though they responded in kind, no one was looking at him. Their attention was reserved for the visitor nearby.

Imam turned to him. "The one you want is now here."

Riddick moved forward, seeming to cross the intervening space between himself and the clerics with barely a step. One by one, he pushed back hoods and examined faces. He had no divining equipment with him, needed none. He knew men better than any machine.

Expecting to recognize the culprit, he was momentarily taken aback when none of the three faces proved familiar. No question: they were all strangers to him. His thoughts churned. Was this some kind of test? Was he being played? And if so, to what purpose? He turned to his host. Imam's face was devoid of duplicity. What was going on here? If these holy men had not been brought here for him to inspect, then why had Imam called them? So *they* could examine *him*? What could be the reason for that? Or was there something more? A second glance in his host's direction suggested as much. But what?

"'Even if I looked,'" he murmured, echoing what Imam had told him earlier.

A twitch drew his attention to one of the clerics. The first one was nervous, unable to meet Riddick's eyes. Though he fought hard against doing so, he kept glancing over the big man's shoulder. Had his first impression been wrong? Riddick mused. Was this increasingly edgy individual the one he sought? Or was he only fighting hard not to look at . . .

Riddick whirled. His blade was out and ready before he finished turning. It halted less than a millimeter from the neck of a fourth visitor. He stared.

"Whose throat is *this*?"

The woman standing under the knife was smooth and supple despite her evident age. Her attire, like her visage, was new to him. She did not seem strong enough to throw words with any skill, much less a knife. She did not show fear, exactly, but neither was she utterly indifferent to the proximity of the sharp-edged tool to her jugular vein. Verging on the maternal, her expression was disarming, yet Riddick sensed this female creature was anything but ingenuous.

He felt Imam coming up behind him, let the man approach. "This is Aereon. An envoy from the Elementals." Tentatively, he reached up to lay a calming hand on Riddick's shoulder. What he felt was more stone than flesh. "She means you no harm."

Riddick listened, but the blade did not relent.

Aereon's voice was notably less ethereal than her appearance. "If you cut my throat, I'll not be able to rescind the offer that brought you here. Nor tell you why it's so vital that you came. There is much more at stake here, Richard Riddick, than trivialities like bounties and personal revenge."

"I make my own definition of what's trivial, thanks. And I'll take the blade off when the bounty comes off."

"I see that additional explanation is in order," she told him.

"I'd say long overdue," he growled softly.

She smiled—just before pirouetting away from him, and vanishing. The knife moved, but too late.

"There are very few of us who have met a Necromonger noble and lived unconverted to speak of it. So when I choose to speak of it, you should choose to listen."

"'Necromonger,'" he murmured thoughtfully. He listened—but he did not put away the knife.

"Be familiar with it," she told him forcefully. "It is the name that will convert or kill every last human life—unless the universe can rebalance itself." In response to his questioning stare she added, "Balance is everything to Elementals. Water to fire, earth to air. We have thirty-three different words for this balance, but today, here, now, we have time to speak only of the Balance of Opposites."

Riddick was one of those rare individuals who was smart enough to know and recognize the extent of his ignorance. "Maybe you should pretend like you're talkin' to someone who's been educated in the general penal system. Places where notions like 'rehabilitation' have too many syllables for the guards to pronounce. Fact, don't pretend. I hear what you're saying, but I ain't following where you're going with it."

"There is a story . . . ," she began. Blade at the ready, arm extended, Riddick whirled repeatedly as he tried to track the voice. The three clerics had withdrawn to the comparative safety of a wall. Imam held his ground, watching Riddick as closely as the Elemental.

She seemed to be everywhere on the veranda without alighting anywhere in particular. Wherever and whenever she materialized, it was well clear of the big man's blade.

Imam took up the tale. "A story, about young male Furyans who, feared for whatever reason, were strangled at birth. Strangled with their own umbilical cords. When Aereon told this story to the leaders of Helion—I told her of you." The way he said it made it sound as if that was intended to explain everything.

The big man's brow furrowed. "Furyans?"

Aereon felt confident enough to move a little closer. The clerics watched her movements in awe. Not Riddick. Always calculating, always thinking ahead of his opponent, he had little time to spare on awe.

"The one race, we calculate, that may be able to slow the spread of the Necromongers." She was eyeing him intently.

It dawned on Riddick why he had been drawn to Helion. Out of touch and glad of it, he had clearly missed hearing about some kind of ominous ongoing conflict. They believed him to be some player in their local drama, some kind of hoodoo hero. He chuckled grimly. He had been called many things in his life, but never a hero. Yet there was no mistaking the intensity with which everyone on the veranda regarded him: clerics, host, and dodgy female visitor alike. Well, whatever. Far be it from him to disabuse the misguided of their consoling delusions.

Sensing his indifference, Imam tried to shore up the Elemental's somewhat distanced commentary. "What do you know of your early years, Riddick? Of your upbringing, your childhood? Of parents and playtimes? What else was told you besides—"

Aereon interrupted impatiently. There was no time to waste, and she sensed that any attempt at nurturing this man would be just that. "Do you remember your home world? Its name, appearance, climate? Where it was?"

"Have you met any others?" Imam pressed him with particular urgency.

"Others like yourself?" the Elemental added.

Many questions, meaningless in the context of his present existence. Why ask such things of him? He had always focused on tomorrow, with little thought for yesterday. What was past was done, dead as he would one day be. His sole undertaking was to prevent that from happening. Each day he survived was another accomplishment. What did it matter where he was from? If he didn't much care, why should anyone else? Yet there was no mistaking the zeal behind their questioning.

You want something from me; give me something first, he mused. He was not the kind to offer up anything freely—not even information. That he did not have the answers to their questions made it that much easier for him to deny them.

"Sister, they don't know what to do with *one* of me."

"If you were to try," Imam persisted, "to think back as far as you can, it's possible that . . . what is it?"

Ignoring his host's entreaties, Riddick had moved to the edge of the veranda and was peering guardedly over the side. The dark street below was no longer empty. Nor did he think the armored and heavily armed figures moving around below were commuters returning from working overtime at their jobs in the commercial sector of the city. Engaged in an active door-to-door search, they were moving swiftly and watchfully. Two would demand attention at a door while their companions covered them with weapons at the ready. Loud, impatient, and insistent, their voices drifted up to him as clearly as he saw them in the dark. A moment later, and they were crowding around the entrance to Imam's house.

Lajjun appeared at the entrance to the veranda. Her eyes went first to Riddick, then to her husband. "They look for a man who came here today. They think he might be . . . uh, what is the local word . . . 'ghesu'?"

"'Spy,'" Imam murmured. Clearly distressed, he turned to the big man. "They must think you're a spy for the—"

His wife interrupted him, speaking sharply to their guest. "Did someone see you come here? Did they?"

The sound of fists pounding on door floated up

from below. It was a decidedly low-tech way of gaining attention, but it worked. Imam spoke to Riddick as he started toward the balustrade. "I'll send them away, but please—one minute more of your time. Will you wait just one minute more to help save worlds?"

Riddick had vaulted onto the railing of the veranda. Now he paused there, like some mythological creature of the night, a muscular gargoyle balancing effortlessly on a narrow perch, ready to depart at his leisure. Though the nearest building was no easy distance away, Imam had no doubt that his guest could leap the gap.

"Or will you leave us to our fate? Just as you left her?"

Not much of a word—"her." In the lexicon of admonitions, a feeble one. But it was sufficient to halt Riddick. He stared long and hard at his host, and then without a word he hopped back down onto the veranda.

Polite inquiry, knocking, and then verbal demands laced with intimations of authority having failed, the edgy soldiers outside had resorted to plasma knives. Slicing through hinges and seals, they made quick work of the front door. It didn't matter that a government delegate lived within. Their instructions included no exceptions. If there was a problem, the owner of the house could take it up later with the bureau that had issued the search orders. Certainly he would be in a position to do so. A year ago, every one of those in the search party would have had second thoughts about forcing their way into the home of so esteemed a personage. But much had changed in a year, and a great deal in the past several weeks. They proceeded without hesitation.

Cut through, the door fell inward and crashed to the floor. The search team swarmed inside, looking for someone to question and, perhaps, to take into custody. Or terminate. Their orders were to take subjects alive if at all possible, but not to take any risks. Fingers tensed on triggers as alert eyes scanned the dim room.

Above, Imam heard the intruders moving around and turned to face his guest. "My associates and I have some sway. Please, stay and let us try and send them away."

Riddick said nothing. But he remained where he was, eschewing the railing. Seeing this, Imam favored his visitor with a small, hopeful smile. Then he and the trio of clerics headed down the stairs, closing the door to the veranda behind them.

It left Riddick alone on the veranda—except for one. Even as he turned, the Elemental moved. He saw her move, but could not follow her. She did not exactly vanish, or dematerialize. She ran, but too fast for him to follow. And if it was too fast for him to follow . . .

Some day, he vowed silently, he would find out just how she did that.

As he listened, the voices beyond the doors gradually subsided. At first, he had heard Imam and the clerics conversing with others. Now there was only silence. Had his host been able to fulfill his hopes? Moving to the edge of the veranda, Riddick peered carefully over the side. He expected to see soldiers leaving. What he saw instead was more disturbing.

There were figures in the street, all right, but only two were armored. They were keeping watch over the people of the house, who had been hustled outside. The clerics were there also, their expressions a mix of anxiety and outrage. He saw Lajjun and Ziza. The woman said something to one of the soldiers. His response was to push her away. Roughly. Riddick studied the scene below for another long moment. Then he moved away from the railing, completely silent, and over to the door that led inside.

The fit between the antique doors that separated upstairs room from stairway was not perfect. Through the narrow crack between the panels Riddick was able to see down the stairs beyond. It was completely dark inside the study—but not to him. There was no sign of movement. To someone like Riddick, that was more significant than the chatter of voices or the pounding of feet. Noiselessly, he backed slowly away.

On the other side of the doors, pressed against opposite walls, the soldiers waited for command. One held a knife to Imam's lips. Despite this, he considered crying out a warning. Had it only been his future at stake, he would have done so. But there were others, two others, waiting for him out on the street. So he held onto his words and prayed for the one who thought so little of prayer.

At a sign from the search party's commanding officer, the soldiers in front responded simultaneously. The doors gave way without much resistance and they surged into the room beyond. It was very dark. The voice that greeted them was perfectly composed.

"Come on in."

There were ten of them. They were well trained, and extremely confident. A few had even been in actual combat, on other worlds. They knew they were searching only for one man. They knew little about him.

It was not nearly enough.

At first unleashed with some control, some concern for their owner's immediate surroundings, weapons began to chew up their surroundings with less and less regard for accuracy as one soldier after another was dropped. Sometimes they thought they saw their target. Other times they saw only a shadow, and began firing at it because it was all they saw. Concern rapidly replaced confidence. This was quickly superseded by its edgier relative, panic. Flashes from the muzzles of rapid-fire weapons strobed the room, illuminating less and less movement as more and more of the intruders went down.

On the pedestrian path below, all that Lajjun and the three clerics could see of the fight were those same muzzle flashes, visible behind windows and doorways. Shouts and screams filtered down to street level between shots. Head tilted back as she stared up at the veranda of her home, Lajjun held her daughter close. Ziza gazed wide-eyed at the second-story confusion. Though she was very mature for her age, it was just as well that walls and railings obscured her view.

Sooner than anyone could have predicted, it was

quiet once again. Though as curious as anyone would have been to view the aftermath of all the fighting, the occupants of nearby houses sensibly kept their windows shut and their heads inside. Tragically, it was often at the end of violent confrontations that the innocent and uninvolved caught the last stray bullet. While the fighting had taken place right next door, sensible neighbors knew it was better to learn the details via the morning news.

At the top of the stairway, Imam and the young soldier charged with restraining him squinted past the shattered doors at the second-floor room. Something was coming toward them. A single figure. The soldier momentarily forgot to breathe. The figure was not armored. It was alone. No one flanked it, no one held a gun to its back. Which meant that except for the prisoner, he was also alone. Of his ten comrades there was no sign. The implication paralyzed him as effectively as any nerve agent.

The remaining figure came closer. The man was not especially tall, but very wide. He filled much of the stairway. For a moment, he stared at the young soldier. Then he reached out and calmly removed the knife from the younger man's grasp. When the soldier did not move, Riddick fluttered an encouraging hand in his direction.

"Shoo, now."

The soldier remembered to breathe. He also remembered his legs. Recalling the incident later, he considered it a matter of some pride that he had not fallen as he had stumbled down the stairs.

Alone with his host once more, Riddick murmured, "You mentioned—'her.'"

Sneaking a quick peek past the big man, Imam scanned the upstairs room. It was filled with lumpy, motionless shapes that hadn't been there a few minutes ago. "She, uh—she . . ." It took him a moment to find his voice. "She went looking for you. Followed your footsteps too literally, I'm afraid. People died."

Riddick inhaled deeply and shook his head. He never wanted that. But despite his best efforts, things had spiraled out of control. No good agonizing over it now. Together, the two men started downstairs. Imam could see that his guest had turned uncharacteristically thoughtful.

"She never forgave you for leaving."

"She needed to stay away from me." Shifting his gaze, Riddick met the other man's eyes meaningfully. "You all do."

They took care exiting onto the street, but the soldiers who had been guarding Imam's family and friends had already taken their leave—inspired, no doubt, by the words of the young soldier Riddick had spared. Whether or if they would return with reinforcements did not concern him. Very soon now he planned to be far, far away.

Everyone was staring at him. With expectation? If so, they were going to be disappointed. Imam would be, too. Knowing Riddick a little, he ought to have known better.

Sensing movement, he glanced up. Aereon was on the veranda, gazing down at him. Tricks. He didn't like tricks. Not when they were plied by others, and especially not when they were directed at him.

The little girl took a step forward. If she had any comprehension of what had taken place up above, it had not visibly affected her. "Are you gonna stop the new monsters now? The human monsters?"

He looked back up at the veranda. The Elemental was still there, watching him. They made eye contact for a moment. Then he turned and moved on, passing the girl without answering her question. In seconds, he was enveloped in shadow. It was his preferred place of abode.

From above, Aereon watched the big man depart. "Sad and difficult, conflicting and sad. He doesn't even know who he is."

A distraught Imam watched him go. Nearby, the clerics were murmuring worriedly among themselves. Imam hardly heard them.

Something made contact. Looking down, he saw that Lajjun had come up beside him to take his hand. She smiled reassuringly, and he smiled back. But he was troubled. It had not gone as he had hoped. Could the Elemental do more? She had not moved to prevent Riddick from leaving. Despite her abilities, Imam was not sure she could have done so. Perhaps she had felt similarly. Or maybe she had another reason for not intervening further. The Elementals were a strange spin-off of humanity. It was always hard to tell what one was thinking.

There was nothing more he could do. He knew Riddick well enough to know that even had they been able to restrain him, they would not have been able to compel him to do anything he himself did not want to do. Easier to move a mountain. That was only a matter of physics.

There was no equation to explain Riddick.

It was a beautiful, clear night. Clear as noontime to Riddick, who shunned the daylight. A quick check behind showed that no one was following him. Imam knew better, he assumed. Not that the delegate or his clerical friends could have stayed on Riddick's track for more than a few meters had they tried to follow him. The big man moved too fast, too silently. He could not disappear in a blur like an Elemental—but it would seem to others that he could come close.

He drew the ship locator without a thought for its original owner. Yesterday's news. It sprang to life when he opened it. Standing in the shadows, he waited for the instrument to lock in and provide him with a return route. This took only seconds. Striding out in the indicated direction, he passed a few citizens engaged in late-night business, or just out for a stroll.

He had covered some distance when he noticed figures on a rooftop. Clearly agitated, they were pointing skyward and jabbering excitedly among themselves. None so much as glanced in his direction.

Turning, he moved out from the darkness until he had a clean line of sight between buildings. The brightness of the comet caused him to squint slightly. It was clear what had unsettled the people on the roof. A *second* head was splitting away from the cometary nucleus. Riddick was able to see certain things those with normal eyesight couldn't. Was able to discern details. His expression did not change—but his direction did.

Near the outermost atmosphere of Helion Prime, the secondary head of the comet began to fracture. These multiple fragments resolved into conquest icons, each as massive and imposing as the next. Ice formed of frozen gases began to crack and flake away from what had formed the head of the "comet." Trailing the flotilla of camouflaged icons were shapes that were small only in comparison to the gigantic structures that had preceded them. Changing course and spreading out, they began to fall toward the planet below. As Necromonger warships, their appearance had been designed with intimidation as much as functionality in mind.

Riddick had been right. Recovering from his temporary paralysis, the young soldier he had spared had reported in. Now other soldiers were carting their dead colleagues out of Imam's house. An officer stood waiting to question the owner and his family. Delegate or not, the senior soldier thought grimly, if some kind of treasonous complicity could be proved, political connections would not save—

The screaming of launching weapons snapped his train of thought. Moving out onto the veranda, he stood with his head back, mouth agape, staring. The family he was supposed to be questioning stood not far away, forgotten. Noticing this, Imam quietly shepherded his small flock toward the stairs. No one stopped them as they descended, passing soldiers both dead and living. The latter were now moving about with greater urgency.

Once back out on the street, the family turned to gaze skyward. The night sky was alive with moving lights that were brighter than stars. High-velocity missiles left streaks of fire in their wake as they soared upward, while pulse weapons blitzed the bowl of heaven with multiple blasts. Their targets were other lights, descending. They illuminated the innocence of Ziza's face as she stared up at them.

"So pretty . . . ," she whispered, seeing but not understanding.

Interior illumination had sprung to life in the buildings that neighbored their own. Ignoring them, Imam lowered his gaze and whispered urgently to his wife.

"We take nothing. Nothing but ourselves."

He sensed they did not have much time. Putting his hands protectively behind his wife and daughter, he guided them away from the only home they had known and off into the darkness of the city night. It did not matter that he was an important member of the government. It did not matter that his financial resources were substantial. Only one thing mattered anymore.

Reaching the shelter on the other side of the river that would protect his family from the lights that were falling from the sky.

V

Disdaining the speed and convenience an internal conveyance would have provided, Riddick had climbed the exterior of a dark building until he reached its roof. Though it would have seemed difficult to anyone else, it had been an easy ascent for him, far simpler than many he had been forced to make on less civilized worlds. Now he stood and looked up, his view and field of vision much improved.

The sky was aflame with flashes and bursts of brilliant destruction, as if two flocks of phoenix were engaged in mortal battle. The fire grew steadily more intense as more and more defensive weaponry was brought online. The noise was overwhelming. Riddick increased his pace, sprinting over the rooftops. While citizens below gawked openly at the aerial conflict, even with his goggles on he was forced to shield his uniquely sensitive eyes from the brightest explosions.

The gap between buildings that loomed before him was clearly too wide for any human to leap. As such, it required extra effort on his part to clear it. Feet first, he slammed down hard on the other side. As he did, atmosphere and ground began to quake all around him. There was something new in the air, and it wasn't the scent of roses.

Unimaginably vast, the dark mass was descending under exquisite control. It loomed above the city, hovering as if with a mind of its own. Within, individual minds functioning as one were deciding where to move first. As Riddick continued to run, the mass shifted slightly toward the center of the capital. Defensive weaponry raised harmless blisters of fire on the object's flanks, deflected by its massive screens.

Perhaps something emerged from the underside of the mass. Or it might have let loose with a wave projection instead of particulate matter. Whatever the source, the result was a shattering concussion. For an instant, the center of the city was lit up as if by sunlight. Seeking shelter, any shelter, Riddick leaped just as the shock wave reached him.

Throughout the city, chaos, as it usually did in such situations, reigned. Panicked citizens scrambled for the imagined safety of strong buildings, monuments, hillsides—anyplace they could think of. One of the first and most natural sources of shelter were the public transit stations that lay underground. It was there that Imam had taken his family, not only to escape the attack, but in hopes of securing speedier transportation to the assembly point than mere walking could provide. To his delight and relief, there was an automated transporter car already in the station. Leading his wife and child, he struggled to force a path through the surging mob, not all of whom were trying to board the vehicle.

Then the effects of the same tremendous explosion that had blown Riddick off his rooftop struck, and the interior of the station went completely dark.

The lights of the capital of Helion Prime were failing, the dominating beacons being extinguished one by one from the center toward the countryside. Hovering above the destruction and devastation was the single black mass. Beneath it, replacing the joyful light of the beacons, was an impact cloud: ominous in its implications, implacable in its spread. After a moment, as if studying what it had done, the black mass began to move again, slowly, but with defined, inimical purpose. Looking for something else to smash.

A lull followed the immense detonation that had flattened the city center, as if the sky itself had been momentarily shocked into silence. There was dust everywhere; the powdered flesh of broken and shattered buildings. Beginning to rise above it all was the seeping stench of death. Having been moved from panic to despair, the citizens of the capital were running in all directions, as if by sheer good fortune they might somehow stumble on a way out of the total destruction that had enveloped them. Bedlam had descended on them without warning, and they were ill prepared for it. Having no idea what was happening or why, screaming, howling, crying, they surged back and forth like ants trapped in a rising pond, their only common denominator the fact that there was a general consensus of movement away from the devastated city center.

One figure was an exception. Keeping to the remaining shadows as much as possible, grateful for the clouds of dust that obscured the brighter lights of distant explosions, Riddick fought the flow, working his way back *toward* the central business and commercial district. Too shell-shocked to care, few of the other refugees thought to wonder why one man was pursuing a single-minded course in the direction of what must surely be certain death. Those who did pause briefly to speculate on the lone runner's bizarre choice of destination were sure he had gone crazy. In that, he certainly now had company. In madness lay one unarguable way out of what had befallen them.

The rising thunder slowed him. Something was happening off to his left. Changing course, he angled toward the sound. Whatever was generating it was big, very big. Rounding the corner of a once-beautiful, now collapsed building, he came to a sudden stop.

Dark dust clouds enveloped the fringes of what at first glance appeared to be a massive, undamaged structure. It seemed impossible that any building of any consequence could have survived the detonation that had obliterated much of the city's center. He was right. What he was seeing was not a building.

Removing his goggles allowed him to clarify the vision. Rising from the ruins of one of Helion Prime's great beacons was a conquest icon. He was impressed, and Riddick was not a man to be impressed easily. That was the purpose of such a construct, of course. The rising crescendo he had heard was still sounding, the rumble of engines reaching release strength as small fighter craft began to detach from the icon and take to the air. Though he did not expect any of them to pay attention to a lone survivor, he nevertheless clung to the shelter of the ruined building. Even a big dog will snap at a bug, if it's in the mood.

On board and within the bowels of the Basilica, uniformed figures worked silently at their stations. Their surroundings were darkly baroque, a reflection of the Necromongers' affection for design as well as efficiency. Believing that everything ought properly to echo their deeply held values—a tenet of the faith that extended all the way back to Oltovm the Builder—even the battle command center had been constructed with these in mind.

One figure in particular commanded attention. Pacing concernedly but unworriedly back and forth, checking readouts and statistics with his own eyes, the Lord Marshal followed the progress of the campaign. Penetrating eyes glittered within a face that was lean without being drawn. As he passed one monitor station, its operator glanced up at him.

"One foot on the ground."

The Lord Marshal nodded tersely. Everything was going as planned. It always did.

Below, squadrons of Necromonger fighters cut through the air, searching for targets. They were met by Helion ships whose pilots were dedicated and well trained but most of whom lacked the kind of actual combat experience that had been mastered by their opponents. Nevertheless, they fought with determination and courage. Kills were scored by both sides.

Like dying moths, ship after ship was struck, to curl and spiral its way finally to the ground.

Behind the Necromonger fighters, the warrior ships were descending. Transports packed with troops and ground vehicles, they rode the first shock wave of success as they dropped toward the devastated city below. It was a scene being played out all across the surface of Helion Prime, as the invaders targeted every major population center simultaneously. To do so required seamless coordination, which the Necromongers possessed in plenty. But it was on the capital, as always, that they focused their efforts. An enemy could always be subdued by repeated stabbings, but victory came far sooner and easier if the head could be cut off first.

Not all of the Helion fighters were intercepted and dealt with by their Necromonger counterparts. The Helion pilots were too good for that. A number of them got through the screening fighter craft to engage the descending warrior ships. Few did any damage against the massive vessels—but one pair did.

An enormous explosion blew off the front of one transport. Unbalanced, its command center destroyed, it lurched to one side as emergency navigation systems struggled to correct and maintain a proper angle and rate of descent. They failed as destruction ripped through the rest of the craft. It promptly blew up, and almost as immediately, imploded as its gravity-defying propulsion system collapsed in on itself. The result temporarily lit the sky around it, blinding everything and everyone not equipped with appropriate protection.

Back out on the increasingly empty streets, a desperate Imam led his family forward on foot. When his daughter, exhausted, slowed to a stop, he picked her up and settled her on his shoulders.

"Hold on, Ziza. Hold on tight, and don't let go." With a nod at Lajjun, he resumed running. He would do so until he, too, dropped. And then, he told himself determinedly, they would crawl.

Across the city, in areas cleared of defenders, the enormous warrior ships were already setting down, disgorging battalion after regiment of helmeted, armed soldiers. Their motivation was simple, their methodology straightforward. It had already been pursued with great success on many worlds, ever since the Necromongers had made their presence and their determination known to the rest of the developed galaxy. Implacable and humorless, they surged eagerly out of their ships, responding to the directives of their officers as they fanned out across the capital in search of resistance.

As always, and as was proper, they envied those they intended to kill.

High above, the Basilica hovered in low orbit. It was well out of range of the majority of independent, ground-based defenses and too well escorted and screened for surface-to-space craft to reach. Not impregnable, but as close to it as Necromonger technology could make it. Those aboard would have felt confident even in the absence of such defenses. When one has been educated and enlightened to have no fear of death, it is easy to go about the business of war.

The tech officer who had spoke earlier turned once

again to the tall, angular figure standing behind him. "Second foot down, Lord Marshal."

The leader checked his own personal chronometer. "Already ahead of schedule. It is as our scouts reported. This system has been too wealthy, too content, for too long. Their equipment is good and their training adequate but no match for those who have been through battles for worlds. Nor for those who are properly motivated."

Wandering to his left, he paused before a lensing port. Not truly a hole in the floor of the great ship, it perfectly duplicated what one would have seen through a hole in the floor, with the added benefit that one was not exposed to temperature fluctuations or radiation from outside. As the battle for control of the planet below raged on, he was joined by a second figure, one even more at ease, and more richly garbed. The two men acknowledged each other with a glance.

"All those poets, on all those worlds: the ones who spoke of battle being such an unsightly thing?" The Lord Marshal nodded at the view presented by the lensing port. "They never stood here, did they? Strange how, from a distance, war can actually be beautiful."

Below, it was as if much of the planet was enveloped in a lightning storm, flashes of light erupting and fading at significant points, some clear and sharp, others muted by cloud. The latter would not slow the forces that had been dispatched to take control of their respective regions, he knew. A Necromonger was happy to fight in any kind of weather.

The flashes had grown noticeably fewer since the last time the Lord Marshal had looked.

Next to him, the Purifier stood quietly as he considered the tiny flickering lights far below. None of it was new to him. He had observed the same on numerous worlds. The end here would be no different. It could not be otherwise.

"Perhaps this time," he murmured, "converts will be easier to come by. It is discouraging when so many die without having known why they have lived. Without having been given the truth." A hand gestured at the port. "Good fighters, these. Not their fault they cannot conceive of what they are up against. Those that survive will make good converts to the cause." Turning away from the scene below, he eyed the Lord Marshal. "Care should be taken to preserve as many as possible."

The Lord Marshal shrugged slightly. "The work must be finished first. And lessons delivered where necessary."

"Very true," agreed the Purifier. "However, it is a wise man who, when cold, seeks other means of warming himself besides setting his clothes on fire."

It was not quite a grin that appeared on the Lord Marshal's aquiline visage. But the Purifier could see that his observation had been duly noted.

"I see it all now," the leader of the Necromonger movement murmured. "This world, this Helion Prime, first. Soon, the rest of this system, for with their primary world taken, the others will fall with nary a fight. Then, battling on through the dwindling outposts of man; world after world, system after system. And then—the Threshold. I can sense it. Rising on the foundation laid by all the previous lord marshals, I shall be the one to at last achieve that goal. Under this regime, we will *all* cross the Threshold." He did not raise his voice. He was only stating what he believed to be self-evident.

The Purifier was more cautious. It was incumbent on him to be so. One of his tasks was to convey reality to the excessively enthusiastic. "Intending no disrespect, but you are not the first to believe thus. Others have had your vision."

"But not with such clarity." The Lord Marshal's gaze rose ceilingward, toward the unseen reaches beyond the Basilica's immense hull. "I tell you, I have seen it! There have been many lord marshals before me. Great men, all, who performed nobly for the cause. There will be none after. There will be one last lord marshal. And he is right here."

The Purifier did not respond. There was no point in trying to apply reason to absolutes. Also, by questioning the Lord Marshal he had performed a useful service. Arguing further with him would gain nothing. Except, perhaps, consideration of a new senior purifier. This man might really be the last lord marshal. His vision might be true. If so, there would be no need for additional purifiers. As for himself, he had no intention of surrendering his office prematurely.

Imam slowed as he neared the plaza. Ziza was walking on her own once again, holding tight to

Lajjun's hand, her small fingers entwined tightly in the woman's stronger ones. The delegate turned to them both.

"Ahead—just ahead."

Exhausted and filthy, they slowed to a walk. The next corner brought the broad plaza clearly into view.

It was empty.

Buildings lay flattened on its perimeter. The trees and flowers that had decorated the broad, open space in patterns of green and gold and crimson had been snapped in half or blown away. A few frantic shapes appeared on the plaza's far side, quickly vanishing into the rubble. Normally crowded with hundreds of strollers and businessfolk on break, the circular meeting place was deserted.

Too young to be intimidated, too bold to keep silent, Ziza tugged on her mother's hand. "Where is everybody? This is *spooky*."

Her father shot her an irritated look, but said nothing. The eerie silence was compelling.

It was almost as silent in a back alley nearby, where debris and dust were rising from the ground, caught in the fringes of a gravitational eddy. Abruptly, armored figures scattered the dust, riding their unloading field to the ground. Armed and ready, the platoon was but one of many being disgorged by the transport craft that was advancing slowly over the rooftops nearby, seeding armored death as it passed.

Once assembled, the platoons split up and headed off in different directions, each on the lookout for resistance. One of them carried a device that was a miniature of the conquest icon. Far too small to serve as a launching pad for warcraft, it had another, equally disturbing function, albeit on a smaller scale.

Blade concealed but ready, Imam took a deep breath and headed out across the plaza. Though the sky was still full of fire and destruction, both had lessened considerably in volume and intensity. Nothing fell on him, nothing descended to wipe him from the pavement. Fast as they had run, he knew that the time remaining to him and his family was finite.

Reaching the central rotunda, he crouched low and performed a circular scan of the immediate vicinity. In better times, music had blared from this small, decorative structure. Better times might come again, he felt, but not soon. And that would not matter, if he and his wife and daughter were not around to witness it.

Satisfied that the area seemed safe, he straightened and motioned across the empty pavement, beckoning Lajjun and Ziza to join him. They could wait in the rotunda until he had scouted out the other half of the plaza. He started to rise.

It was difficult to tell who arrived on opposite sides of the plaza first: the platoon of Necromonger soldiers or the brigade of Helion fighters. Though outnumbered and outgunned, the Necromongers did not hesitate. Nor did they attempt to take cover. Instead, they unlimbered their sidearms and rushed straight toward the much larger number of Helion defenders. To someone trained in conventional military tactics, it would have looked like a suicide charge. Initial developments did nothing to dispel the validity of such an observation. In no mood for a display of politesse, the Helions opened fire immediately.

Ignoring the burst of gunfire and waving his arms wildly, Imam started toward the ruined building where his family awaited. "No!" he screamed as loudly as he could. "Keep back, stay there, don't—"

The furious fire from the Helion defenders would have tracked and eradicated him as a possible enemy combatant had not a pair of hands grabbed him and pulled him down. He fought briefly against the pull, and futilely. It was as if he had been caught and dragged down by limbs of metal instead of flesh. Effortlessly, but with care, they slung him into the deep shadows of the rotunda. He still held the knife. Rolling furiously, he started to come up and face whoever had tackled him. A flash of dim light on goggles stopped him. He knew those goggles.

Crouching opposite Imam, Riddick quietly contemplated his old acquaintance. As always, it was impossible for Imam to tell if the big man was irritated, angry, or merely indifferent.

"Are you following me?"

It would not have mattered if Imam had been able to come up with a sensible answer. Anything he might have said would have been drowned out by the roar of gunfire as the Necromonger platoon clashed with the much larger Helion force.

Attacking with what seemed to be more bravery than military sense, the Necromongers pushed in on the Helion soldiers—and were cut down, one by one, as repeated shots reduced armor and bodies to ruin.

In the end, only the soldier carrying the small conquest icon survived—just long enough to plant his burden in the ground and deploy a release mechanism. There was a soft *poomph* as the head of the icon cracked open. Something missiled out and up, to pause overhead.

Wary but increasingly confident, the Helion soldiers advanced beneath it. Spinning, levitating, the lambent orb of pale energy resembled some kind of aerial marker, or perhaps a distress signal. If the latter, it had been deployed too late. Every member of the Necromonger platoon lay dead or dying on the plaza. Watching their perimeter, the Helion force continued to advance across the devastated plaza.

Within the shadows of the rotunda, Imam struggled to rise. "Lajjun and Ziza—they're out there."

"Out there where?" Riddick asked him.

Restrained in the big man's grasp, the delegate could only flail helplessly in his family's direction. "Southwest side, under a broken roof. I've got to get to them. They don't know what's happening, don't know where I am. Just let me—"

Riddick held him back, the way an owner would a puppy. "When it's over."

"When it's over? *When it's over?*" Rising as much as Riddick would allow, Imam gestured in the direction of the recent firefight. "Didn't you see what happened? This group of invaders, they're all dead. It is over, at least for the moment." He struggled to rise. "*Let me go*. I need to be with—"

"When it's over," Riddick repeated. Despite what Imam implied, the big man had seen what had happened. And it hadn't made any sense to him. No thinking fighter, however well motivated or brainwashed or drugged, went marching stoically into the face of visibly superior firepower without some purpose in mind. Distraction, perhaps. Something more—they would know, as he had told Imam, when it was over. Which to Riddick's way of thinking was Not Yet.

The rotating energy orb did not dissipate, nor did it change position. Increasingly convinced that, whatever it signified, it might be something more threatening than a distress signal, the officer in charge of the Helion unit ordered his troops to back off. They would go around the plaza. Standing out in the open any longer than was necessary was an invitation to attack. Voices crackled in his suit communicator. Something about something—behind them.

The Necromonger soldiers who had appeared behind the Helion brigade had materialized as silently as their comrades in the plaza had died. Now perhaps a hundred of them blocked the street the brigade had used to enter the plaza. A check of another street revealed another hundred or so of the enemy had already taken up defensive positions there.

Approaching from across the plaza came a third group. Threatening and unexpected, but not invincible. All they had to do, the Helion commander realized, was attack any one of the three columns and reduce it while defending themselves against the other two. They were outflanked, but not outnumbered or outgunned. Inclining his lips toward the pickup in his helmet, he prepared to issue the necessary orders.

At the front of the Necromonger column that was advancing on the plaza, a senior officer halted. Vaako was a favored commander, unusually young to have achieved such a high rank. For an instant, he observed the preparations taking place among the Helion force. It appeared that they were going to make a charge, in his direction. Another officer in a similar battlefield situation might have been concerned, might have rushed to prepare his own troops to withstand the frontal assault.

Instead, Vaako removed from one pocket a compact signaling device. It was small in size, but not in import. Unhesitatingly, he raised his gaze until it was focused on the pale orb of energy that continued to drift above the plaza. It was significant not for what it displayed, but for what it represented. He pressed the single button on the mechanism, transmitting a certain signal to his assembled troops.

Strange thing, gravity. Abstract in concept to all but mathematicians and physicists, when wielded by guiding instrumentation it could move mountains. Or crush them. The Necromonger soldiers who had encircled the area fired—not on the Helion defenders they had surrounded, but toward the hovering orb. Absorbing the combined energy of the discharged weapons fully activated the device. When the sphere of now massively increased gravity descended, it punched a neat, perfectly round hole in the plaza to a uniform depth of half a meter. Within its circumference, everything was crushed to a thickness of less than a millimeter. It was as if the ground had been painted with a smeared combination of metal, pavement, bone, and blood—an abstract vision of ghastly color gratefully muted by the night sky. Within that circumference had been decorative paving stones, railings, and every one of the Helion soldiers. Now all that remained was a multihued stain barely thick enough to scrape.

Having raised his head just enough above the rim of the rotunda to witness the shockingly sudden massacre, Imam found himself stunned and sickened by what he had seen. In contrast, Riddick was nodding slowly, his expression neutral, his opinion of what he had seen wholly unemotional and professional.

"Beautiful. Clean, quick, no mess."

Sitting on the hard floor of the rotunda, his back pressed against the curving inner wall, Imam stared at his companion. He really didn't know anything about this man, he realized. Drawing him here had been an expression of desperation leavened with faint hope. A last-minute thought before the darkness descended, as it was doing even now. And very possibly, a waste of time.

Time. Time was something he had always had, but was now rapidly running out of. But what to do next, how to proceed? Especially given the horror he had just witnessed.

Unexpectedly, Riddick had a suggestion. He was not one to dwell on the past, even if that past was only a matter of days. Understanding, if not sympathizing, with why Imam had conspired to draw him here, he rested an arm on one knee while dividing his attention between his companion and the mob of Necromonger soldiers that was forming up to leave the plaza.

"I've got a ship; she's ready to roll. Come ride bitch if you want."

Didn't the man realize he had other concerns? "No, no, I'll stay to fight. This world has been good to me, and I owe it that much. But I just need to get my family across the river first. There's an underground facility there, built to shelter citizens displaced by severe weather, where they'll be safe."

Impatient, Riddick interrupted him. "You'll never get there." He jerked his head in the direction of what had once been the Helion system's center of power. "Too many ships, too many scans. Too many guns. If one of them doesn't shoot you, one of your own's liable to."

Imam looked at him: pleading not with words, but with his eyes. "I have to try. I could go with you, but they can't."

The unspoken implication behind the man's words being, Riddick knew, *You take too many chances, I don't really trust you with my family, and what kind of existence would they have in your company anyway even if you could make it out of here?* The big man was not offended. Reality never offended him.

"You know, I'm sure God has his tricks. He plays them often enough. But getting outta hellified places no one else can? That's one a' mine." He smiled thinly. "I prefer practice to prayer." He glanced briefly over the rim of the rotunda before nodding tersely in the other man's direction. "Get your family,

Imam. Stay low, move fast, and tell 'em to keep their mouths shut."

No one thought to recheck the rotunda that sat in the center of the plaza. It was too small to provide a refuge for Helion soldiers, and civilians were not yet a prime interest of the invaders. Having assembled an appropriately impressive ground force from the three columns of soldiers, Commander Vaako was now leading it across an approach bridge. On the other side lay the capitol dome, purposely left intact by his forces. An appropriate place for accepting the capitulation of the planetary government.

He could have surrounded the place with dropships, but marching up in good order across the bridge would be far more dramatic. It would also serve to testify to the complete dominance of the Necromonger force, and to its indifference to any defense the locals might still think of mounting around their capital. Show was important, Vaako knew. The idea was to crush resistance as quickly and ruthlessly as possible, so as to preserve as many enemy fighters as possible. Preserve them for purification and incorporation. A good many of the troops now formed up behind him—armor glistening, weapons at the ready, were converts from previously conquered worlds. Soon Helion Prime, too, would contribute its share.

A quick, efficient glance at his surroundings showed several gravity orbs still circling above different parts of the city. From time to time, a deep-throated booming would echo over the streets as one was activated and dropped. The Helions were good fighters and there was still some resistance. All the more reason to secure the government's unconditional surrender as rapidly as possible.

He checked his posture, straightened. It would not do for the man inside the armor to appear less impressive than his suit. It was important to make a good first impression. It was important that the locals fear him on first sight.

Time and time again Riddick found himself having to slow down to allow Imam and his family to catch up. While he was not even breathing hard, they were sweating profusely and gasping for breath. To her credit, the little girl did not complain. Only once, when she stubbed her foot. As her mother brushed at her tears and tried to quiet her, Riddick came over and stared down. Meeting his eyes, Ziza quickly went silent.

Lajjun looked up at him uncertainly. "Do you have a way with children?"

He shook his head curtly. "Only with real people. She qualifies." Turning, he resumed leading them onward into the night.

They moved as fast as the woman and the girl could manage, avoiding obstacles that included ruined buildings and dead soldiers—the latter mostly, but not exclusively, Helion. Imam felt they were making excellent progress, when Riddick suddenly spied something approaching and motioned them to move back. There was an urgency to his gestures that barred dissent.

Well hidden in the rubble, they did not see the

creatures that came loping slowly up the cross street. Riddick had spotted them just in time. While he was not familiar with and did not recognize their specific physical configuration, he had seen enough in that split second to suspect their purpose.

First one lensing Necromonger and then a second appeared, followed by a specialist squad of soldiers. The lensors were troops who had lost their faces, or parts thereof, in battle, but who through the application of modern military medical technology remained—salvageable. Eyes and ears gone, mouths replaced by injectors, even noses blasted away, they had been converted into tracking devices whose melding of human biologics and electronic enhancements could not be equaled by equivalents that were either purely organic or wholly mechanical. Eerily silent, they led the way along the thoroughfare, single-mindedly searching for survivors. In ancient times, humans had used specially trained dogs for such purposes.

Leading this particular mop-up team was a Necromonger warrior of singular size and reputation. He was not called Irgun the Strange because of his distinctive facial features, his manner of speech, or even his sometimes peculiar personal affectations. Rather, he had acquired the name because during one especially intense battle on a long-since conquered world, he had received a knife in the middle of his back. This very low-tech manner of attack had importunely struck and penetrated so close to his spine, the blade curving slightly but critically as it entered, that even Necromonger surgeons felt it could not be removed without considerable risk. That, however, was not what had inspired the singular nickname.

It was the fact that he had chosen to leave the knife—blade, hilt, and all—where it was. It protruded from the center of his back like a flag, a rallying point for his fellow soldiers and a warning to any enemy. *Here is my pain,* it declared for any and all to see. *I welcome it, I embrace it, in the service of the faith.* In its utilitarian appearance, in its owner's indifference to its presence, it was more frightening to an adversary than any deformity of face or body. On observing the injury, the Lord Marshal himself had praised Irgun for his defiance of pain, and had insisted that the blade remain forever where it lay.

As Irgun and his squad swept their surroundings with waiting gun muzzles and sharp eyes of their own, the lensors scanned everything in range or sight of their enhanced senses. Streets, windows, doors, cracks in the ground—all were subject to the same remorseless scrutiny. Occasionally, they found something. Some feeble sign of life. Wounded soldiers being more trouble to the cause than they were worth, they were efficiently finished off by Irgun's team.

Instantly divining the source of the squad's leadership, Riddick determined to start there, before the busy lensors could find him and those who had consigned themselves to his care. Working the darkness and the shadows as only he could, he slipped out of his hiding place and advanced. As he moved, the blade he carried shifted from hand to hand. In an instant, he had drawn close. Should he do it now? Or should he wait, hoping the lensors' senses would overlook the only active life-forms within blocks? He decided to wait.

The squad moved on, lensor heads moving slowly from side to side, soldiers watching, waiting, but not taking aim. Imam and his family stayed where Riddick had put them, holding their breaths. Trying to hold their heartbeats. The Necromonger team was rounding a far corner. Except . . .

There was another lensor. Trailing the squad, it hesitated. Perhaps Lajjun breathed too strongly and it detected the sudden rise in carbon dioxide. Possibly Ziza inhaled too sharply and the working of her small lungs was overheard. Or it might have been the pounding of Imam's heart. Whatever the reason, the creature turned. Locking on, it began to move directly toward the family's hiding place. Noticing their bloodhound's sudden change of direction, several of the soldiers changed direction to follow. One proceeded to alert the others.

Seeing the Necromongers coming toward them, Imam reacted without thinking. Bolting into the open, robes flying, he sprinted as hard as he could for the ruined buildings on the other side of the street. As a gesture worthy of a parent bird or rabbit seeking to draw sniffing predators away from its nest, it worked. Irgun and his troop immediately gave chase. They could have cut him down immediately, but they were curious. A single Helion, in civilian clothes, running from them at high speed, constituted an unusual encounter in this part of the devastated city. He might be worth interrogating. While killing him would take only seconds, questioning would not take much more. Irgun was curious. So he and his troops pursued, but did not shoot.

It might be a diversion, of course. Any such sudden, unexpected action might be a diversion. So one soldier and one lensor remained behind, to keep watch, and to see if there was anything else that might have drawn the first lensor's curiosity.

Lajjun and Ziza huddled in their hiding place, pressed back as far as they could among the rubble. It was very quiet. It remained quiet even when the lensor's distorted, sensor-filled skull appeared above them. There followed a muted, cracking sound, but it was not the sound of gunfire, or even of sensors rendering confirmation. The lensor's head twisted around 180 degrees, its faceplate catching the starlight. Lajjun had never seen one of the creatures before, but given its otherwise human body she did not see how it could be capable of such a feat of skeletal dislocation.

It was not. The turn was entirely involuntary, forcefully induced by the man who now stood behind the slumping figure. With distaste, he let it fall to one side. It landed not on the ground, but on the body of a Necromonger soldier, dispatched recently and with equal efficiency.

Ziza's eyes were very wide, but to her credit the child somehow managed to keep silent. As for her mother, Lajjun could only whisper desperately. "Imam—can you find Imam and—bring him back?"

Life was simple, Riddick mused. It was always

people who complicated it, messed things up. Turning, he vanished into the night.

Expecting to feel his back explode at any second, Imam ran on, amazed by his continued existence. Could he have lost them? It seemed improbable, unreasonable. He did not slow down to ponder the unlikeliness of it. Still unwilling to accept that he was going to live through this, he thought he might have a chance if he could just reach one place, one special spot. After all, he knew the city, knew where he was. His pursuers did not. And Riddick remained behind, to look after his family.

It lay just ahead of him: a small pedestrian bridge. In normal times busy with strolling couples or exercising bureaucrats, it loomed like a darker slash against the night. There were places on the other side, a warren of pathways and tunnels through a nearby city park, where one might successfully hide even from trained trackers. If he could just get across it . . .

Something flashed through the air to one side. He wasn't sure if it leaped, or ran, or was propelled by some mechanism beyond his understanding. All he knew was that in one moment the narrow bridge stretched out empty before him, and the next.

The next, a single figure stood blocking the way. Slowing, Imam regarded the Necromonger. The man was huge, his armor designed to intimidate, his expression pitiless. All the humanity had long ago been drained out of him, lubricant for the soul that had never been replaced. Yet he did not shoot. Instead, he smiled encouragingly and beckoned for Imam to approach. The smile was as genuine as the rest of the man's expression.

Exhausted from running, frustrated at the events that had overcome him, in agony over what had happened to his innocent, beautiful home, Imam knew instinctively that whatever the soldier wanted, in the end they would not just let him go. He knew it as surely as he knew his faith, and his destiny. There was only one more thing he could do, and that was to try and extend for as long as possible the diversion that had sent him running from his family in the first place. He wanted to tell that to Lajjun. He wanted to tell it to Ziza, too. To try and explain what had happened to their life. It would not have mattered if he had been given the opportunity. Because he had no explanation. Maybe Riddick would discover one, he thought. Only that would not matter, because Riddick wouldn't care.

Locking eyes with the slowly advancing soldier, Imam pulled his plasma blade. Surprised, Irgun stopped. He continued to beckon, to encourage. Wondering which way he was facing and hoping it was the right one, Imam murmured a silent prayer. Then he attacked.

Moving fast, Riddick heard the distant guns discharge. He accelerated, keeping to the shadows. It would do no good to move faster. Better to stay out of sight and get there alive.

He slowed when he reached the bridge; scanning the span, both ends, the ruined buildings nearby, the destruction that dominated the far side. The only thing moving were a few insects, the ultimate survivors of any combat. In the distance and fading fast, he heard the sound of retreating boots. A distant glimpse of soldiers double-timing it away, dominated by one figure that towered over all the others, and then they were out of sight.

Cautiously, he moved out onto the bridge, stopping only when he saw moisture at his feet. He did not have to taste the blood to recognize it. The trail of dark liquid led to the opposite side. In a single leap he was on the parapet, balancing there easily. A solitary shape on the pavement below caught his eye immediately. He could not see the face, but he recognized the robes.

Should have killed them when I had the chance, he told himself angrily, thinking back to the initial encounter with the patrolling platoon. He had been too cautious. Because of the child? Should have trusted his first instincts. Death invariably followed hesitation.

The child. With a last glance to make sure all of the Necromongers had left and that there was nothing in the immediate vicinity capable of following him, he jumped down onto the bridge and rushed off into the night.

VI

Eventually, mercifully, dawn came to Helion Prime. The sunlight washed out the light from the fires that continued to rage throughout the capital and other major cities. Locally, the last pockets of resistance were being overwhelmed and mopped up by Necromonger forces. Outside the centers of commerce and industry, all was relatively quiet. Unable to affect their own destiny, country folk listened and waited to learn of their fate. They had nothing to say about it. Having not participated in the fight, they would be equally shut out of the peace.

Like a gigantic black beetle, something massive and dark squatted in the center of the capital. Come to ground, the Basilica was even more impressive than it had been suspended high in the upper atmosphere. It towered above the surviving government structures, dominating them as easily as a lion would a pack of cowed foxes.

Preparations for the armistice had been prepared as meticulously as the battle plan. The Basilica faced the damaged but still intact capitol dome. Flanking it were the warrior ships. Soldiers lined up on both sides of the towering doors at the bottom of the Basilica. The doors had been proportioned to impress onlookers, not because the command vessel was crewed by giants. As martial music flared, the barriers parted.

Backed by his field commanders and principal advisers, the Lord Marshal stood staring out at the battered surface of Helion Prime. Even from his interior vantage point he was able to make out the capitol dome and the ranks of hovering warships. At his appearance, the heads of the ranked vessels began to dip in perfect unison: an aerodynamic bow. The aerial ballet could not fail to impress any who saw it.

Eminently satisfied, he started down the wide steps. "It is time. Let's go replenish the ranks."

Commanders Vaako, Scales, and Toal trailed him as he exited the Basilica and strode toward the waiting capitol dome. The Purifier was there, too. Falling in alongside Vaako was a woman who held no formal military rank, but whose attention everyone sought. That she was partnered with Vaako did not keep others from trying to insinuate themselves into her good graces—and elsewhere. Vaako was aware of such efforts. They did not rouse him to anger because he understood the motivation. Having seen, or more properly, been exposed to Dame Vaako, most men and not a few women could do little else. That she had chosen to partner with him was a matter of some pride.

"Never fails to inspire, does it?" she commented

as they marched side by side. "Each time a dynasty falls. So much expenditure of effort, so much waste of treasure, all for naught in the end. As it always is, so it will always be."

Leaning toward her, an annoyed Vaako whispered tightly, "This is the Procession of Conquest. Mark your words and remember your place."

Unperturbed, she hooked her arm through his and nodded in the direction of the Lord Marshal. "Why? Do you worry *he* will overhear? He is too full of the moment of victory, too full of himself right now, to notice anything that does not reflect on his glory. As for my place, that is at your side, dear Vaako. From now till the UnderVerse come. Never doubt that."

"I don't," he replied with conviction. Raising a hand, he pointed. "Look. The ceremonial final."

A pair of Necromonger fighter craft had zeroed in on the huge symbol that crowned the capitol dome. A few perfectly placed charges smashed through its base. The symbol teetered unsteadily. Then, falling as if in slow motion, it toppled and spilled to the ground, cratering the surface where it landed. Digging its own grave literally as well as symbolically, Vaako mused. He did not think the intentionally violent gesture out of place. As an experienced warrior, he knew well the importance of symbols. In case any still doubted, it was visual confirmation of the fall of Helion Prime.

In the central meeting chamber, the leaders of Helion waited uneasily. Politicians, bureaucrats, ministers, clerics, they waited and whispered while surrounded by an elite corps of Necromonger fighters led by Irgun the Strange. Some of the representatives had come willingly, hoping to negotiate the best possible terms of surrender for their people. Others had arrived with hopes of working with the conquerors. Still more had been rounded up and chivvied along against their will, unable to escape or turned in by the first of the inevitable collaborators.

Silence fell as the Lord Marshal and his retinue entered. Without fear or hesitation, he started down the stairs toward the central dais. No one had to part the milling Helions for him. That he advanced alone, without flanking security, was not lost on the onlookers. Backing away, they gave him plenty of space, as if the radius of fear that surrounded him was a palpable thing and not just an impression.

Mounting the dais, he took time to study his surroundings as the Purifier joined him. The interior of the capitol dome was impressive—in the usual transitory, meaningless way of the ignorant and misguided. Like everything else, that would soon be corrected. As the Purifier began to speak, his words were heard clearly all the way to the back of the circular auditorium. The voice of the senior spiritual adviser of Necromonger society had no need of amplification.

"Leaders of Helion! Harken unto me and learn of the true reality. In this 'verse, life is antagonistic to the natural state of being. Here, humans in all their societies and sects are but a spontaneous outbreak, as Covu realized, an unnatural occurrence, an unguided mistake. Our purpose in coming among you is to correct this mistake. Because of the nature of the truth, we are compelled to bring forward our message of understanding and deliverance by those means that cannot be argued."

It was certainly not the speech the assembled had expected to hear: no talk of paying tribute, of installing satraps and governors over the existing provinces of Helion Prime. No thundering denunciations or threats of reprisal against the stiff resistance that had been put up by the planet's defenders. Some of those who had gathered in fear now began to relax ever so slightly. Others maintained their guard, as wary of what they did not expect as they were of that which they did not understand.

The Purifier continued, his voice rising, cajoling, persuading. "But let me tell you of another 'verse. A 'verse where life is welcomed. Cherished. Appreciated for what it represents. A ravishing, wondrous, all-encompassing new place called the UnderVerse. All one needs to reach this place is to walk the road that crosses over the Threshold."

"The Threshold," the assembled victorious troops intoned rapturously. *"Take us to the Threshold."* It was difficult to tell which was more unsettling to the assembled leaders of Helion: the volume with which their menacing guards thundered the request, or the massed unison with which they declaimed it. It smacked of political and religious philosophies long discarded in this part of the galaxy. As the sagest among them knew, technology had a way of granting new life to discarded dogmas. Technology, and promise.

"The Threshold," the Lord Marshal explained for the benefit of the confused—which at that moment included every non-Necromonger in the chamber—"is what you happen to call 'death.' Sadly, it is a term that throughout human history has been as misused as the condition itself has been misunderstood." He stood a little straighter on the dais. "We have been privileged to see through these historical misconceptions, and to find the one true road."

Nodding, the Purifier continued. "So you see that it is our 'verse—and not the one popularly thought of as the beyond or the end or any one of a number of other equally inaccurate designations—that must be cleansed of life so that the UnderVerse can populate and prosper."

The threat of the circle of watching soldiers notwithstanding, rumbles of discontent began to rise from the assembled Helion leaders. Not only from the clerics, whose own deeply held faiths were being so casually disparaged, but from their secular counterparts as well.

"I know the true name of your 'verse," someone shouted from within the crowd. "The perverse!"

Muting the rising discontent through the sheer force of his personality, the Lord Marshal stepped forward and replied. "*Look around you.* Look—are you afraid?" He waited while the sullen eyes of the subjugated scrutinized their vanquishers. "Every Necromonger in this hall—every one of the Legion Vast that just swept aside your planetary defenses in one night—was once like you. Fought as feebly as you. Commander, officer, soldier. Supporter, technician, adviser. All came from elsewhere, from elsewhen. From other empty, meaningless lives. From worlds not conquered by us, but liberated by us. From ignorance and delusion. Because every Necromonger who lives today and who serves the cause is a convert. A convert from ignorance and delusion."

His speech did not have the intended effect. The roiling sounds of discontent filled the chamber even louder than before. Why was it always so difficult? he wondered. Why were there always those who felt compelled to resist? He had come to think of it as a reflex action, no more planned than it was predictable. Some worlds were worse than others. He had not yet decided about Helion Prime. But it was always the leadership that was the most difficult to convince. Perhaps because they felt they had the most to lose. If only they realized that they had the most to gain.

It would not matter. The end would be the same. As it always was.

"*We all began as something else,*" the Purifier boomed, his voice rising above the swelling clamor. "I was once no different from you. No less resentful, no less angry. And no less uninformed. It was hard for me to accept, too, when I first heard these words. But I listened, and reflected, and in listening and reflecting I was changed. I let the words take away my pain. Just as you will, too, when you realize and accept that the Threshold to the UnderVerse will be crossed only by those who have received the Necromonger faith. For those who will, for those who are willing to challenge accepted ignorance on behalf of revealed truth, right now, drop to your knees and ask to be purified." Lowering his head, he stretched out his arms toward the crowd, as if willing them to give a positive response.

Emboldened by the semiconciliatory nature of the words that had been spoken, more and more in the crowd began to give voice to feelings that had been suppressed since the inevitability of their military collapse.

"You cannot expect us to do this, or to ask it so brazenly of our citizenry. So much has happened so quickly. They need time to recover, to consider, to discuss and debate the fine points of what you assert. Do you really expect all of us who believe, to on such short notice—"

"Renounce our faith?" a Meccan cleric interjected in disbelief.

"No one here will do what you ask," another well-known, well-respected politician declared boldly. He did not back down as the Lord Marshal descended from the dais and came toward him. Eyes locked on the approaching armored figure, the politician continued, making sure that everyone around him could hear.

"It's unthinkable. This is a world of many peoples, many religions. Our diversity is our pride. We simply cannot and will not cast all that aside, not even on the word of a military conqueror. You may triumph by military means, but your philosophy is alien to us, as it is alien to common sense, to reality, to—"

He gasped and sucked in his breath, his speech cut off in mid-sentence. Something had emerged from within the Lord Marshal. It was red and ethereal yet very real. It resolved itself for all to see into a third arm that plunged deep into the body of the politician. The man twitched, clutching at himself, his eyes threatening to pop from their sockets. When the astral limb reemerged it held something that writhed and twisted and all but screamed. The essence of self? A human soul? Never having seen the like before, none of the shocked and stunned onlookers could say for certain. They could only stare, and surmise.

The ethereal arm threw the torn, convulsing thing onto the floor. Even before it struck, the empty husk of humanity that had been the defiant politician was collapsing. He was dead before he hit the floor.

Content with the effect his action had produced, the Lord Marshal struck a pose and turned to survey the traumatized crowd that surrounded him. "Anyone else believe that our philosophy is alien to reality? Or that what you have just witnessed did not occur?" The silence that greeted his challenge was deafening. "Who will now bow and beg to, someday, cross the Threshold as one of the Select?"

Man by man, woman by woman, row by row, the leaders of Helion Prime dropped to their knees. They could not be defeated by words, but the brutal action of the Lord Marshal had served to subdue them completely. One could not deny the evidence of one's own senses. Who knew what other marvels these people could command? All of them wanted to know, to learn for themselves—but not by means of a personal demonstration. It was a mass capitulation that seemed final and complete.

Except for one figure that remained standing by the main entrance.

Vaako rolled his eyes. There was always one. One too obstinate or ignorant to conform. It appeared that the lesson was not quite over. As the nearest senior officer to the mulishly defiant one, he took it upon himself to cross the floor and confront him, halting with his face barely an arm's length from the man's own.

"Well?"

Leaning casually against the massive doorjamb, Riddick replied nonchalantly, "I'm not really with them."

Vaako frowned, unsure he had heard properly. No matter. "This is your chance. Your one chance to accept the Lord Marshal's offer. Consider yourself privileged. The Lord Marshal is being generous. Most times, such blatant displays of defiance are simply disposed of."

Riddick did not move. "I sign with no man."

Conscious of his larger audience, Vaako chose to exercise tolerance. For the sake of the defeated, it was useful to show that the reluctant could be persuaded as effectively with words as with weapons. One could blame this fool standing before him for his obduracy, but not for his ignorance.

"He's not a man," the commander explained patiently, as one would to a child. "He is the holy Half Dead who has seen the UnderVerse. He is much more than a man." He gestured toward the central dais, where the dead husk of the impertinent politician still lay. "Did you not see with your own eyes the palpable demonstration of his abilities?"

Riddick eased away from the wall, just enough for

Vaako to twitch in response. But the big man made no move toward the commander. "Tell you what. I'm not much into the bow-and-beg thing. Just doesn't do anything for me." He jerked his chin toward a massive figure that was rapidly approaching, recognizing the shape if not the face. "But I *will* take a piece of him."

A smile of expectation split the face of Irgun the Strange as he lengthened his stride. No one had asked him to silence this arrogant blasphemer. No one had given a formal order. But, sensitive as he was to the moods of his commanding officers, he knew that if he took the initiative to do so, no one would interfere to stop him. Raising not one but two ceremonial war axes, he knew that at this point, no one *could* stop him. His sole regret was that he was zeroing in on only one opponent. It would be over much too quickly, and he needed the exercise. Perhaps, he thought hopefully as he advanced, he could make it last long enough to be entertaining.

Seeing Irgun draw near, recognizing the look in the assassin's eye, Vaako stepped back out of the way. "A piece you'll have," he informed Riddick coolly.

Apparently unarmed, the intruder held his ground. Seeing that Irgun's quarry was not about to break and run, Necromonger soldiers and Helion politicians alike strained for a better look. Taking the measure of his opponent, Irgun saw nothing to give him pause. The prey even had something wrong with his eyes that forced him to wear some kind of special goggles; a maggot with shades. Irgun was not in the least ashamed to slaughter someone with a visible handicap. He was very much the egalitarian executioner.

Slowing slightly, he crossed the two axes he was holding in front of him. A few preliminary cuts—here, here, and here, he decided. Then a leap, perhaps with a twist, and he would bring both blades down and across simultaneously, neatly severing the foe's head from his neck. If the double stroke was delivered cleanly, blood should fountain from the severed neck for several seconds before the decapitated body collapsed. He intended to do right by the killing. Though more than slightly mental, Irgun took pride in his work.

Without preamble, he rushed forward. His target was big and muscular, therefore slow. Both axes came down and around to slice through . . .

Empty air. Faster than a scream, his target had moved to one side, twisting and spinning. As Riddick wisped past the charging assassin, one hand reached out, grabbed the hilt of the dagger that protruded from Irgun's back, and pulled it free. As he wrenched the shaft out of his attacker's flesh, the blade brought with it blood and bits of nerve.

Twin axes still gripped firmly in both hands, Irgun straightened. His expression of grinning expectation was replaced by one of surprise. He looked astonished. Then he looked dead. Falling forward like a tree cut straight through at the base, he formed an impressive heap on the floor—weapons, armor, communications gear, and all.

Those Helions in a position to see everything that had transpired let out a collective gasp. Among the

Necromonger soldiers there was a disbelieving shifting of bodies and raising of weapons. Murmured conversation among dissimilar groups traveled along similar lines.

Indifferent to the reaction he had provoked and satisfied with the statement he had made, Riddick turned and headed for the gaping portal. A single word boomed behind him.

"STAY."

Riddick paused. Abandoning the central dais, the Lord Marshal was moving toward him. As before, citizens of Helion and Necromonger warriors alike stepped back to give him more than ample room to pass. The radius of fear he projected seemed lost on the man he was approaching. Riddick held his ground before the Lord Marshal as stolidly as he had when faced with the onrushing Irgun. This fact was not lost on the Lord Marshal, nor on the Purifier who accompanied him.

Halting before Riddick, the Lord Marshal wordlessly looked him up and down. Riddick responded by doing exactly the same to the Lord Marshal. Like the man's indifference, this bit of calculated insolence did not go unnoticed by the Lord Marshal. He filed it for further reference. Every reaction of the defeated, even the disrespectful, was useful.

With one armored hand he indicated the nearby corpse. "Superbly trained. Utterly converted. A true believer and a dedicated servant of the cause. One of my best, Irgun."

Riddick didn't bother to look in the dead man's direction. His tone as well as his attitude indicated that he was singularly unimpressed. "If you say so."

The Lord Marshal was intrigued, as he was by anything out of the ordinary. At the moment, whether the man before him was supernally brave or supremely stupid did not really matter. What was important was his novelty. That, and his fighting ability. The former was a diversion. The latter might prove useful.

"Rare, isn't it? The knack for turning your enemy's strength into his fatal weakness? Quite rare. Usually a talent found in machines, in predictors. Not in individuals. You're an unusual man."

Riddick was moved to repeat himself. "If you say so."

The Lord Marshal almost smiled. With a nod, he indicated the bloody blade gripped with apparent (and only apparent) indifference in the man's hand. "So you like that blade?"

Riddick considered the weapon, testing it with a few speculative flips and whirls. They might have been performed by a magician, for all that those nearby were able to follow the movements. Vaako was grudgingly impressed. The Lord Marshal watched with silent appreciation.

"Half-gram heavy on the back end." Flipping it around, he considered it thoughtfully. "Not so good for throwing. Good metal, though. Unusual alloy. Never seen the like." He indicated the body of the dead Irgun. "Obviously no problem penetrating bone."

"In an age of high-speed compacted explosives,

energy weapons, and internal guidance systems there is something comforting about a killing device as ancient yet reliable as a knife." The Lord Marshal reluctantly watched the holder pocket the blade with one hand. "Yours, not mine. In our faith, we have a saying. 'You keep what you kill.'" He leaned forward, squinting intently, studying the impassive face of the man standing before him. "Are you familiar to me? Did we meet before, on some distant field?"

Riddick met the other man's gaze. And it was just a man's gaze, he had already decided—holy Half Dead or not.

"You'd think I'd remember."

The Lord Marshal nodded slowly. "You'd think I would, too. There's an inkling there I can't shake, but one I can't place, either. I don't like ambivalence. There's no room for that in one who seeks the Threshold. I think perhaps further investigation is in order. Nor, in such matters and despite my position, am I so vain as to eschew assistance." He looked to Vaako. "Bring him before the Quasi-Deads." The interview over, he turned and stalked away.

Functioning as one, Vaako and the elite soldiers nearby coalesced to form a tight, threatening ring around Riddick. Had he been a cat, his hair would have bristled. As it was, the only visible sign of any reaction was a slight tightening of his fingers around the haft of the knife. A couple of the soldiers pushed toward him. At a glance from their intended prisoner, they promptly stepped back. Uncertainty hung over the incipient confrontation like one of the rotating gravity orbs that had remorselessly flattened sections of the city.

A slim figure pushed through the ring. She was unarmored, at least in the conventional sense, and carried no weapons—at least in the conventional sense. That did not make Dame Vaako any less dangerous than the soldiers who flanked her. On the contrary. She stared with unabashed interest at the axle around which the soldiers wheeled.

"Perhaps the breeder would do it if someone just asked him, instead of threatening him with dozens of weapons." She advanced. Riddick's goggles lowered as he studied the new arrival with interest. His grip on the knife did not slacken.

"It's a rare offer," she continued. "For a nonbeliever to pay a visit inside Necropolis." Full of inscrutable promise, one finger rose to her lips and hovered. "Would you like to see me there?"

On his way back to the Basilica, the Lord Marshal now paused in the great portico. He frowned slightly. This was not a matter for Dame Vaako, and he disliked seeing her inserting herself in the middle of it. But being pragmatic, his primary interest was in results. He did not interfere.

Within the circle of soldiers, Vaako found himself liking even less the turn the confrontation with the insolent one had taken. Without an interjection from the Lord Marshal, however, he was obliged to let the scene play itself out.

Riddick was doing some investigating of his own. As he let himself be led onward, he inhaled deeply of the scent of one member of the party whose presence he was currently sharing. Anyone present would have had little doubt about whom he was referring to when he finally commented.

"Long time since I smelled beautiful."

VII

As a congealed celebration of death made of metal and stone, the interior of Necropolis was a daunting achievement. Designed by Oltovm the Builder and situated in the heart of the Basilica, the Necromonger command ship, it was a cathedral of the dead, a place to worship and salute the end of life. Towering and vaulted, it would have constituted an imposing enclosed space on any ground. That it existed and had been transferred whole and intact *inside* a starship only added to the effect it created on those who were allowed into its presence.

The sculptures that decorated its high walls, many commissioned by the great Kryll himself, were designed to make an indelible impression on all who looked upon them. Like the vast open space in which they were set, they were intended to impress upon visitors the inevitability of the final passage. Within its tomblike aura, dozens of the penitent and the hopeful trod the nearest thing to the Threshold the mind and skills of man could create. The overall result was to humble, to shrink, to reduce in stature any who passed through.

Riddick strode along coolly, taking it all in, his face betraying no clue to what he might be feeling. Flanked by Dame Vaako, the Purifier, and others, he followed the Lord Marshal without comment. The place was an absolute and unapologetic celebration of death, an embracing of biological termination that was almost loving. To almost anyone else, the sheer scale of it was nothing less than mind-boggling.

Riddick's mind was not easily boggled.

Dame Vaako had acted as guide and interpreter ever since they had entered the ship. A fusion of fiery pepper and thick honey, her voice tended to stir more than academic curiosity in anyone it favored. With Riddick, however, only the words themselves penetrated.

She gestured at the imposing surroundings as they advanced deeper into Necropolis. "Six regimes of Necromongers have called this home." She pointed to a row of imposing statuary. "Past Lord Marshals. All of them have crossed the Threshold. As will all those who believe, eventually. Magnificent, isn't it?"

"Kinda dark, even for me," Riddick replied, taking it all in. "I mighta gone a different way."

"True of us all," observed the Purifier candidly. "One's fate cannot be predicted at birth. Only time, circumstance, and study can properly prepare one for a life. We never know until then which way we will be asked to choose. All too often, no choice is given, and that way is forced upon us."

Continuing on, they passed beneath a suspension

bridge of living figures. Clamped into coffinlike assemblies of wires and tubes and instrumentation, their expressions ran the gamut from the tormented to the beatific. At a glance from Riddick, the Purifier explained.

"Converts. Some have difficulty adapting to what they have chosen. Here they learn how one pain can lessen another."

"Yeah," Riddick murmured. "This place is a real cradle of education."

They continued on, until a side passage emptied into a circular grotto that was as austere as the previous portion of Necropolis had been adorned with the lavishly macabre. It struck Riddick immediately that he had been allowed to take the lead and that no one had followed him in. He turned a slow circle. Dame Vaako stood in the portal through which he had entered. There was no sign of the others.

Too focused on the extraordinary to notice the ordinary, he chided himself, waiting for whatever might come. What came first was the voice of Dame Vaako, her tone as serpentine as her shape. It was unbending, but tinged with sympathy. Sympathy for what? he found himself wondering. What did he need her sympathy for? He had a feeling he was about to find out.

"Relax," she advised him. "Don't try to fight it. The more you resist them, the greater the potential damage will be."

"Them?" he thought to himself. *"Who the hell is 'them'?"*

He looked around sharply. Those were his words, his thoughts. But they had sounded aloud in the grotto, echoed by voices as wraithlike as they were distinctive. There was no one else in the chamber but him. Nothing else but floor, ceiling, and walls. Walls indented with dark hollows. He chose one, peering hard into its inky depths. Behind him, a door closed, shutting Dame Vaako away from view. He had been brought here for something more than a tour intended to impress him with the might and endurance of Necromonger society. There was something else in the grotto with him.

"Something in here that's—" He stopped. Or rather tried to. Easier to stop talking than to stop thinking. *"Who's saying that?"* His own mind was betraying him. Something was present; stealing his thoughts, repeating them out loud in a voice that was quavering but comprehensible. This was not something that could be shut down or cut off by the edge of a blade.

Peering at the single figure within, the Lord Marshal nodded to the Purifier. "Touch is established. Any time." Turning, the Purifier passed a hand over one lens among many that was set in a control panel.

Inside the grotto, focused gravity caught Riddick in its invisible grip and shoved him to his knees. The weight of his own body had suddenly become barely bearable. Hands pushing against the smooth surface, he fought to keep from being crushed all the way to the floor.

From a balcony above the chamber, elite soldiers watched the drama unfolding below. No matter how effective the tightly focused gravity or how helpless it appeared to render the subject, they had been instructed to be on full guard at all times. While privately questioning the need for what seemed to be excessive vigilance, they silently obeyed the orders they had been given. Standing opposite the guards, Vaako and his consort followed the play intently, knowing it could only have one ending.

In the center of the grotto Riddick struggled against a bond he was not only unable to break, but one he could not even get a grip on. As he struggled to keep suddenly heavy lungs working, he caught a change of light and shadow out of the corner of one eye. There was movement beyond the gravity lens that restrained him. Movement within the dark hollows that lined the far wall.

The shapes that came sliding out were tall and rounded. Whorls and inscriptions decorated their sides. They resembled the ancient ammonites of old Earth, but there was nothing primitive about the technology that drove them. Each supported, both physically and organically, a single body draped in a diaphanous shroud. Symbols and signs on shrouds and motile disks testified to the importance of the bodies they bore.

The bodies themselves did not move. They existed in a condition difficult even for accomplished biologists to properly describe. Commonly, they were known among the Necromongers who revered them as the Quasi-Dead, representatives of a unique order founded by Kryll himself. The same technology that preserved their bodies from final decay allowed the desiccated remains to serve as housings for minds that were as ruthless as they were insightful. All but freed from their physical forms, these minds were capable of inserting themselves into the mental pathways of others. They were able to view—and to search.

A wary Riddick tracked the apparitions as they trundled into place, forming a circle around him. Visually nothing more than a bunch of creepy corpses fastened to supportive platforms, mentally they were far more impressive. Almost immediately, they commenced their probing of the single subject pinned down before them.

"Wondering," the voices chimed. Looking at them, appraising them, Riddick was unable to tell whether they were all male, all female, or a mix thereof. It did not matter. Inside his head, they were all the same.

"Wondering about us . . . realizing now that we're in his mind. Beginning to fathom the Dark Thought. Trying to shut us out, shut down the here-and-now. Resisting—anything to resist. But vainly, so vainly. Cannot think not to think without thinking about it. The inevitable conundrum. It will fade and fail, as they all do."

Eyes shut tight, Riddick flinched as a mental thrust tore through his brain. Doing everything possible to resist, he quickly realized there was nothing he could do. If not restrained by the gravity lens, he could have run headfirst into the nearest wall and knocked himself out. But that would have been a foolish defense. Unconscious, he would be safe from the prying, from the probing. And then he would wake up, and it would start all over again. That much was obvious. He could not outwait his silent interrogators. The almost dead had an infinity of patience.

So he remained conscious and cogitating, trying to mute and protect his thoughts while simultaneously striving, searching for a way to fight back. Restrained in both body and mind, he found himself wilting under the relentless assault from multiple minds. Sensing growing weakness, they probed harder. They were not worried about damaging the subject. The body was resilient. Besides, they were much experienced at their work. A dead subject was a useless subject. So while they pushed, they also moderated their intrusion. The process of dragging information out of an unwilling subject was always an adventure.

"Thinking of escape now."

"Always an opening." Riddick tried, but was unable to keep from hearing his own thoughts repeated aloud for any who might be listening. And he had no doubt that many were. *"Wait for the chance and attack it. It'll come, it'll come. . . ."*

"Having many ideas now," the collective Quasi-Dead voice intoned solemnly. "All swirling, chaotic. A conscious attempt to confuse. As admirable as it is ineffective. An interesting specimen. An interesting mind. But still a mind; human, organic, unable to hide . . ."

The Lord Marshal had expected resistance. Subjects always resisted, at first. Some lasted only a few seconds before succumbing to the inevitability of the Quasi-Dead's probing. Others managed to fight for minutes. A few, a very few, went insane before the desired information could be extracted. He had ample confidence that this man would not go that way. Not until the Lord Marshal had learned what he wanted to know, anyway. He hoped the subject would survive intact, both mentally and physically. If not dangerous, he could be useful, as every good fighter was. Provided just enough of his mind was preserved.

"Regress," he ordered via a special pickup. One did not converse with the Quasi-Dead as one did to visitors across a table, with drink and food at hand and music playing in the background. But communication was possible.

There was a brief pause as the unique minds repositioned themselves mentally. Then, "New mindscape. Just hours old. Relevant image indistinct. Particularly strong retention factor. Wondering about some 'visitation'—who she is. Where she is from. Her purpose in appearing before him. Wondering what her appearance means for— Wait. Subject attempting to dissemble. Overcoming. Wondering what she means by—**Furyans?**"

The Lord Marshal twitched slightly. The scene being played out within the grotto of the Quasi-Dead now had his full attention. "Again," he ordered. "Regress again. Further. Distant past. Not hours, but years. All the way. Anything related. Seek significance. Seek clarification. Seek *link*."

The Vaakos were monitoring not only the interrogation within the grotto, but the questioning from without. Now Dame Vaako turned to the man next to her.

"Curious. The unusual intensity. Have you ever seen him this way? The Lord Marshal?" Her attention was shifting back and forth between the session taking place below and the two men responsible for its direction.

Vaako had been wholly absorbed in studying Riddick's attempts to fight off the inexorable intrusion of the Quasi-Dead. He glanced over at her irritably. "What's that? What 'way' is that?"

"Oh, I don't know," she responded casually. "Concerned. Worried."

Vaako shifted his attention to where the Lord Marshal and the Purifier stood talking together. "I don't see it," he replied finally.

She lifted one shoulder slightly. "I must be mistaken."

On the floor below, Riddick fought the regression as hard as he had battled the initial intrusion. It was a door in his mind he did not want to unlock. Not only for the relentless, probing Quasi-Dead, but for himself. He was not going to be allowed the privacy of self. Questing thoughts ripped and tore at his past.

It took the form of a visual metaphor. From nothingness, a hand reached out and extended through space. Seemingly endless, it terminated in thick, powerful fingers. A world appeared, green and lush. Was it the same world he had seen in his recent dream, while locked in cryosleep? The fingers plunged downward and tore into the surface of the planet as if its granitic crust were skin. The fingers dug for a moment before emerging with thousands of life-forms in their grasp. Minuscule wriggling shapes, near microscopic human life-forms no more than hours old. Oozing through the massive fingers as they clenched into a fist, the figures fell away screaming and crying into the great void of space—until only one remained. One child shape, infinitesimally tiny, dangling from between two fingers. Hanging on, fighting for life, screaming in pain. Screaming infant defiance. Screaming, screaming . . .

Abruptly, Riddick's eyes rolled back in his head. His body, already crunched beneath the force of the gravity lens, slumped forward. Outside the grotto, readouts unexpectedly went flat. Restless and disturbed, the Lord Marshal spoke forcefully from his position above.

"Bring it back. There is more I need to know. Where did he come from? His birth world? His subsequent history? These are things I need to know, and I need to know them—"

He broke off. Something was wrong. Leaning forward, he peered down into the grotto. The Quasi-Dead were shuddering atop their support platforms. Near-dead bodies twitched erratically. Legs virtually devoid of muscle spasmed atop their smooth, curving supports. Beneath ceremonial shrouds, sunken faces grew agitated.

"Something—new," the unified voices were chorusing uneasily. "Feedback in the dark thought. Not resistance—something more. Not receding—coming out. Coming forward." The sense of disquiet increased. "Need to stop. Stop the feedback before—before—"

Shifting his attention from the Quasi-Dead, the Lord Marshal focused intently on the subject.

"Keep him out. Out of the mind loop." The volume of their voices increased. Suddenly, there was a sense of panic. "Shut down the dark thought! Shut it down! Keep him away from us. Just keep him—"

Awed, Dame Vaako gave voice to her thoughts. "It's not possible. Not possible. He's scanning the Quasi-Dead. . . ."

"Kill the breeder!" the unearthly chorus was now shouting shrilly. "Kill the Riddick. Kill the Riddick! KILL THE RIDDICK!"

Within the grotto, the Quasi-Dead were jerking on their platforms as if an electric current had suddenly been applied to their supports. Cadaverous faces contorted, vacant mouths gaped wide. Bits and pieces of nearly decayed flesh and bone flaked from bodies one step removed from the dust.

In the stunned echo of the Quasi-Dead's rising dirge, the Purifier reached out and fired a hand over the console before him. Instantly, the gravity lens that had restrained the subject disappeared. Was it the correct reaction, or simply the first that came to mind? Clearly, the Purifier was reacting to the wailing of the Quasi-Dead. Whether he had reacted properly remained to be seen. But no one observing the unexpected turn the interrogation had taken could deny that something had to be done, and quickly.

Riddick did not waste time contemplating his restored freedom of movement. As soon as the agonizing pressure that had kept him pinioned in place was removed, he straightened. All around him, beleaguered Quasi-Dead were moving away, sliding backward on their mobile supports.

Outside the grotto, everything the Lord Marshal

had seen and heard compelled him to agree with the conclusion reached by the Quasi-Dead. Though he had not received all the information he sought, neither was he of a mind to go against their assessment of the subject. Without hesitation, he addressed himself to the nearest pickup.

"Kill the Riddick."

In response, three of the elite soldiers in attendance on the balcony leaped into the grotto. Vaako himself was not far behind them. Fighting to put themselves as far from the subject as possible, physically as well as mentally, the psychologically battered Quasi-Dead continued trundling unsteadily backward toward the hollow places in the walls, seeking the safety of their lightless sanctuaries.

Riddick did not have time to watch them go. He was busy.

The most active and eager elite was the first to go. Wanting to make it personal, he charged with blade in hand, a comrade close behind. As the first to make a mistake, he was also the first to die. Riddick blocked the blow, twisted, and sliced. As the blade was emerging from the soldier's already crumpling form and his colleague was raising his own weapon to strike downward, Riddick saw that the third soldier and Vaako were not about to engage in similar primitive foolishness. Both were leveling guns in his direction. He grappled with the second soldier.

And flung himself, dropping and rolling, just as Vaako and the other soldier fired. The shaped charges of their weapons arrived simultaneously, on opposite sides of the second soldier, and crushed his armor as if it was a can. With its owner inside. A mess resulted.

Four of the five Quasi-Dead had reached the safety and sanctity of their hollows. As Vaako and the surviving elite realigned their weapons, and as other soldiers came pouring into the grotto, Riddick picked up one of the dead soldiers' weapons, grabbed at the transport of the one remaining exposed Quasi-Dead—and let it drag him backward.

Fearing for the safety of the revered Quasi, Vaako got there fast. Just in time to see it slide into the security of its dark cubicle—preceded by Riddick, who held back the approaching soldiers with their dead comrade's own gun. Crouching, the frustrated commander tried to take aim. But the darkness within rendered any shot uncertain, and he could not risk hitting the Quasi-Dead. As he tried to decide what to do, the armored portal slammed shut—and sealed.

The subject was gone.

Above, her garb of rank draped around her, Dame Vaako stared down at the milling soldiers on the grotto floor. Everyone was shouting, moving, trying to decide what to do next. Outside, the Lord Marshal and the Purifier were engaged in deep, intense conversation while technicians swarmed around them. Her gaze moved to the sealed doorway through which the last Quasi-Dead and the only subject had vanished.

"Who is this man?" she found herself muttering. Who—or what.

The interior of most starships, the working sections not seen by interstellar travelers but only by the technicians who occasionally had to visit to service problems the automatics could not handle, were a maze of conduits and channels, life-support systems and electronics, engine components and proactive apparatus. A difficult realm through which to travel and a harder one for a stranger to puzzle out. Always one for seeking the simplest solution to a problem, Riddick used the gun he had taken from a passing soldier to punch his way through one level after another. Knowing his pursuers would try to predict which of several possible passageways he would take, he chose wherever possible to make his own.

Tenders working engine support were startled to hear a pounding over their heads that was not associated with their work. Eyes turned upward toward the source of the sound. Several technicians tracked it as it moved slightly to the right. They drew back when a hole was blasted in the ceiling. Shredded metal lined the edges of the new opening, through which a large man promptly dropped. Landing on his feet, gun in hand and knife secured, Riddick looked around to get his bearings. Aloud, he said nothing. Attitude-wise, it was very much "Don't mind me—just passing through."

Though every Necromonger was trained in the arts of war, technicians on the Basilica had no reason to carry weapons and went about their duties unarmed. No one moved to challenge the man with the gun. Even had they been armed, they would not have been inclined to do so. Clearly, the intruder was a problem for soldiers to deal with. And speaking of soldiers, where were they? One tech moved to sound an alarm and call for assistance.

Riddick ignored him just as he ignored the others. Moving fast, he found what he was looking for: the gap bordering one of the many stabilizers that kept the huge Basilica ship level on the surface of Helion Prime. There was more than enough room for him to drop through the opening to the surface below. He moved toward it.

And halted when a gravity orb intercepted him. If he hadn't seen it coming, it would have taken off his head. A smaller version of the one he had previously watched smash dozens of Helion soldiers in the city plaza, it positioned itself in the gap, blocking his exit like a live thing. No doubt similar orbs had been deployed to prevent his escape at other exposed locations throughout the ship.

There was noise and commotion behind him. Elite soldiers were pouring into the engineering room, drawing weapons as they ran. Seeing them, Riddick pulled the pistol he had appropriated. But instead of firing at the oncoming troops, he turned and threw it as hard as he could, directly into the slowly rotating orb.

Programmed to attack anything that impacted on its field, the orb promptly contracted around the weapon. The result was that, where a moment before a solid sidearm had been spinning through the air, a piece of compacted metal no bigger than a fingernail now fell onto the stabilizer housing, landing with a tinny clink. The way now clear, Riddick leaped for the opening and threw himself into the gap. Landing on a portion of the stabilizer housing, he clambered down it like a gibbon. Above, soldiers arrived and gathered around the opening. A few pointed their weapons downward at the retreating figure, but did not fire. Their line of sight was not good, and there was too great a risk to the stabilizer mechanism itself.

With the vast bulk of the Basilica looming above him, Riddick emerged in the rubble of buildings that had been crushed beneath the great weight of the Necromonger command vessel. He was free. If the craft above him shifted even a centimeter or two in any direction, he would probably be crushed. But that would require reprogramming its position. By the time anyone might think to do so, he would be gone.

And he was, out from beneath the ship and clear of its threatening mass in a matter of minutes, disappearing into the ruined warren of streets and blasted buildings that had been the Helion capital.

Settling on a suitably inaccessible basement for a hiding place, he waited there for nightfall, when his unique eyes would once more give him an advantage over his ordinary, day-sighted brethren. Emerging only then, he was gratified to see that he was not alone. Numbers of citizens were about: moving fast, not wanting to be picked up for questioning, rooting through the rubble of their city in search of anything useful. They reminded him of ants scrabbling over the remains of a picnic. As he looked on, men and women stumbled out of the ruins carrying all manner of goods, from small valuables to still functioning electronics. He shook his head disapprovingly. Within a day or two, they would be trading such trifles for food and water.

Only one artifact interested him. Pulling the ship locator from a pocket, he activated the device and waited. He did not quite hold his breath. As it developed, he did not need to: the unit was working perfectly. The merc ship was right where he had left it, buried in the dunes, sending out a strong locator signal as it awaited the return of its crew. Him. Even if the Necromongers had by chance happened to have found it, he didn't think they would bother with the hidden vessel. So far, that was apparently the case. Small and unarmed, it posed no threat to their invasion.

Aligning himself with the route the ship locator helpfully suggested, he started off purposefully through the destruction.

A few, but not all, of the survivors paused to glance in his direction. That was all they did. They were too busy trying to decide what to do next, how they would greet the following morning. That is, those that were not wandering aimlessly, still in shock.

One who seemed to know what he was doing wore the concealing robes of a Meccan cleric. The figure paused longer than others to plot the big man's path. As it was doing so, a small Necromonger transport appeared. Lensors hung from its flanks, sweeping the surface, scanning, scanning. Both cleric and Riddick rushed for cover.

Concealing himself, Riddick found that his move had not gone unobserved. Eyes were staring at him, eyes that were all at once wide and pleading and confused. The little girl standing out in the open and crying softly was about the right age, the right height. His gaze narrowed slightly. It couldn't be Ziza. Not here. Not alone. But the girl was about the right age, the right proportions. He fought to put it out of his mind. Doubtless there were a lot of children wandering the streets of the capital this night, homeless and alone. It wasn't any of his business.

But it looked just like her.

The thrumming sound of the transport's engines was fading into the distance. Making a decision, he emerged from his hiding place and approached the girl. Her back was to him, and he had to turn her around to see.

It wasn't her. Actually, on close inspection, the poor child didn't look anything like Ziza. His eyes had been playing tricks on him. Except, his eyes never played tricks on him. Never. As he held her, the girl started to cry harder than ever.

The transport reappeared far more quickly than it had gone. Whether the scanning lensors had picked up on the girl's crying or on his presence he didn't know. It didn't matter. Only two things mattered now: him moving fast, and the fear on the little girl's face.

A blur of motion, he dumped her in the safety of a ruined doorway and ran on. Hopefully, her parents would find her, or a relative, or a friend—if any of them were still alive. Those piloting the transport had definitely homed in on him now. The vessel was descending in his direction, troops gathering within in preparation for dropping down on their single running, swerving target.

Perhaps those aboard were so focused on their quarry that they neglected to follow proper defensive procedures. Perhaps they simply overlooked the threat. Whatever the reason, Riddick's eyes registered the three bright streaks of light that pierced the night at the same time as did those aboard the transport. The important difference was that the streaks were aimed at the ship and not at him.

On impact, they blew the rear section of the transport to bits. Bodies flying, flames and secondary explosions turning night into day, the crippled ship retained a dangerous amount of rapidly falling forward momentum—in Riddick's direction. He barely had time to dive for cover as the fatally wounded vessel passed directly over him. Slamming into the base of a standing structure, it finally ground to a fiery, burning stop. Within the flaming, crackling wreckage, nothing moved.

As Riddick rose from his hole, the sound of cycling armament made him turn. Four black-garbed figures stepped out of the shadows. All were carrying weapons, one of which was a still smoking missile launcher. Leading them was the figure garbed as a Meccan cleric who, along with Riddick, had also taken cover at the initial approach of the Necromonger troop transport.

All of the weapons, including the missile launcher, were now pointed in Riddick's direction.

Pausing, the cleric took a moment to study the ruins of the Necromonger craft. His attitude was not sympathetic. Then he came toward Riddick, pushing back his cowl as he did so. Their eyes met. Their was nothing of the spiritual in either gaze.

It was Toombs.

Behind him, one of his new associates was intent on his instruments' readouts. "'Nother one circling. Not focused yet, but closing. We should move. We should move *now.*" Looking up from the device, the mercenary glanced at the night sky.

All five of them looked uneasy. They were well armed and well equipped but not as experienced as their predecessors. Nevertheless, they were competent enough; the best at their jobs Toombs had been able to find.

Despite the warning, the leader of the mercenaries lingered amid the rubble. As was his style, he wanted to crow a bit before running. But this time he kept his distance, remembering the little trick his quarry had pulled at their last meeting.

"Two things you coulda done better: first, find and trash the locator beacon inside the ship you jacked. But that woulda meant taking the time to locate the locator, wouldn't it? You musta been in one shit-fired hurry. Second—and this is really the more important part—you shoulda dusted my dick when you had the chance."

Reaching beneath his appropriated cleric's robes, he brought out a pair of cuffs and tossed them to Riddick.

"Let's do this one more time. One last time. Any questions?"

Riddick considered the four sets of weapons aimed

in his direction. He could take out Toombs and one or two of the others, but not all four. They might be edgy, but they weren't unskilled. *Wait for the opening.*

"Yeah," he said flatly as he started putting on the cuffs. "What took you so long?"

VIII

The surface of Helion Prime fell away beneath the accelerating merc ship. From space, it was impossible to tell that the dominant society on the planet had been battered and torn, that devastation and destruction on a massive scale had occurred at all. Oceans still rolled, clouds still scudded, plant life still stained multiple continents with swathes of muted green. At a distance, the works of man, whether benevolent or malign, shrank to insignificance.

Aboard the ship, the last lingering vestiges of concern had given way to preliminary celebration. There was much whooping and yelling. Despite the unusual challenges and dangers, they had pulled it off.

"In and out, unsuspected and undetected by either side!" one of the mercs was hollering. "Damn, I love a good smash and grab!"

While equally pleased, the copilot was busy carrying out essential piloting functions. They might be out of the woods, but they weren't out of the system.

"Stand by, stand by," she muttered earnestly.

"Picking up fields here. Frequencies all over the place." Her fingers worked the instrumentation, her eyes darting from monitor to monitor.

Seated alongside her, the pilot worked his own necessities, methodically analyzing readouts and totaling up what the numbers meant. "Shit, here it comes. . . ."

The copilot was shaking her head dubiously. "Some kinda scan. Readin' our drive spit, maybe." Her attention was riveted on half a dozen readouts. "I dunno, I dunno. . . ."

Toombs didn't hesitate. He who hesitates was one dead motherfucker, as the ancient saying went. Or something like that. "Don't wait for detailed analysis. Let's drop one."

The pilot complied, assaulting the appropriate instrumentation.

As the ship continued to accelerate, a portion of its exterior appeared to break away and spin free. It tumbled only for a moment, until independent internal self-guidance and operations systems took over from the master control on board the mother vessel. As the merc ship sped spaceward, the liberated engine's own internal backup drive kicked in. This was a particularly messy, undisciplined drive that spewed indications of its presence all over the immediate spatial vicinity. Kicking off at an angle to the merc ship's course, it sped away at its own impressive speed. It did not possess the onboard resources to do so for very long, or to enable it to reach another star system, but that was not its purpose. Its purpose was to make fools of whoever happened to be tracking.

Aboard the mother craft, the merc crew held their breath as they watched the tracing field indicators on their respective screens dropping, dropping—and finally going dead flat line. Both pilots sagged in relief. Whether it was a scanner or missile or inertialess projectile that had been tracking them, it had changed course in pursuit of their clever decoy. In a very little while they would be able to make the jump to supralight speed, and should be safe from any pursuit.

Satisfied that they were not going to be boarded or blown out of the rapidly darkening, star-filled sky, Toombs made his way to the lock-up located directly behind the cockpit. It had been designed and built with enough strength to contain a pack of rabid Sinurians. As such, it ought to suffice for one human prisoner. Even one named Richard Riddick.

Tightly bound, secured to the wall, and pretubed for jump, Riddick did not look up at Toombs's approach. His attitude remained one of languid indifference. Someone other than Toombs might have been infuriated by the prisoner's attitude. Not this time. The mercenary leader was not stupid. Riddick was static and serene in the same way as a coiled snake. Having been badly bitten once, Toombs had no intention of repeating the mistake. Despite the prisoner's bonds, the merc kept his distance. His opinions, however, he was always ready to share.

"So," he began conversationally, "where do we drop your merc-killin' ass?" He feigned thoughtfulness. "Maybe Butcher Bay, darkside."

Riddick considered the proposal, responded immediately. "Butcher Bay? Thelriss system? Ten minutes every other day on the dog run. Good protein waffles, too. Fauna, not veg."

Toombs acted as if whatever the prisoner said had no effect on his train of thought. He would not admit that Riddick had derailed it slightly. "Or, hey, how 'bout Ursa Luna? Nice little double-max prison. Small, secure, compact. Civilized. Penal boutique."

The big man shrugged. "They keep a cell open for me."

Toombs nodded as if he had expected to hear something just like Riddick's retort. "Real predictable, you know that? You know what I'm thinkin' *now*?"

"That if your mother had known your father you'd be raising fruit on Bannkul IV?"

A muscle twitched in the mercenary's cheek, but otherwise he showed no reaction. "I'm thinkin' that all these joints are health clubs for waffle-eatin' pussies. Just not right for an elite guest like yourself. Wouldn't be doin' you fair to let you off somewhere lotus land–like, where they might stick you doin' somethin' really hard time like clerical. Maybe we should think about uppin' our game here. Someplace truly diabolical." He stared down at the prisoner, in his own quietly sadistic way thoroughly enjoying himself. "Fine word, 'diabolical.' Five syllables, all of 'em totaling up to narsty."

Up forward, the crew was listening. The copilot turned to her colleague and commented, keeping her voice down as she did so. "What the hell's he thinking? *Now.*"

Riddick answered, since the pilot could not. But

while his words were directed forward, his attention remained casually focused on Toombs. "He's thinking triple-max. Only three of those slams left. Used to be more, but 'civilized' folk raised a stink, wouldn't have 'em in their planetary backyard. NIMS—not in My System. Where there's a demand, though, there's always money to pay for it. Just keep it out of the sight of enlightened folk, that's all. Out of sight, out of mind, but be sure an' keep the minding part strong.

"Two of 'em way out in the borderlands other side of the Arm. Too far out of range for a shitty little undercutter like this with no legs. That leaves just one."

Now Toombs did look irritated. He'd intended to shock Riddick with the destination, only to have the prisoner steal his thunder. While he dithered over how to recover the conversational high ground, Riddick finished the thought for him.

"That *is* what you had in mind, right? Crematoria?"

Toombs muttered something under his breath. "Fuck you. Feelin' warm, yet? If not, soon enough." Turning, he snapped an order over his shoulder. "You heard him. Dope it out." He looked back at Riddick. "Good place to sweat some of the smart-ass out of a man. Or sweat him out, period."

Forward, the pilot groused over his instrumentation even as his fingers were moving. "I hate this run. . . ."

"Just *do* it," Toombs growled. The game wasn't playing out as he'd intended. Unlike most of the runners he had tracked and brought down for the money, this prisoner wasn't any fun.

Watching, evaluating, Riddick read the meaning behind the mercenary's gamut of expressions. "Dunno about this new crew, Toombs," he commented with false sympathy. "Skittish. Like they're kinda worried about something. Need to take their mind off whatever it is they're worrying about. Hey, I know: did you tell 'em what happened to your last crew?"

Even though it was the prisoner who was bound and he was the one walking free, Toombs had the weirdest feeling that their respective condition had somehow become reversed. He struggled to regain mastery of the situation.

"You know, you were supposed to be some slick shit—an' here you are, all back of the bus. Don't know how to finish. But don't worry—I'll handle it for you." Turning away, he gestured to one of his crew. "Getting on time for jump. Change his goddamn oil." Clearly annoyed, he walked to the front of the cockpit to converse with the pilots.

After making doubly sure the prisoner's bonds were intact, the merc Toombs had given the order to begin activating the standard cryochill that had been hooked up to Riddick earlier. He did so while only occasionally meeting the prisoner's gaze.

"So, uh," he murmured with a precautionary glance in Toombs's direction, "what *did* happen to the other guys?"

Tired of conversation that was to no purpose, and not inclined to deal with junior employees, the prisoner lowered his head and went dead mouth. Disappointed, the merc worked a little more roughly on the tubes and monitor lines.

"Ohhh—he don't wanna talk to me. You know, Riddick, I'm gonna be awake a lot longer than you."

Letting it hang in the air as a threat, the merc finished his work, concluded by leaning over to boldly give the prisoner's cheek a firm slap-pat as if to say "Nighty-night." Riddick might have reacted, but he was not a man to waste energy without a definitive payoff in sight.

Especially if it was not one that he favored.

That there was still some sand and rock mixed with the telltale vitrification was clear indication that the ship that had taken off from the spot was designed to leave as little evidence of its passing as possible. Anyone charged with carrying out a casual scan of the area might well have missed it. The Necromonger search team did not.

Having been summoned by the team that had found the place, Vaako ran a hand over the seared surface. Satisfied, he turned to the lensor standing nearby. The creature was signaling that it had divined something from the immediate surroundings, and not necessarily just from its inspection of the ground.

The tap at the base of the lensor's spine broadcast directly to the handheld unit in the commander's right hand. There he saw, and read, what the lensor had computed: a suggestive lingering in the sky of a departing vessel. This had been merged with a series of reports from orbital monitors put in place just prior to the main assault on Helion Prime, most particularly a recent one that told of a fleeing, fast, small craft that had deployed a fairly sophisticated decoy to throw off any pursuit. Taken together, they were combined with reports from soldiers and citizens on the ground who had observed a small group of armed civilians traveling in this direction with a single distinctive, unarmed man in their midst.

All the replies to all the questions added up to a pretty good approximation of an answer. That, and the fact that there had been no other sightings of the singular prisoner since his remarkable escape from the Basilica added up to a reasonable conclusion: there had been a small vessel hidden here, and it had departed in a great hurry, most likely with the man Vaako was after on board. Who had taken him and why was not important. All that mattered was the probable presence on the departed vessel of the individual the commander sought.

Rising, he turned to a subordinate. "Take my Galilee team, the one with the most acute lensors, and see this done. I'll make the composite report myself, in person."

In the control room that was the neural ganglion of the Basilica, the Lord Marshal was consulting with his general staff. Toal, who had led the assault on Jeranda, was there. So was Scales, famed for his ruthlessness in the service of the faith. And the Scalp-Taker, who needed no addendum to his reputation.

Together, they were gathered around a malleable extrusion map of Helion Prime. At present it showed, in full and flexible relief, the central portion of that world's western hemisphere. As fingers were pointed and words were spoken, features flowed and re-formed on the map, responding automatically to both gestures and commands.

Toal was busy delineating the current bump in the Necromongers' path to complete conquest of Helion Prime. Under his words and moving fingers, all manner of defensive weaponry was conjured up, only to vanish and be replaced by others as his hand moved on.

". . . just south of the equator, within this central land mass," he was saying. "They've pulled back from the centers of population and concentrated a good deal of their remaining primary forces and reserves here, here, and here. Defensive energy projectors, still fully powered and active. An unknown number of fighter craft." His hand moved rapidly, efficiently. "All along this continental rift. Well protected and deeply dug in to several interconnected mountain ranges."

Even while deeply engrossed in analyzing the situation, the Lord Marshal could venture homilies. "The body flails, even after the head's been chopped off."

As the field commander responsible for the area under discussion, Toal was less inclined to wax philosophic. The Necromonger forces were extensive, but they were not infinite. The quickest and most assured way to subdue an entire world was to obliterate its principal defenses as swiftly as possible and then install a converted, cooperative native administration.

Otherwise, it would prove impossible to move on to the next world, and the next. Because all your troops would be tied down occupying a world or two. Local cooperation was crucial to the success and growth of the Necromonger cause. Securing that cooperation was impossible so long as significant resistance persisted.

"If we don't act soon, this area will become a magnet for continuing resistance elsewhere on the planet. It could even reach off world and draw reinforcements from the outlying inhabited worlds of this system, the ones we hope to intimidate into submission."

Scales grinned wolfishly. "Give it to me. I'll go straight into their teeth. It'll take twenty thousand converts and two warrior ships, no more. I swear it. A week, maybe ten days, and this problem will be disappeared."

No one looked over from the map as Vaako entered. Their backs were toward him, their attention focused on the rippling and changing display. He stood there, unnoticed, watching. There was something he had long been curious about but had been reluctant to investigate. Others, especially one other, felt he had put it off too long.

Why not now? he asked himself. When better than in an innocuous moment when the subject of his curiosity appeared engaged not only by the flow of information but also by the words of subordinates?

No cat could have made an approach as silent and fluid as Vaako. He advanced as if motivated by some grave internal purpose, gliding across the floor on well-worn boots that made no sound. All of his attention, all of his focus, was on the figure who lay at the terminus of that experimental approach.

"While I do prize brute force," the Lord Marshal was saying, "there are times when a more artful, subtle approach may be more valid. While every convert is willing, a convert lost here is lost to us the next time." His hand moved over the map; altering positions, viewpoint, locations.

"Go in with smaller forces first. Instead of a frontal assault and landing whose effects can only be judged by the number of our people who survive it, pick off these defensive positions first, one by one. If moves are made to defend them, so much the better. We can ramp up each attack in proportion to the increase in defense. Before long, they will be so busy trying to defend their multiple individual positions that their forces will be scattered. When they are dispersed, not when they are concentrated as they are now, will be the time to initiate your major attack. If they do not disperse, then we can take out their defensive positions one at a time.

"Remember," he said, turning to Scales, "whether one is mounting a defense or an attack, it is important to dictate the flow of battle, to keep control. Not only for strategic reasons, but to maintain morale among the converted. Every defense, every offense, has its blind spot. Finding and exploiting it is the key to victory, not the mass sacrifice of one's own forces." He gestured at the map one more time. "These Helions are no different. As with most, their blind spot . . ."

As the Lord Marshal declaimed on the merits of military subtlety, Vaako moved closer and closer. Was such a thing as complete surprise, after all, possible? Was he about to secure proof of what he had long wondered about? He was there, almost there, almost within an arm's length.

The visage that turned toward him was vaporous, but clearly defined. It was the facial equivalent of the third arm that not long ago had ripped the soul from a defiant politician in the middle of Helion's capitol building. It stared unblinkingly at the approaching Vaako, who halted sharply as the physical face caught up and merged with its astral predecessor.

". . . is right behind them," the Lord Marshal concluded without any change in tone.

To his credit, Vaako recovered quickly, betraying no sign of his purpose in approaching so stealthily. "We found a launch site and witnesses. There is no proof the sought-after subject was aboard, but the weight of evidence would seem to support such a conclusion. An intercept was attempted, but failed. However, orbital units were able to make a pick subsequent to the indicated craft's supralight jump. That is only sufficient for an initial destination, of course, but having escaped the intercept, those on board should be full of confidence. Since they do not know we have the capability of making a course pick, it seems unlikely they would go to the expense and trouble of dropping out of supralight to make a course correction. In lieu of confirmation, all is supposition, of course."

"If the subject has gone off world," the Lord

Marshal replied, without in any way alluding to Vaako's unusually furtive entry, "then you should be off world, Vaako."

The commander stiffened slightly. It was not a reprimand, but neither was it praise for good work already done. "I've already ordered a strike team to follow as far as needed. It is well prepared and well led. I have the greatest confidence in its ability to—"

The Lord Marshal interrupted him. "My confidence lies in those closest to me." Was that a sly comment on his entrance? Vaako could not tell. "Wherever the Riddick has gone, it falls to you to lens him out and cleanse him. You. If I wished another officer to take charge of this matter, I would already have designated one."

Vaako was more confused than angry. There was no glory to the cause in following and tracking down one lone malcontent, whatever his perceived abilities. The real action was here, in the Helion system, doing battle with sturdy planetary defenses and hordes of the unconverted.

"Forgive me, but—isn't my place here? Participating in the planning and execution of the remainder of the Helion campaign? My training, my experience, has led me to the command of dozens of ships, thousand of converts. Surely it's not necessary for me to be present at the takedown of one man? Isn't this where I'm most—?"

The Lord Marshal spoke with disarming softness. "Are you questioning my judgment in this matter, Vaako?"

The expressions on the faces of the other senior officers in the room spoke volumes. Toal, for his part, actually moved a couple of steps away from Vaako. Scales favored his colleague with the kind of look one reserves for an acquaintance who has suddenly been diagnosed with a rare, incurable, and highly contagious disease.

"No, my Lord Marshal," Vaako responded hastily. "I would never think to question your judgment."

"Then don't," the supreme leader advised him. His attitude softened. "Take it on faith."

Stepping back smartly, Vaako bowed sharply. His participation in the strategy session was over. He was fortunate, he realized as he retraced his way out of the chamber, that that was all that was over.

She was waiting for him in the quarters they shared. As befitted his rank, it was comparatively spacious—private space being a luxury even on a vessel as commodious as the Basilica. At the moment, she was applying makeup, a ritual unchanged among humankind since self-consciousness first appeared among the species. Befitting the culture to which they belonged, such artificial epidermal enhancements were more foreboding than cheerful or illuminating.

Casting off bits and pieces of his duty uniform, he paced furiously behind her. Though aware of the emotions surging through him, she did not pause in her work. Like sweat, the anger and uncertainty he was clearly experiencing would soon evaporate.

"It's a fool's run, suitable for a mid-level officer and a squad or two of Elite. Why the need to assign a Commander of the Faith to supervise? For that matter, why care about one man, one breeder? A good fighter, to be sure. Quick and fearless. But still only one. And a full alive, at that. No mysteries there, no hidden threats.

"Meanwhile, we have a war to plan, a faith to spread, a stubborn system to subdue, and here he's ordering me off to—" A new thought made him pause. He stared over at her. "Am I falling from favor? I have done all that has been asked of me, both personally and professionally. What could I have overlooked that would lead him to treat me this way?"

Dame Vaako continued to apply her maquillage. Cloaked in the calm tone of reassurance, her actual words were disquieting. "He's always been unsettled, the current Lord Marshal. Unsteady. There are more whispers than you can imagine. Some say he's too artistic for the job. Others that his ambitions exceed his abilities. Megalomania, and worse. Of course, extremism in the service of the faith is no vice, but when it threatens to overwhelm good judgment . . ."

Judgment. Was her use of the word just a coincidence? How could she know of what had transpired in the strategy room? He did not pursue the question. Long since, he had learned to value and respect the innate cunning of his current partner, and to make use of it without examining her methods too closely.

"In such situations," she was saying, "one never knows what will happen. What the immediate future may bring. Wouldn't be surprised if someone promoted him soon—to Full Dead."

That was going too far. To voice such a thought,

even in the privacy of their own supposedly screened and secure apartments . . .

"Take care what you say."

She turned to him. Her beauty was legendary, her sensuality overpowering, her intelligence tangible. He was reminded, yet again, why he had partnered with her. "Should I say it softly?"

Was she teasing him? He muttered a reply. "Sure, say it softly. So it sounds *more* like a conspiracy."

She rolled her eyes. She was not teasing him, then. He felt a combination of embarrassment and inadequacy. In all Necromonger society, only she, only this one woman, could make him feel like that.

"Why is it that if you so much as *breathe* about the demise of him on the throne, everyone assumes a conspiracy? Why isn't it considered prudent planning? If he's as profoundly gifted as everyone insists, isn't it the sort of thing he would be expecting and preparing himself for?"

"He is occupied with other concerns." Vaako's defense of his superior was unquestioning and admirable, even though no one else was present to hear it. "The business of eventual succession is a complicated one. By this time in a lord marshal's career someone has usually moved to the fore and positioned himself, whereupon any other pretenders accept the reality and retire any personal ambitions they might hold in that regard. That has not yet happened, nor has the Lord Marshal given any indication that he favors any one of several among those who are qualified. There's Toal, Scales, even the Purifier himself. It would be unusual, but not unprecedented, for a purifier to accede to the role of lord marshal."

She was nodding slowly, as if intimately familiar with both procedure and candidates. "Yet none of them," she finally declared, "with the simple elegance of 'Lord Vaako.'" Rising fluidly, she moved toward him, her voice falling to a husky whisper. "You can keep what you kill."

Vaako swallowed. A trio of approaching enemy armed to the teeth he knew instantly how to deal with. This woman, diaphanously cloaked and sensuously madeup, represented an entirely more complex challenge.

"Stop," he muttered.

Her voice was soft in his ear, sugar in his mind. "It is the Necromonger way."

"STOP!" Having momentarily turned away, he spun around and grabbed her, his fingers sinking into her receptive flesh. He struggled to control himself. "His passing will come in due time. And not a moment sooner."

"Why?" she wondered, her personality a blend of coquette and assassin.

Vaako straightened as if on parade. Which, in a sense, he was, even there in their private rooms. "Because I serve *him*—we all serve *him*. That is also the Necromonger way. It represents how we have managed to become what we are, how we have succeeded in growing and spreading our creed. It's called fidelity."

"It's called stupidity."

Always one to reduce the exalted and the complex

to an oversimplification, he thought angrily. As linked as they were, there was a point beyond which he would not be pushed. He replied with the front of his hand across her face, hard.

It did not have the intended effect.

She smiled, an entirely carnivorous manifestation. It was fortunate that Vaako was intimately familiar with it. Another man might have been frightened. "Well—finally, some attention."

She did not so much move toward him as strike, attacking him with the kind of coiled, primal sexual energy normally held in restraint beneath her noble poise. Knowing it was futile to do so, he made little effort to resist. Knowing also that he did not want to do so. Though as adherents of the Necromonger faith it would be counter to their beliefs to procreate—and their reproductive systems had been modified accordingly—the enjoyment of the act was not forbidden to them.

Then, just as abruptly and unpredictably, she was stroking his face, cooing at him like a lover on their wedding night. "You have such greatness in you, Vaako. So much potential. Everything you ever strove for, everything you ever wanted, is right there, yours for the taking. But it will not be given to you—you have to take it for yourself. I just wish you could see it like I do." She kissed him again, not biting this time, her lips hot and moist as they traced abstract patterns against his skin.

"You know what I want?"

Vaako was present physically, occasionally returning her kisses as she continued to caress him, but a part of his mind was not. That part of him was remembering. Calculating.

"He was meeting with the other commanders," he murmured wonderingly, staring off into a distance only he could see. "They were completely occupied with what they were discussing. Everyone's back was to me. I was very careful. I came up behind him in perfect silence—not a squeak of boots, not a rustle of clothing."

For all that they continued to speak aloud, they were not having a conversation. They were each of them lost in their own worlds now, their own private thoughts.

"I want to go down to Necropolis, right now," she whispered throatily.

"And he knew," Vaako muttered, recalling the incident with disbelief. "He knew I was there even though he never turned till the last instant. His astral self sensed I was behind him, and communicated my presence."

Her hands were moving now in counterpoint to her tongue. "And if no one's around, when no one is looking, I'll get down on my knees. . . ."

Vaako was shaking his head. "You can't surprise him. It's impossible. He knows everything. And if the living half of him doesn't, the dead half of him does."

". . . while you sit on the throne," she finished. In a frenzy of bacchanalian expectation, she clutched his arm and pulled him toward the door. He did not resist, his startled expression showing that he had hardly heard her—and didn't care. Whatever she wanted right now, it didn't matter. While his thoughts were confused, hers clearly were not. Might as well then, he reasoned, let her forge ahead.

On their way down to the center of Necropolis, they were greeted by soldiers and technicians, support personnel and life support staff alike. As they drew nearer and nearer to the traditional inner sanctuary of Necromonger belief, however, they encountered fewer and fewer citizens. This was a place for ceremony and contemplation, not for those with daily tasks to perform.

To ensure privacy, she detoured to the sweeping balcony that overlooked the central sanctum. Unexpectedly, the floor below was occupied. Only three people there, conversing in low voices. When she saw who they were, her initial intent in coming was quickly forgotten. Her abrupt change of attitude did not appear to make any difference to Vaako, especially after he also recognized the reason for it.

On the main floor, the Lord Marshal and the Purifier were interrogating a third figure. A stranger in more than one sense of the word. Or was it more of an interview than an interrogation? At a distance, it was difficult to tell. Certainly the visitor was not visibly restrained. Wishing for better powers of hearing, she strained to catch a phrase, a word. Next to her, Vaako crouched low against the balustrade, staring and listening.

"An Elemental," she murmured. "Here. But why?"

Vaako essayed a guess. "Helion Prime is something of a junction system. Those who prepared the way for us reported the presence of many visitors, some who came from a considerable distance. They as well as locals were taken captive." He nodded toward the distant Elemental. "She might be one of them."

Or not, Dame Vaako reflected as she observed. There was something between the Elemental and the Lord Marshal that was difficult to discern at a distance. Tension, certainly. That was to be expected. But she thought she could detect indications of something else, something more. A familiarity, perhaps. Or something even deeper. Possibly—a history?

"How unexpected," the Lord Marshal was saying out of earshot of the two observers. So focused was he on the female standing before him that even his half-dead self did not notice the pair crouched behind the balustrade. Though they did not know it, they were just far enough away to be outside the range of his casual detection. "That on this particular planet, of all the inhabited planets in the known galaxy, we turn up an Elemental on the very same day we find, of all things, a male Furyan." He leaned toward the subject of his mock surprise.

"Just why is that? And why, of all Elementals, would it be you?"

Outwardly unperturbed, Aereon stood before him, making no move to flee. For that matter Vaako wondered, being as he was somewhat familiar with the singular abilities of the Elementals, how had she been brought aboard in the first place? Or had she been brought? Was it possible she had come of her own free will? If so, to what purpose? A complicated and confusing day was only becoming more so.

"Helion Prime is a crossroads world, a center for trade and exchange. Given the speed with which your kind has been moving through this part of the galaxy lately, the odds are not so against it."

The Lord Marshal was less than convinced by this argument. "Try again. And this time, make me believe you."

If Aereon was intimidated, she did not show it. "It's no secret that Elementals are interested in the balance of things. When that balance is disturbed, we have been known to travel far to observe cause and effect."

"As you've been known to know more than you usually tell," the Lord Marshal riposted. "You'll have to do better than that. I'm not one to be manipulated by clever evasions and reluctant half-truths."

Dame Vaako's sinuous mind was working overtime. "Doesn't regard her as a captive, though. A guest reluctant to speak forthrightly, maybe. No weapons in view. That suggests neither is afraid of the other." She shook her head, hating that she could not understand. Then she smiled over at Vaako.

"You be a good soldier and go after the Riddick. The Marshal hasn't given you much of a choice, anyway. Do your job and terminate the breeder, or bring him back. Meanwhile, I'll find out why the Lord Marshal is so threatened by him. And what the Elementals have to do with all this. There are wheels within wheels here, my dear commander, and I need time to translate the squeaking."

Leaning toward him, she thrust her tongue toward

the back of his mouth while her perfect teeth simultaneously nibbled teasingly at his lips. Her hot exhalation surged down his throat.

In the face of an argument like that, he could do naught but comply.

IX

It was a stark and blasted world, wobbling uncomfortably on its axis. Too close to its sun, one hemisphere was presently roasting in the heat of Hades while the other shuddered in the death grip of mortal cold. In between lay the terminator, a band of tolerable twilight that was wider and moved more slowly than on most human-inhabited worlds.

Approaching from the night side, a small ship descended through an atmosphere incapable of holding moisture and therefore devoid of comforting clouds. No markings identified it, the insignia of no system flared proudly from its flanks. The same might be said of its crew.

Automatically, cryotubes retracted from selected arms and legs. While the rest of the mercenaries slept, the copilot detached herself from remaining monitoring links and life-support conduits. Rising from her place of repose, she stretched until the air in her joints popped. Forcing herself through the prescribed regimen of wake-up exercises, she then proceeded to check on her colleagues. They would be reviving soon. A quick run-through of systems showed that everything aboard the compact little craft was functioning normally. Pleased, she was about to signal their presence to the ground prior to initiating preliminary procedures for touchdown when she remembered there was one other on board whose status she ought to check on.

As was proper, their cargo was still out. Of course he was. It was absurd to think he might have emerged from cryosleep on his own. An interesting specimen, even if he did represent nothing more than a quick and satisfying cash-out. His origin was a mystery to her. Toombs might be their leader, but he hadn't provided much in the way of information about their captive. Just that he was one more in a long list of the recovered. Toombs was nothing if not boastful.

Not that it mattered to her. All that mattered was payday. Which, assuming no trouble with the authorities on the ground, ought to be forthcoming very soon.

Still, she could not entirely repress her natural curiosity. There had been that intriguing but brief verbal interplay between the prisoner and Toombs, for example. And those goggles the man wore: she'd never seen a pair quite like them. Much more than simple sunshades, of a design that was new to her and a composition that suggested a need to do more than merely dampen sunlight, they intrigued her almost as much as the comatose man who was wearing them.

Edging closer, she reached out a wary hand. There

was no movement, no response to the approach of her fingers. Were the inside of the lenses as distinctive as their exterior? She lifted the goggles.

And nearly fell backward and down. A pair of eyes was staring straight back at her; a pair of eyes that glinted with a hint of the kind of devious surgical modification that in polite society was more often whispered than spoken about. So calm and controlled moments earlier, her breath now came in sudden, short gasps.

Riddick turned his head ever so slightly to one side. "Do you know that you grind your teeth when you're in cryosleep? Makes one wonder what you're dreaming about. Sexy."

Though it was right behind her, she fled to the safety of the copilot's seat and the unchallenging familiarity of the console's instruments.

Gradually, one by one, the rest of the crew slowly emerged from the extended rest and biochange that were required to allow the fragile human form to endure the rigors of extended supralight travel. Disdaining the health of his own body, or maybe completely confident in its ability to handle anything that might come its way, Toombs ignored the appropriate, recommended rehydration regimen in favor of gargling with a bottle of tequila.

What was wrong with his copilot? There seemed to be an uncharacteristic trembling in her voice as she reported on their status. He did not press for an explanation, however, and as they continued to make their descent, it soon went away.

"I make almost seven hundred degrees on the

hemisphere in daylight," she was reporting as she scanned readouts, "and maybe three hundred below on the night side. Vacation heaven."

Knowing from Crematoria's reputation what to expect, Toombs stood next to Riddick and nodded slowly. "Lemme tell you: if I owned this place and hell, I'd rent this out and live in hell. At least in hell, the climate's consistent."

Something beeped within the forward console. Checking the readout, the copilot announced evenly, "We've got permission to land." She eyed her colleague. "What's with the caution? I don't recognize the code."

The pilot was busy disengaging specific instrumentation. "Means no automatics permitted. Security measure. Don't ask me why. I wasn't the nutcase who decided to put a slam here." He flipped off another series of contacts, activated others. "Switching to manual control as per ground directives." The ship responded with a slight jolt.

"Coming up on terminator," the copilot announced briskly.

"Running behind sked. They won't like that, down below." The pilot adjusted his own attitude as well as the ship's. "Let's line this up fast, and get it over with." He eyed the solar monitor. The readings there were much, much too high for his liking. As a pilot, he valued the information sent back by hara-kiri solar probes. He just didn't want to become one himself.

It grew very quiet within the little ship. Riddick said nothing, missed nothing, his eyes taking in the readouts, the monitor screens, the pilots' technical back-and-forth. Clocking everything. Filing it for later.

"Destination lock on," the copilot announced tightly. "One, two . . . *go*."

The pilot jammed controls forward. Usually, all he had to do was sit back, watch, and monitor touchdown. Not here. Not out in this deity-forsaken backwater piece of hell itself. For a change, his life and that of his passengers resided in his own hands instead of a bunch of unfeeling circuitry.

Coming in to almost any other world, it would have felt good.

Riddick felt himself slammed back into the rear of his prison as the ship dipped into atmosphere. His situation differed little from that of his captors, who were similarly pressed back into their chairs. A couple of the mercenaries howled with bravado, trying to cover the fact that they were struggling not to soil their shorts.

On the desolate landscape below, something was moving. It was active, but not alive. Among obsidian mountains and fields of cracked and cooled glass, safely distant from volcanoes whose lava flowed downslope in other directions, a pair of doors were opening. Fashioned of a special alloy of ceramic and titanium, they parted to reveal an underground hangar that marked the terminus of a specially fabricated runway. Within the area open to the atmosphere, nothing moved.

A towering pillar of natural stone marked the general location of the hangar. The pilot nosed for it, wishing he could use the automatics, knowing that if he did so those on the ground were likely to react unkindly, and perhaps lethally. The ship dropped steadily—not quite fast enough.

The sun came over the horizon.

Stunned atmosphere shocked the descending vessel. Unequipped with the special stabilizers used on regular Crematoria resupply ships, the mercenary craft heaved wildly. Recoiling from the sun despite the special goggles he was wearing and the muting effect of the foreport's automatic polarizers, the pilot fought to maintain control. Behind him, someone uttered a panicked obscenity.

The hangar was coming up way too fast. But if they slowed gradually, they'd be subject to more of the brutal solar effect. Without waiting for instructions, the copilot slammed her open palm down on a large, red plunger someone had hand labeled PARTY POPPERS.

Instantly, a pair of emergency atmospheric engines deployed behind the ship. Gulping atmosphere, they burned it and solid fuel in twin blasts that fired in the opposite direction the ship was taking. Immediately, it began to decelerate and drop faster.

They cut out just before the ship slid to a hard stop—in the center of the runway and slowing to safety inside the hangar. Wisps of smoke and vaporized hull protection rose from the side that had been sun blasted. Inside, nervous laughter mixed with expressions of relief.

Sighing heavily, the pilot tiredly removed his protective goggles and rubbed at his eyes. "And *that's* why I hate this run."

One of the other mercs asked hesitantly, "What happens if you miss the first approach and have to go around again?"

The copilot squinted up at him. "You like fried food?"

There was no one to greet them. No reason for anything organic that valued its water to hang out in the vicinity of the runway and landing hangar. Exiting the ship once the soaring doors had shut behind them, they made their way to the small underground transport terminal. On other worlds, such a locale was often decorated with murals, photonic projections, adaptive flora. Like the rest of the installation on Crematoria, here it was wholly prosaic. The tunnel wall was bare stone that had been chiseled and melted out of the surrounding bedrock. The transport vehicle itself was a flat, utilitarian slug of a sled. Two of them, actually: main in front, secondary smaller one in back, for cargo. Their sole function was to go from one end of the line to the other while breaking down as infrequently as possible. That was the extent of the designers' intentions, the ultimate aim of its exceptionally well-paid builders. Importing labor to Crematoria was even more expensive than importing raw materials.

"Get in, meat!" The mercenary who shoved the tightly bound Riddick into the cargo sled might have received a murderous glare from any other prisoner, or at least a mumbled curse. Riddick said nothing, not even when the merc followed the push by landing hard himself on the big man's chest. The others took seats on the main sled.

Reduced to basics, the sleds had neither roof nor doors: a necessity of design since it was used for transporting goods and material as often as people. At a touch from the pilot, the lump of metal and plastic began to accelerate. Before long it was racing beneath the wretched surface at speeds approaching 300 kph. On the very rudimentary console, an odometer was ticking off kilometers. Long-lasting hanging lighting fixtures fastened to the ceiling of the tunnel kept it reasonably well lit.

Riddick's attention was focused on these fixtures as they flashed past overhead with almost hypnotic effect. Perhaps the evenly spaced lights had a similar effect on the merc who was sitting on his chest. Perhaps he was already bored. Maybe he was convinced that the man on whom he was sitting was going to cooperate and ride quietly. After all, what else could he do, chained and pinned to the bottom of the cargo sled?

What Riddick did was arch his entire body in one single, convulsive muscular spasm. It boosted the startled mercenary upward. Not far. Just, however, far enough.

The next lighting fixture caught the back of the startled mercenary's head before he could so much as utter a startled shout—and removed it, simultaneously sending the decapitated body flying over the back of the sled.

By the time anyone else in the speeding vehicle noticed the absence of their comrade, many kilometers had passed. It was the copilot who happened to glance back and, espying Riddick seated calmly and alone in the last row, raised the alarm.

"Where's Dahlven?"

Her companions joined her in searching for the missing merc. It took about twenty seconds to ascertain that he was nowhere on the sled. Toombs stared hard at Riddick. With those damn goggles he wore it was impossible to tell where the big man's attention was focused. But he did shrug a response, as if to say, *beats me.*

Toombs hesitated, then burst out in a screaming cackle. "Four way! Four-way split!" Hell, he'd never much liked Dahlven anyway. Dumb ass had a real dangerous tendency to react before he thought. Though the mercenary leader didn't know the details, he had a strong feeling that was just what might have happened. As the sled began to decelerate, he turned and sat back down in his seat.

It docked hard, the exceedingly low-tech absorptive bumper at the end of the line sucking up the last of their forward momentum. Toombs leaped up onto the platform and headed for the containment door that led, if memory served, to the prison control center. Douruba, the slam boss, was there to greet him. Beyond gruff, he snapped disappointedly at his visitor as the other mercenaries unloaded their cargo.

"This is all you bring me? After coming all the way out here? Just one?" Practiced, experienced eyes studied the prisoner, sizing him up.

Toombs was not put off. He'd anticipated the reaction. "One expensive piece of highly-priced ass. Got room, don'tcha?"

In the distance beyond the control room doors, something unearthly howled as if in expectation. Douruba shrugged. "Oh, we always got room for more. Nobody likes to admit that we're here, and nobody wants to do without us. Always a place for a setup like Crematoria." Turning, he led the way into the control center. Toombs and his comrades followed, cargo in tow.

"How's business?" the head mercenary inquired conversationally.

"Pretty good," Douruba replied. "Just enough residents to keep things running smoothly, not too many to impact adversely on the bottom line. A good balance." He looked over at the merc. "Your one boy won't upset things."

Toombs grinned. "Wait till you see the line on him. You might think different."

The slam boss pushed out his lower lip. "Can't cost that much."

Unpleasant as ever, the mercenary's grin grew more crooked. "Wait till you see."

Runaway Nature had provided the basis for the prison in the form of a gaping volcanic throat whose subterranean source of lava had long since shifted elsewhere. Multiple levels had been sliced into its circular sides. From there, tunnels and accessways, storerooms and cells, punched deep into the solid rock, forming hollow spokes that extended outward from the central cavity. One side of the old volcano had been devastated by a small, rogue lava flow that had broken through and poured into the depths below. Now hardened as solid as the untouched rock around it, it entombed more prisoners than the supervisors had been able to count. But that had been a long time ago.

Prison control was located at the top of the circular hollow. At the bottom, several guards noticed the ceiling aperture grinding open. One never knew what might be coming down. Since it was too early for a shift change, the lift might be sending down supplies, tools, extra rations—or something new. Numerous eyes regarded the expanding opening with interest. On Crematoria, anything new was worth studying.

A single figure rode the service hoist. Unusually, it was suspended from its wrists instead of riding down on a platform. A bit out of the ordinary, but not unprecedented. Either the newcomer was being punished for something, or else he was being handled with extra care. If the latter, the guards would be taking special interest in him.

The figure was only part way down, however, when its progress came to a jerking, unexpected halt.

In the control room above, Toombs had just moved to halt the winch that had been lowering Riddick. The mercenary did not look happy. Behind him, his crew looked confused.

"What in the bowels of Christ are you talkin' about? 'Seven hundred K'? Where on this bare arse of a dirt ball did you come up with that figure?"

Relaxing near a control console, Douruba glanced at his first assistant. "Remind him."

In between popping and masticating some kind of

light green nut, the other man proceeded to elucidate. "Look, you know how it works, Toombs. The Guild pays us a caretaker's fee for each prisoner, each year. We pay mercs like yourself twenty percent of that total fee, based on a certain life expectancy and work output. Out of that, there are all manner of peripheral costs that have to be deducted and . . ."

An angry Toombs took a step toward the lethargic speaker. "I wired this in at eight-fifty. Nobody at that time said anything about 'peripheral costs.' I know as well or better 'n you how the system operates." He gestured in the direction of the unseen sky. "Any other slam in the Arm would deal me that much right now, no shit." One finger pointed in the direction of the prisoner, who had not descended very far from the control level.

Douruba was not impressed. "This isn't any other slam, is it?"

Across the room, a guard tech glanced up from the console over which he had been laboring. "Don't take this one, boss."

The slam boss nodded at his subordinate, then smiled at his increasingly irate visitor. "How about that, Toombs? Anatoli here has a nose for trouble. What I'm reading from him is that this one"—he jerked a finger toward the silently dangling prisoner—"this 'Riddick' guy, is—"

"Big trouble," the guard tech finished for him. Turning back to his console, he perused the latest readout. "He don't come with a record, this one. He comes with an encyclopedia."

Nodding appreciatively, Douruba restarted the

winch. Like so much else in the prison complex, like the sled transport system, it was intentionally low-tech. Advanced electronics and similar devices did not survive long on Crematoria. Where a seal applicator might easily clog or overheat and fail, for example, a simple hammer would not. It was a design philosophy that not only saved money, it kept the prison going.

"Seven hundred K is good money," Douruba reminded Toombs.

Outside the control station and once more dropping steadily again, Riddick glanced up and barked at his captor. "Better take it, Toombs." The mercenary just glared down at him, watching his former prisoner winch farther and farther out of reach.

On multiple levels, guards and techs and prisoners watched the newcomer descend through the center of the volcanic throat. As depth increased, mobile lights supplied additional illumination within the impressive open space. Riddick took it all in silently, surveying his new surroundings, ignoring the emotional range of the stares that tracked his descent. At the moment, they were irrelevant to his needs.

Above, Toombs had turned away from the cylindrical cavern to once more confront Douruba. "I got a better idea. How's about this?" He nodded at something behind the slam boss. "You open the safe hidden behind that console there, pull out the *real* books." Jerking his head sideways, he indicated the guard tech. "Not the electronic crap you can manipulate with an eyeblink. The hard copy backup you maintain in case of total systems failure and memory wipe. Show me what you shitniks are gonna bank for a guy like Riddick: all killer, no filler. *Then* we'll figure out my cut. *Then* I'll be on my way."

Douruba could not have been more shocked had Toombs suggested they go for a casual stroll out on the surface. At noon.

"Open my books? Let you roam through the hard copy? This is what you suggest?"

The mercenary had taken a step backward. The movement appeared casual. It was not. "Wasn't a suggestion."

It was enough to charge the atmosphere within the control room. Guards and mercenaries alike stiffened. Within holsters and attached to fastsnaps, sidearms were prepped for quick release. Slam boss and merc leader locked eyes.

Moving slowly and keeping his hands in clear view, Douruba walked to a nearby cabinet. Standing to one side as he opened it, so that Toombs had a clear view of the interior, he reached in and removed an exquisite bottle of cut crystal. Half full of some glistening crystalline liquid, he placed it on a flat portion of a nearby console, then brought out a couple of glasses. While everyone else in the room looked on enviously, the slam boss carefully filled the two small glasses. They were the only shots in the tension-filled room.

He handed one to the wary mercenary leader. "This is not the time for confrontation. Not when you hear what is happening elsewhere in the Arm. These are dangerous days for everyone, if you believe the talk." Raising the glass briefly, he sipped at the contents. Heat that was not of Crematoria coursed down his throat and warmed his belly.

Accepting the other glass, Toombs eyed it for a moment—then nonchalantly poured it down an open hatch, much to the slam boss's obvious disapproval. Toombs's free hand continued to hover in the vicinity of his sidearm.

"Talk. What talk?"

Douruba turned introspective. "About some army. Appears out of nowhere. No indication of origin, no warning or quarter given. Not robots, but its soldiers fight like automatons. Absorb any healthy survivors. Strange beliefs—you wouldn't believe some of the rumors. About dead planets, societies reduced to ashes. About 'them.'"

The slam boss's final word seemed to hang in the air, casting a further shadow over the already stressed negotiations.

Toombs refused to be distracted. "Here's one for you that ain't no rumor. Am I gonna get my money?"

Douruba sighed, downed the last of his drink, set the glass aside. "I can see that your interests are typically narrow. Tell you what: I'll run the numbers again. Isn't as simple as it sounds. Have to figure in how this new meat will interact with the system, what it might produce, stats *in re* potential disruption. It will take some time. Meanwhile, you and your team can stay as my guests. No hotel here, but it'll get you off that little ship for a while, let you stretch your legs. At least here we're all safe, yes?" He smiled thinly. "Just tell your people not to go for any long walks in the countryside."

"They know," Toombs replied. "Everyone saw, coming in." He knew full well that the slam boss was stalling for time so he could look for an out. Preferably, but not necessarily, a legal one. The mercenary was not concerned. His formal filing and notice of intent to deliver had carefully complied with every relevant guild regulation. Let the boss have his math toadies run the regs. They wouldn't find any holes. And as much as he wanted to be off and away from this miserable hot rock, a night in a real bed instead of the soggy slog that was cryosleep would do his body good.

"I'll give it a day," he finally announced. "One."

The first assistant grinned. "And our days are fifty-two hours long." Toombs did not smile back. He knew that, and had factored it into his offer.

Douruba seemed pleased. "Fair enough. Anatoli," he instructed the guard tech, "find our new friends some slots. Someplace comfortable. Someplace cool." Having defused the looming confrontation, he returned his attention to the main console.

X

The winch that had been steadily lowering Riddick jerked to a halt about three meters above the floor of the cavern, leaving him still dangling in midair. Since it provided a good view of the lowest level of the prison, and never one to waste time that could be put to use, he utilized the opportunity to study his latest surroundings. It also helped to take his mind off the ache in his wrists.

The encompassing environment was less than salubrious. Sulfurous steam rose from fissures in the ground. Illumination was weaker here than higher up, adding further to the Dantesque aura of his new surroundings. At first, there was little sign of life.

Then three figures appeared. Emerging from a sizable fissure, they immediately spotted the man hanging from the lift chain and started toward him. Riddick eyed them with interest. They were completely covered in yellow dust. Clothes, exposed skin, hair—everything except their mouth filters was coated in a fine and apparently permanent layer of powdered sulfur. In the lightweight netsacks they carried, Riddick saw the outlines of small, sulfur-coated crustacean-like forms. Something to eat or maybe something to barter.

Tracking downward from Riddick's face and special goggles, the attention of the flavescent trio eventually came to rest on the big man's boots. This was not surprising, since the footgear of the recently emerged three was shabby, torn, and in certain spots, actually melted from the intense heat of the ground on which they walked. Brandishing their homemade collecting pickaxes, they moved into position beneath him and took up expectant stances, making no attempt to disguise their intent. It was usually food that came from above, but this was the first time in a long, long while something as appealing and useful as Riddick's boots promised to do the same. Pickaxes in hand, they waited for him to drop the last three meters. With a resigned, internal sigh, Riddick prepared to do so also.

Moments later, the latch above his wrists gave a soft click and disengaged.

As he fell, he flipped and twisted. Bunched muscles torqued open his bonds. It was a trick he could have done earlier, on the merc ship or while being transported to the prison. But while he could force open his restraints, he would have still have had to face three or four guns. Get all, get free. Get three, get dead. He wouldn't call the shots until he could also call the odds.

But there were no guns aimed at him now, and he

had no compunction about finally releasing his hands.

As he stuck his landing, he caught the first blow, parried it, dislocating the first attacker's shoulder and driving the pickax-wielding arm so far backward that the aft end of the pick pierced the man's spine. Almost immediately, he whirled to confront a second assailant.

The crystal scavengers were not slow. As Riddick was taking apart his second attacker, the third slipped behind him and started to swing his axe. Halting in mid-swing, he dropped the tool, both hands grabbing at his neck, around which a chain had just wrapped itself. As Riddick disposed of his hapless second assailant, he watched the chain being yanked back. Following it led him to a deceptively slender, lithe figure. The figure's slimness did not surprise him. Its lines did.

As he removed his goggles, the woman disappeared into the stone rubble that littered the bottom of the cavern. He would have followed; perhaps to thank, certainly to question, but was distracted by a voice from above. A deep, male voice that boomed off the surrounding walls.

"There are inmates and there are convicts," it declared with the conviction of the long converted.

Two tiers up, a formidable group of the latter were working their way downward. Leading them was an older individual whose face was as worn, battered, and tough as the surrounding volcanic rock.

"Who says so?" Riddick called upward.

"The Guv says so," came the reply from the man.

"*I* say so. A convict has a certain code. He learns the corners, he learns the pulse of the prison. A convict knows to show a certain respect when it is warranted. Respect to his fellows, respect to the system. The convict system, not the prison system. *Our* system."

Arriving at the bottom, the Guv approached, halting a mutually respectful distance from the newcomer. His retinue formed up behind him, ugly and prepared, but also willing to give the new arrival a chance to define himself. Eyes studied Riddick. Expressions granted grudging respect.

"An inmate," the Guv continued solemnly and meaningfully, "on the other hand, is someone who pulls the pin on his fellow man. Who does the guards' work for them. Who brings shame to the whole game." It did not seem possible, but his voice lowered even further. "And in this slam, inmates get someone right up in their mouth. Might be right in the middle of breakfast, might be in the middle of the night. But it's damn fucking straight righteous inevitable."

Advancing once again, he drew close to Riddick, unafraid and challenging. As he did so, one of the yellow men started to get up. Without breaking stride, the Guv kicked him in the mouth and put him right back down. He did not like interruptions.

"So," he inquired emotionlessly of the newcomer, "which would you be?"

"Me?" Riddick slipped his goggles back into place. "I'm just passin' through."

With that he stepped past the Guv and strode

away, swallowed up by a hissing wall of steam, ignoring the intense eyes that followed him.

Later, food was provided, if you could call it that. That afternoon it came in the form of some large, boiled arthropod hailing from a family and species Riddick didn't recognize. But if the knobby, spine-sporting exterior was a horror, the meat inside was pale white and perfectly edible. Settling himself outside an empty cell, he studied the ongoing activity within the vaulted cavern while cracking shells and sucking out the contents. Stringy, but nutritious, he decided.

As he was walking back inside the cell, a shape materialized behind him. Alert, lithe, and livid, the newcomer eyed him with quiet intensity.

"Should I go for the sweet spot? Left of the spine, fourth lumbar down; the abdominal aorta. What a gusher . . ."

Turning, Riddick removed his goggles to stare clear-eyed at his visitor. He said nothing. What could he say, to this woman?

"How do I get eyes like that?" she muttered at him.

He shrugged. "You gotta kill a few people."

The woman nodded knowingly. "Did that. Did a lot of that." She moved closer. It's unlikely anyone else would have noticed the small knife concealed in one hand. Riddick caught her before the hand could swing forward, swung her around, and slammed her into the bars of the cell. Not hard enough to break bones but roughly enough to make her drop the shiv. He continued talking as if nothing had happened.

"Then you gotta get sent to a slam."

Her body might be pinned against the bars, but there was nothing restraining her mouth. "Where they tell you you'll never see daylight again. Only there wasn't any doctor here who could shine my eyes. Not for twenty cools, not for a quick bang off, not for nothing." Her voice dropped slightly, but the words were as hard-edged as before. "Was there anything you said that *was* true?"

She wrenched upward, fighting to break free, trying to catch him in the wrong hold. It only made him boost her harder.

"Remember who you're talking to, Jack."

She seemed to spin within her own skin, whirling around and popping forward the miniature blade she kept concealed inside her mouth. Just like Riddick's hold, it didn't keep her from talking.

"'Jack' is dead. She was weak, just couldn't cut it." Lashing out with the concealed blade, she slashed his cheek before he could completely draw back. It did not make him let her go, but he did so anyway. He followed her as she vanished into the steam and sweat-soaked murk outside.

"I'm Kyra," she called back to him, her voice still trembling with cold anger. "A new animal."

The frigate represented the epitome of Necromonger science and adaptive technology. Swift, sleek, stunning in its size and overawing in its mass, it swept through deep space like a wasp searching for a world to paralyze and feed upon. Within its dark depths, her crew operated in shifts: some in cryo-sleep, others emerging from time to time to ensure all was operating optimally and that the vessel remained on course. As yet, few aboard knew that the urgency with which they had departed orbit around Helion Prime was inspired by the disappearance of a single man. They did not need to know, nor would it have affected the efficiency with which they went about their work if they had.

At present, the command team was out of cryo-sleep for several days. Time to exchange thoughts, eat real food, drink, and stretch underused muscles. Then they would return to the embrace of cryo travel while automatics and a skeleton crew watched over the vessel. But for now, they talked.

Vaako was engaged with his navigators. The process of trying to track another ship through deep space was a complicated one. Without advanced computational predictors, it would have been impossible. But with people as dedicated to their work as to the cause, the commander was confident of eventually finding what they were looking for.

The Purifier entered and stood off by himself, observing. Occasionally, his gaze would travel from the distorted stars visible beyond the port to the converts busy at their stations—and eventually, to Vaako. It unsettled the commander more than he would have cared to admit.

It was better when the Purifier came toward him. At least the man wasn't standing off by himself, lingering in the background, piercing everyone with his critical gaze. Talking to him reduced Vaako's feeling that he had been weighed and found wanting.

He did not know the half of it.

"Long journey." Standing behind the commander, the Purifier peered past him, his gaze focused on the glistening firmament ahead. When the commander did not reply, the other man continued. "They can be a test, these deep runs. A test of our inner selves as well as of crew and vessel. Difficult to be so long away from the comforting confines of Necropolis. Yet sometimes they must be done. Long and lonely they are." His attention shifted to the martial figure before him. "Do you find that to be true, Vaako?"

"I know some do," the commander replied without admitting to anything. Unlike the Lord Marshal or his fellow commanders, the Purifier could sometimes be frustratingly cryptic. When beset with questions that were enigmatic, it was best to provide answers that were equally nonspecific. Vaako considered it only tactful. Dame Vaako would have called it self-preservation.

Not that he felt any threat from the Purifier. On the contrary, he was usually quite relaxed in the other man's presence. It was only when the spiritual head of the cause was standing behind him, out of sight, that he found himself wondering about the nature of the other man's thoughts. What did he think of Vaako? Of the Lord Marshal? Of their respective abilities, for example? It would be useful to know.

He couldn't ask, of course. That would have been worse than tactless. Such a blatant need to know would have suggested uncertainty: a dangerous trait in a high commander. But the fact that he dared not ask such things did not keep him from wondering about them.

"Just being so far from the armada," the Purifier was saying, "your head can fill with strange thoughts. Doubts. Don't you ever have doubts, Vaako? About the campaign? About our Lord Marshal?"

Was the Purifier trying to bait him? If so, the transparency of the attempt was an insult to the commander's intelligence. Surely a wise, knowledgeable adviser like himself could do better than that. It was a good thing Dame Vaako wasn't there, he knew. She would have been hard-pressed to keep from bursting out laughing at such obviousness. *There* was a woman, he knew, from whom even the most cunning diplomat could take lessons. Not for the first time, he found himself thinking how glad he was that she was on his side.

As for the Purifier's questions, he was able to respond straightforwardly and without hesitation.

"If you're here to test my loyalty, you succeed only in testing my patience. I have a task to perform that allows little time for such barefaced nonsense. Take your testing elsewhere and annoy others with it, Purifier. I am Vaako: first and always a Necromonger commander, a defender of the faith, and a leader of converts new, old, and always."

To this the Purifier only nodded, giving no indication whether he was satisfied or disappointed by the response. "Well spoken, noble Vaako. 'First and always.' Have you ever paused to consider the full meaning of the words we all speak? For myself, I have always wondered what that really signifies . . . 'always.'" Without another word, he pivoted and headed out of the command center.

Vaako watched him go. Peppered with queries, left in custody of a riddle, he was more disconcerted by the fleeting exchange than he had been when the Purifier had been staring at him from behind. What was the meaning of the brief confrontation? If the other man was not checking his loyalty, then what had been the purpose of it all? Amusement? Somehow that did not fit with what he knew of the Purifier's personality. The interpreter of the faith was nothing if not somber by nature.

A navigator was pressing him for a decision. Reluctantly, he abandoned the mystifying line of thought to return to the business at hand. *This was what was important,* he reminded himself. The work. The task that had been set before him. Not the philosophic ramblings of a solitary theologist. He respected the Purifier for his learning and for his devotion, but that did not mean Vaako had to admire him slavishly, nor pay close attention to everything he said.

There was no shower, no UV room where dirt could be removed and potentially infectious organisms destroyed. What the bottom level of the slam did have, however, were several streams of geothermally heated water. While they smelled of sulfur, the odor would soon wear off, and the minerals dissolved in the liquid actually made for a healthier soak than an equivalent amount of purified dihydrogen monoxide. The problem was not an insufficiency of hot water but an oversupply. Prisoners desiring to take a bath had to time their immersions carefully, as the temperature of the flows frequently jumped according to unpredictable variations in subsurface magmatic levels. Hop in too soon, and the flow might stop entirely. Linger too long, and you could find yourself parboiled redder than the last dinner delivery of unidentifiable alien arthropod. Or you might not emerge at all, until the guards came to fish out your boiled, blistered corpse.

Right now Riddick found the temperature just about right. Soaking away layers of grime and sweat was about the only real pleasure available to prisoners on Crematoria, and he relished the opportunity. There was no soap, but the mineral content of the water rendered unnecessary the need for artificial epidermal abrasives. The water stung the small gash on his cheek: a departing kiss from the woman who now called herself Kyra. The thought, or something else, made him turn and peer out from beneath the sweltering flow.

She was there, watching him from across the way. Watching and sharpening something reflective, edged, and pointed. Her expression was unreadable, her thoughts concealed. He kept an eye on her as he started to dry himself. A different voice greeted him, coming closer.

"Still passing through, I see."

Though outwardly studiously neutral, there was a twinkle in the Guv's eye. The possibility that at any moment it might turn to uncontrollable rage did not escape Riddick. He listened politely without letting down his guard.

Unexpectedly, the older man held up one hand. The fingers looked as if they had been run over by a transport sled. Several times. But they were all there, which spoke volumes about the man's ability to take care of himself even in the worst surroundings imaginable. A gold band glinted on one finger. It was nearly as scarred and beat-up as the flesh it encircled.

"I remember how gorgeous she was—well, gorgeous in the right light. But for the goddamn death of me, I cannot remember her name anymore."

Compressed in the quiet observation was an entire personal history: one the Guv chose not to expound upon. Instead, he motioned to another nearby convict. The second man was squatting around a particularly hot spot in the cavern floor. Suspended above the hot spot was a crude but serviceable setup for brewing liquids. In this case, Riddick suspected, the local variety of slam tea. Ingredients varied from prison to prison, but it was always something conjured out of fragments of edible material that was not part of the regular slam diet. In its own quiet, scalding way, seeping slam tea was a means of one-upping the guards, who were never granted access to it. If one was intrigued enough to come nosing around, the teapot was always empty—even if it had to be "accidentally" knocked over and its laboriously prepared contents dumped on the ground.

"Have one on me," the Guv offered. "Since we're all going to be here for the rest of our unnatural lives.

Not exactly the kind of welcome drink you get at the better outsystem hotels, but brewed with more honesty and care than you'll find anywhere else. And the price is right."

Riddick nodded. "Where do you get the water?"

The Guv gestured upward. "Distill it ourselves. Anytime you got this much water and this much heat, it ain't difficult to put together a still." He moved off, but stayed within earshot.

Displaying a certain coarse pride, the brewmaster offered a steaming cup to the new arrival. "Tobacco, syrmoss, bits and pieces of this and that. Sweetener when we can get it. Nothing harmful." He grinned, showing an impressive deficiency of teeth. "Nothing diuretic. Tastes better than you think." When Riddick kept his hands down and continued to eye the cup, the brewer's attitude changed instantly. "What, you don't want to drink the Guv's tea?"

At this, a number of the other convicts in the immediate vicinity began to gravitate closer. In a moment, they had surrounded Riddick. A prisoner could go solo if he wanted to, but violating hospitality—that was something that could not be allowed to pass unremarked upon. Preparatory to making any remarks, several of the convicts had picked up fist-sized rocks or hand-made utensils.

"Maybe he knows nothing's free in slam," one of them commented.

"Got nothing to sell, nothing to trade." Another greedily eyed Riddick's boots and goggles, even though he had no idea of the special nature of those dark lenses. "Nothing he'll give over *voluntary,* that is."

"We can *make* him comply," a third insisted, shuffling the sharp rock he held back and forth between his hands.

"Information," exclaimed still another member of the gathering pack. "First newcomer in months. Information for tea. That's a fair trade."

"What kind of information?" the one who envied Riddick his boots snapped.

"News." Two of the inmates voiced the wish simultaneously. "Outside news. Outsystem news. Like about the rumors."

"Guards' rumors," growled a bigger man. "Shit and spittle."

"No," insisted his companion. "Too much natter about the same matter." He looked hopefully at the still silent, attentive Riddick. "We hear things. Even down here. Visitors talk to the boss, boss talks to the guards, guards bitch among themselves. Talk about some kind of widespread invasion. Multiple worlds, not just one. Some kind of spirits, or spirit-infested folk."

"More like gods, I heard," another inmate chipped in uneasily.

"What planets? Which ones?" the second speaker demanded.

"They can't be killed," the one whose concern had prompted this line of talk insisted. "At least, it's said that their leaders can't. Because they're already dead."

Initially skeptical, the biggest of the convicts now

found himself peering uncertainly at Riddick. "Is it true? Any of it? Or is it all interplanetary bullshit?"

Riddick let his gaze travel slowly over each and every one of them. "They call themselves Necromongers. And it sure as fuck was true on Helion Prime."

Now he accepted the tea and drank thirstily from the metal cup. While he did so, the news rippled through the assembled convicts and rapidly passed up the rings of tiers all the way to the top of the uppermost prisoner level. Whispers winged from cell to workstation and back, traversing the prison like a bad wind.

"Helion Prime—they're on Helion Prime. . . ."

One of the convicts who had spoken first stepped forward, his tone and expression a confused mix of pride and fear. "I'm Helion Four. You're not just sunning us, newcomer? These people really exist, and they've taken Helion Prime?"

Riddick peered over the rim of the cup. "I was there. I saw it. I smelled it. Bunch of mercs snatched me clear." His goggled eyes dropped back down to the cup. "Right now, not much difference between there and here. One hell's noisier, the other's hotter."

Another inmate presented himself. "Helion Six—dammit. Still got family there." His eyes pleaded with Riddick even if his voice did not. "You think these freaks are gonna take Helion Six, too?"

Riddick said nothing. Stating the obvious would only make the two men feel that much worse. It was transparently clear that if Helion Prime completely went under, the entire Helion system would fall to the

Necromongers. He knew military strategy, even if these poor cage monkeys did not. There was no need for the Necromongers to attack Helion VI, or IV, because both secondary inhabited worlds relied on Helion Prime for the basics necessary to keep their commerce and societies functioning. The Necromongers knew this, too, hence their bypassing of the outer worlds to launch a straightforward attack on Helion Prime itself.

Faces turned to the Guv as the other convicts waited for him to announce the name of his home world. Whether he would have done so or not no one knew, because they were interrupted by the sound of multiple doors opening somewhere overhead. And another sound, different entirely.

To the prisoners, an all-too familiar, unearthly, and bone-tingling howling.

It was new to Riddick, however. Head tilted back, he stood and listened with interest. Meanwhile, the Guv put an end to the conversation. "Doesn't matter where anyone's from. Not here. There's just one world now: this one. And we didn't get to pick it."

Above, security doors opened and shut as the detachment of guards entered the prison proper. Working quickly, they unfastened bridles and removed muzzles. As soon as the latter came off, they stepped back fast. No matter how much experience one had with the hellhounds, it was impossible to predict their initial reactions at being released. Usually, the beasts followed their training. Usually. It was the occasional, rare, but not unknown psychoflip you had to look out for. More than one guard bore physical evidence of this in the form of scars not even modern medicine could completely erase. There were also a couple of ex-slam employees buried Outside. One had not reacted soon enough to his animal's drastic mood shift. The other had made the mistake of teasing a large male by withholding its food. The enraged hellhound had eaten the guard's face instead. That was a gaffe every other guard handler was careful not to repeat.

The name of the creatures derived from their appearance, which was vaguely caninelike without possessing so much as a single strand of earthly doggy DNA. At times they could also appear strikingly feline, though there was no more cat in them than dog. They were wholly alien, imported from a world noted for the ferocity of its native fauna. That they were manipulatable at all was a tribute to a few small dedicated families who had settled on their home world and made quite a nice business out of training and exporting the animals. In nowise, however, could the hellhounds be called domesticated. Their inherent and unsuppressed wildness made them that much more useful in such occupations as prison work.

Occasionally, as a special treat, they got to eat a prisoner.

Just watching them deploy was a lesson in vertebrate efficiency. Flying over a walkway, their scaly, slate-gray skin changing color as the chromatophores within reacted to the animals' heightened emotional state, they were a perfect image of racing terror. Seeing them, the last thing anyone, down to the toughest of inmates, would want to do was get in their way. Relaxed and at ease, knowing that the path ahead would be cleared for them by the eager patrolling beasts, armed guards followed.

Word traveled quickly throughout the prison. Shouts of warning made the rounds of the ranked tiers, descended to areas inhabited only by those who scavenged for food in the sulfurous depths. Cell doors slammed shut; not to keep prisoners in, but to keep four-legged berserker carnivores out. The inquisitive crowd that had gathered around Riddick evaporated as convicts sought shelter in open cells or among the rocks.

"Here they come!" The shouts rained down. "Slot up, slot up! Get off the tiers!"

Head back, the Guv all but shook a fist skyward. "A herd! A goddamn herd. *Is that all we are to you?*"

Pushing frantically past his fellows, the man who had first questioned Riddick scrambled around him toward safety. "Flee now, talk later! The cull is on!"

Lowering his gaze, the Guv turned to Riddick. Without saying so, he had apparently come to a decision regarding the new prisoner. "Just don't let the howlers catch you out. Find an empty cell, a crevice, anything. Make sure it's solid—you can't believe how strong the bastards are. If they think they can get at you, they'll try to bite their way in right through the rock. And if you're confronted, do not—*do not*—make eye contact. Play deaf and dumb and you *might* get away with it." He started off in the opposite direction. "Or you might get to be lunch."

Above, more guards were descending via the lift. One hound was giving its handler added trouble.

Snarling and hissing, it snapped at the guard's maulstick but was finally jabbed into compliance. Its ear tag identified it as #5, but the nameplate it wore was considerably more evocative: Thrash.

Circling the prison singly and in pairs, hellhounds did their work, making sure level after level was clear of prisoners. To their disappointment, it usually was. The slam on Crematoria had no need of elaborate scan and check systems, no need for guards to inspect every cell and hiding place individually. The hellhound pack did it for them. Furthermore, the pack could not suffer from systems failure, or electronic breakdown, or a power outage. Should any of those events take place, either as a result of an escape attempt or naturally occurring breakdown, all prison administration had to do to secure the entire complex was release the hellhounds and let them run free.

Years earlier, a trio of prisoners had tried just that. They had succeeded in shutting down all electronics in the hope of reaching the landing hangar and overpowering the crew of the regular supply ship. They were found in the transport tunnel, barely ten meters from the prison access station, with half a dozen snarling hellhounds on top of them. By the time the handlers managed to pull the pack off the would-be escapees, there was nothing left but a pile of bones, cracked and broken to extract the marrow.

That was the one and only time anyone had tried such a stunt.

Continuing on their patrol, multiple animals leaped gaps between tiers that no human could manage without mechanical aid. One brute, hungrier and more hopeful than its fellows, disdained the ramps in favor of sliding down the solidified lava fall. Its claws left grooves in the rock.

The overall effect was one of controlled panic, if that wasn't a contradiction in terms. Stumbling over one another, shoving fellow prisoners out of the way, grim-faced convicts scrambled to find cells with doors that closed tight. Caught out far from their chosen abodes, one group resorted to grabbing a de-hinged door off the ground and frantically propping it into place, wedging it tight with rocks and whatever other materials they could find.

Loping along one of the lower levels toward her own residence, Kyra found herself cut off. Ignoring the ramps, one of the hounds had come down a service chute. Half crazed with longing for the taste of human flesh they might be, but they weren't stupid. Repetition prompted learning. One day she would not be surprised to see members of the pack using the lift in an attempt to beat unlucky prisoners to their cells.

Spotting her, the hellhound lengthened its already impressive stride, then leaped. Instead of trying to dodge the animal, she accelerated straight toward it. At the last possible instant she dropped, sliding feet-first beneath it, and was up and running on the other side before the creature hit the ground. It turned within its own body length, but by that time she was on a rope and rappelling her way to the bottom of the cavern.

One group of guards was methodically patrolling the upper tiers, whistling menacingly as they walked.

The second group made its way downward via the central lift. A couple of them carried powerful spotlights. These were used to pick out prisoners foolish enough to remain out of their cells. Whether it was done for reasons of security, to provide a quick snack for the hellhounds, or simply for the guards' amusement it was impossible to say. It was just the way it was in Crematoria slam.

At the bottom of the cavern, a pair of sulfide scavengers vanished into a fissure so rank with the smell of sulfur-laden steam not even a hellhound would enter it. Not far away, a prisoner who had hatched the crazy idea of waiting in hiding in hopes of grabbing onto the bottom of the lift and finding himself hoisted to the half freedom of slam control found himself confronted by one of the remorseless creatures. He turned to run but wasn't nearly fast enough. The sounds of human shrieks mixed with delighted snarl-hisses drifted upward through the cavern. Fortunately, the accompanying crunching sounds were too subdued to be heard more than one tier up.

Riddick had sequestered himself behind one of the geothermal cascades the prison population used for bathing. The steaming rush was loud enough to mute any sounds, the sulfurous stink strong enough to mask any body odor. Droplets of heavily mineralized water beaded up on his goggles as he stared silently into the surge.

They did not prevent him from seeing the approaching hellhound. He lifted his goggles in an attempt to obtain a clearer view. Head sweeping back and forth over the ground, the creature would occasionally lift its muzzle to sniff at the air, then drop its jaws to the surface again. As it strode past, Riddick had the opportunity to observe the muscles rippling along its flanks, the razor teeth that flashed in its jaws, the feral glint in its predatory alien eyes. Powerful and lightning fast, it was capable of easily overwhelming any human.

It continued past the cascade—and stopped. Maybe it sensed movement not generated by water. Maybe some smell lingered in the air. Whatever the reason, it turned sharply, growling deep in its throat, and approached the waterfall. Pushing through the aqueous veil, it nosed steadily deeper within. Rising up on its hind legs, it was even more impressive than it had been on all fours. As it probed, an identification tag jiggled against one ear. Number five. Piercing, animal eyes flashed menacingly.

And came face-to-face with Riddick. Eyeshine to eyeshine.

XI

The Guv's chosen living quarters lay nearby. While the majority of prisoners preferred to live on one of the upper tiers, near the control center, he and the other, more wizened convicts had made their homes at or near the bottom of the cavern. There was no sky to be glimpsed from the upper levels, anyway, and the guards got to you sooner. Sure, the air was a little fresher, but for a lifer that was only a tease best avoided. It wasn't really fresh air, anyway, a commodity that was sorely lacking on Crematoria. Down bottom, a man or woman had time to think. And to forget.

In his convoluted, troubled, difficult life, the Guv had seen it all. Or thought he had, until that moment. Moving to the bars of his self-sealed cell, he gaped in amazement at what he thought he was seeing. It was hard to tell, at a distance and with all that falling water. There was Riddick, that was for sure. And there was a hellhound—that was a surety also. It was the interaction that caused him to blink and rub several times at his sulfur-stained eyes. Because it could not be happening.

Riddick was petting the hellhound. Toying with it, slapping it playfully back and forth across its lethal muzzle. Once, the Guv could have sworn he saw the newcomer put his clenched fist *inside* the predator's mouth. Instead of snapping off the morsel in one bite, the hellhound gnawed on it affectionately. The Guv would have doubted it all, attributed what he was seeing to age and delusion, except for one thing: as he stared, the hellhound's flushed skin changed from an energized deep red to a neutral slate gray.

Within the mist-shrouded cascade, Riddick continued to play with the carnivore. As he did so, he noted the deep scars on its muzzle and body, the dark slashes that were the mark of a maulstick applied at maximum power. He chucked the hellhound under its chin and it snapped at him playfully.

"Yeah," he muttered. "Know how it feels."

Outside the cascade, a sharp whistle sounded, piercing the unwholesome air of the cavern. At its sound, the hellhound dropped to all fours, backed off, and departed.

With reluctance.

As the lift touched bottom, the quartet of guards that was riding it jumped off. Adjusting breather units and checking weapons, they headed for the base of the lavafall. Periodically, it was necessary to perform a comprehensive sweep of each part of the prison. One never knew what kind of fiendish deviltry the prisoners might get up to if left too long to their own devices.

Today, it was the turn of the cavern bottom, the top of the volcanic plug that had choked off the flow of magma to the now empty core. There wasn't much to it. Anything resembling a permanent, functional installation had been pretty much ruined by the surprise lava flow of decades before. But with convicts, you never knew. Better to regularly scan every centimeter of the prison than to wake up one morning to find out the system had overlooked something potentially dangerous.

The area around the base of the lavafall was exactly where one might expect to encounter such problems. Full of nooks and crannies of tormented stone mixed with the remnants of the prison installation that the lava had destroyed, it was the perfect place for a convict to dwell in self-imposed isolation, away from guards and prison routine. A place where plots might be hatched. While the handlers and their hellhounds cleared the tiers elsewhere, the four-man team began probing places where sedition might lurk.

What they found was Kyra. Light beams joined together to focus on the single figure, momentarily blinding her.

"And just when you thought the cull was over," one of the guards commented as the shape of the prisoner was identified. A nice shape, too, he thought to himself. Of course, down here, you never knew whether a protrusion beneath prison clothes was part of the prisoner, or a portent of something potentially treacherous. So even though there were four of them and only one of her, the guards still advanced with caution.

"Runnin' solo." The nominal leader of the group let his light sweep their immediate surroundings, search for scat or urine. "Hounds ain't been through here. Could be she's trying to hide something. Which is why we're here." He used his light to gesture at the unmoving figure. "Check her out, make sure she's clean." Alongside him, his three colleagues hesitated, looking at each other, avoiding their superior's gaze.

"C'mon," the senior member of the foursome chided his comrades. "What're you afraid of? What is she, fifty kilos? Search her."

Taking the lead, one of the other guards warily entered the open cell where Kyra had retreated. Making himself as large as possible, he gestured with his maulstick.

"Let's go, sweetheart. You know the routine."

Without a word, she turned, placed her hands against the wall, palm forward, and spread her legs, assuming the classic, age-old search position. Her compliance was more than encouraging: it was stimulating. Thus motivated, the other guards edged forward to join their colleague.

"Too bad Pavlov couldn't see this," one of them murmured.

The guard who had been bold enough to approach moved closer. Close enough for her booted foot to rub up and down his lower leg. The action simultaneously calmed and encouraged him. This wasn't going to be so difficult after all. Some of the female inmates, now, they made a habit of being troublesome. That was what the maulstick was for. But this one . . .

Eyes closed, Kyra was repeating some private mantra. "'Sokay . . . it's okay . . . it's okay. . . ."

The guard thought she was murmuring to him: mistakenly so. But, momentarily mesmerized by the inviting sight spread out before him, that part of his brain that should have been on full alert had turned to tapioca. Advancing the rest of the way, he put one hand on her back. It was well muscled, of course. Young or old, male or female, there was no fat on any of the inmates. Crematoria's diet was not conducive to the accumulation of excess avoirdupois. His other hand reached up between her legs . . .

At which point a pair of steel spurs snapped out of the heel of her boot, driving upward and back, gaffing him like a trapped fish. The way his eyes bugged out was pretty piscine, too. He was too startled to scream.

That would come later, when he had time to fully comprehend where the steel had struck home.

Rabbit quick, her head snapped straight back to break his nose. Whirling around, she grabbed the maulstick and slammed it into him, driving the already half-unconscious mass into the cell bars. Libido literally crushed, he slid to the hard ground as limp as a sack of Jello.

It was the best she could do. Her intent, her hope, had been to break through and escape to the other side of the cavern, where she could take refuge in the sweltering hideouts of the sulfide collectors. She was not quite fast enough. One of the remaining three guards caught her as she dodged past the other two. Despite taking a solid whack from the purloined maulstick, he held on long enough for his companions to pile in. She crumpled beneath the sheer weight of massed muscle and raging testosterone.

The maulstick was wrenched from her fingers. Behind, as the three of them wrestled her toward a smooth patch of ground, the guard she had gaffed had lapsed into unconsciousness. Too bad, the leader of the remaining trio thought grimly. He was going to miss all the fun. They would make it last as long as they could, of course. But of one thing he was certain: this was one convict who by tomorrow morning would no longer be around to collect her food ration. She'd earned that end for what she'd just done.

Two of them were putting her down on the ground, pinning her with their weight. They ignored her curses and involuntarily moans of pain, not caring if they broke anything in the process. They were all three of them plenty mad: mad at what she had done to their colleague, mad that she had managed to get away with it, and particularly mad that they had been so easily put off their guard. That wouldn't happen again.

The guard holding her left arm down frowned. Something was hovering in the shadows behind them, in the direction of the central cavern. As he stared, it emerged from the darkness. Just another convict, drinking calmly from a metal cup. Well, no matter how long he lingered or what he saw, the intruder was not going to get any. If he was lucky, the guards would let him disappear back the way he had come, instead of making him disappear permanently. Not that the slam boss was likely to raise an eyebrow over the death of one more prisoner. Especially after being told what she had done to a member of his staff.

The figure spoke. "You should take your wounded and go." The newcomer nodded in the direction of the guard lying unconscious and bleeding in the cell. "Chalk it up to lessons learned. Take him and get out. While you can."

Slowly, the guards rose from the slender shape they had been pinning to the ground. Raising her head slightly, Kyra lay there, not getting up. Not wanting to meet the business end of another maulstick. The three guards formed a small semicircle facing Riddick. They were not happy at having their fun interrupted.

The biggest of them sneered at the would-be knight with no horse and no shining armor. "Is there a name for this private little world of yours? The one you seem to be living in at the moment? And what happens there when we don't just run away, huh? You kill us?" He gestured. "With your soup cup?"

His friends snickered, appreciating their colleague's wit. For his part, Riddick contemplated the metal cup, as if sizing up its potential.

"Tea, actually," he murmured.

The big guard frowned, uncertain he'd heard correctly. "Whazzat?"

"I will kill you with a teacup."

Inverting the container, he set it down just soooo on a nearby rock. No guest at a formal dinner could have been more precise. Unnerved, but not unduly so, the big guard's eyes flicked between convict and cup, cup and convict. A part of him insisted that he was missing something. Another part insisted that it didn't matter. The latter won. He looked over at his superior.

The leader of the trio shrugged indifferently. "You know the rule. They aren't dead if they're still on the books."

The big guard nodded, then seemed to lapse into introspection. What he was actually doing was slipping the illegal blade from its sewn-in scabbard in the back of his pants. Once the point cleared his ass, he charged.

Even before he started forward, Riddick had picked the cup up again—and slammed it down. Hard and sideways, at a carefully precalculated angle. The rock it scraped was ragged and broken. It imparted a similar edge to the rim of the cup. A serrated edge, though not one that would win any prizes at a tool-sharpening competition.

It didn't have to. The result was not neat, but it was effective. As the big guard reached him, Riddick blocked the slicing knife strike. Instead of retreating, he lunged ahead, right into his attacker. His right hand jammed the jagged rim of the cup forward, driving it in and down with tremendous velocity. The metal was thin but well-forged and composed of a particularly tough alloy, designed to take a good deal of rough treatment and last. Despite the force behind it, it did not snap and break.

The muscles of the guard's belly were composed of

less sturdy stuff. The ragged cup rim ripped through them, making a very impressive hole. When Riddick drew his arm back, the hole filled with blood and bits of some slick, colorful internal organs. Stunned, the guard grabbed at himself. Riddick threw him back into his comrades.

Dodging around the flaccid body, they leveled maulsticks and other devices designed to subdue unruly prisoners. As they did so, Riddick removed a food-tin key from a pocket, showed it to them, and set it down on a prominent rock. Just soooo.

The two survivors hesitated, exchanged a glance. Then they started backing up. It wasn't easy for them to lug their surviving wounded colleague from the cell. But they managed.

It was less debilitating than the alternative.

Slowly climbing to her feet, Kyra sauntered over to the guard Riddick had killed, bent, and with an effort, yanked the bloody cup from his body.

"Death by teacup. Damn, why didn't I think of that?"

Ignoring the fact that she was now in possession of the lethal cup, Riddick turned and looked back the way he'd come. "Wouldn't have worked for you. Insufficient mass behind it. Wrong kinetics."

"Another time, other circumstances," she replied sharply, "that might be taken as a compliment."

"Yeah, yeah," he muttered, searching for any indication that the guards might have already managed to summon reinforcements. "Not that I mind playing Who's the Better Killer, but it might be a good idea if we move along to the next thing."

"Oh, you don't get off that easy. Not when you started it. 'Sides," she whispered into his ear as she darted past him, "it's my favorite game."

She started to whirl away from him, but he was too fast. A viselike hand whipped out to catch her and spin her around. He was tired of games. Tired of riddles.

"Did I hear right about you? That you came *lookin'* for me?"

Her expression was half smile, half snarl. "If that's what you heard," she shot back rebelliously, "then you missed the good part. I hooked up with some mercs out of Lupus Five. Said they'd take me on, teach me the trade, give me a fair cut." Turning briefly away from him, she spat at the ground. "But first job out, they flipped me to a pack of 'Golls. They slaved me out, Riddick." She stared at him, seeing her own face reflected in his goggles.

"You know what that can do to you? When you're that age? When you're twelve years old?"

She was selling the sympathy thing, and Riddick wasn't buying. He never did. Life was a bitch, you looked out for yourself or you didn't, and the galaxy was a cold, cold place. Not all the steam that was rising came from the vents around them.

"I *told* you to stay in New Mecca. Why didn't you listen to me?" He added, almost to himself, "Why doesn't anyone ever listen to me." His voice returned to normal and he was in her face now, at once accusing and advising. "I had mercs on my neck then. I'll *always* have mercs on my neck. And then you go and sign up? With those no-good wannabe *badges*? The same guys I was steerin' away from you?"

Seeking a release for his frustration, he turned away and slammed a fist into the nearest wall. The solid mass indented beneath his scarred knuckles. She knew he was doing it instead of pounding *her*. His fury cowed her—for about two seconds. She had long ago passed beyond being intimidated. After all, she had come to realize, all anyone could do was kill you. She had lost her fear of that along with her youth. Or maybe before. Sometimes, it was hard to remember things. Oftentimes, it was better not to.

So she continued to confront him. "What're you pitchin' at me, Riddick? That you cuttin' out was a good thing? That you had my scrawny twelve-year-old ass covered from halfway across the galaxy?" She snorted derisively. "I was supposed to take that on faith, huh? That was supposed to be my salvation? A few words from you and then bam, you're gone, gone."

He was muttering to himself. She knew he must have heard her, but he did not acknowledge it. "Mercs. She signed with mercs."

The knife she twisted in him had no blade, but it cut deeply just the same.

"There was nobody else around."

Up above, in slam control central, word of the confrontation far below had yet to work its way up to the notice of the slam boss. Right now, he and everyone else in the room had more important things on their minds. An important ritual was about to take place; one of the few daily activities of any real importance on Crematoria. Things were about to happen in swift succession that would brook no error. That they occurred once a day did not mean they could be taken lightly. Everything depended on certain equipment, certain instruments, working flawlessly day after monotonous day. The alternative was possible death: not monotonous perhaps, but to be avoided nonetheless.

Having been given the run of the facility (perhaps in Douruba's hope that while doing so they might run afoul of some fatal encounter and save him the trouble of further bargaining), Toombs and his copilot had just entered the control room. Immediately aware something of importance was taking place, he and Logan moved off to one side. Out of the way, they kept to themselves and watched. All information, Toombs knew, was potentially useful information.

Certainly the slam boss and the guard techs in the control room were sufficiently preoccupied with what they were doing to ignore the visitors. The chief tech was monitoring a dozen different readouts. One supplied, among other stats, the external temperature. Presently, it was minus one hundred and rising fast. Toombs's pilot eyed it with interest. The only other place he had ever been that showed such numbers was out in deep space itself, and there they didn't fluctuate as rapidly as this.

"Terminator approaching," the chief guard tech was reporting methodically. Throughout the control room, readouts changed by the second, screens flared, and alarms began to beep for attention.

The temperature readout suddenly went green. A bell rang, sounding above the multiple beepings. Douruba straightened and regarded his team.

"Clock's running, people. Let's pop the cork."

Another tech moved hands over console. Toombs and his colleagues grabbed for the nearest unmoving object as the whole control room shuddered slightly. But it was a light tremor. What was unusual was that it continued, a steady vibration in the floor, in the walls.

The control room was rising out of its hole, a slow mechanical mole preparing to peek out at the surface. It ascended on massive, solid alloy screws. The mechanics seemed primitive, but even sealed hydraulics couldn't survive long on Crematoria. If the control room happened to get stuck topside when the sun came up, simple screw mechanisms would behave a lot better than hydraulics, and presumably survive. That was the theory, anyway, tested and verified through computer simulation.

By technicians and designers who had never actually set foot on Crematoria, the prison staff knew. None of them had any desire to test the validity of that particular mechanical thesis.

This morning, like every other morning, everything worked as intended, however. Simple in design but sound in practice, the screw and lift system elevated the control room until it was well above the surface. Equally rudimentary, the huge vents on the lower, uninhabited sides of the control room louvered open. Multiple fan-powered exchangers whirred to life and began the vital process of swapping the old, sulfur-impregnated air inside the prison with recently chilled, fresh air from outside.

Along with meals, it was one of the few eagerly anticipated moments of the day. Prisoners back in their cells moved to doors and bars to suck in as much of the fresh outside air as possible. Concealed oxygen generators supplemented the nitrogen and argon that dominated the planet's atmosphere. That was the reason for the hellhound-policed cull. With the control center elevated, it was theoretically possible for a wily prisoner to slip beneath it and gain access to the outside. Why any fool would want to do so, no one could imagine. But rules were rules. Even futile escapes would mess with the count, and despite what Toombs might think, Douruba prided himself on his bookkeeping.

Mixing with the rising steam and hot air from below, the cool, descending wind greeted Riddick as he made his way back up to the prison's middle tiers. He stopped outside a cell that had opened early. To no surprise, it belonged to the Guv, who was not above defying prison regulations if only to show that he could. But though he might look longingly at the gap between the underside of the control room and the rock rim that marked the beginnings of the actual surface, the other man made no move to ascend in its direction. He knew all too well that what awaited outside was not freedom but only a different kind of hell. He did not look in the newcomer's direction as Riddick approached, but he knew the newcomer was there.

Riddick followed the older convict's gaze. "So they

do go topside—to swap out air." He was nodding to himself, thinking hard. "'Lot simpler and cheaper than installing full-term recyclers."

"That ain't the only reason," the Guv told him dourly. "See, they wanna make room for more." His expression twisted. "This place has a reputation to maintain. The one slam nobody escapes from. Not even the dead."

Up on the surface, being careful where they stepped, a group of guards bore the bodies of the two inmates who had been unlucky enough to be caught outside their cells during the last cull. The unfortunate pair would soon have company, though. Their bodies were unceremoniously dumped on the pile of dust and lingering bones reserved for those not holding a ticket off Crematoria. Unlike with their previous burden, a fellow guard, this time no one suggested taking the time to sprinkle words over the remains.

The terminator passed quickly. Inside the control room, relevant instrumentation signified that a full air exchange had been accomplished. Without waiting to double-check the validity of the claim, technicians swiftly adjusted controls and issued orders. A computer could have done it faster, and easier. But software was prone to glitches, computers to breakdowns. Crematoria was one place where the reliability of hand-operated, old-fashioned mechanics was more than prized: it was deemed essential to continued survival. So levers were pulled and buttons pushed, while advanced voice-operated instrumentation was reserved for preparing food, providing entertainment, and prison operations less critical to the business of surviving another day.

Vents began to close and seal as it grew lighter out on the surface. Exchangers shut down and locked in position. As rapidly as it had ascended, the control room began to lower on its support screws. Through the ports, the sun-shattered terrain outside began to vanish from sight, giving way to smooth-sided walls of solid rock. Moments later, there came a slight jolt as the room docked in its home position. Latches secured room and screws. Their work done for another day, unseen engines and their backups went dormant. Having followed the entire procedure with interest, Toombs nodded appreciatively.

"One way to clean house . . ."

He eyed the largest of the temperature gauges. The control room had only been docked for minutes when the readout broke two hundred and kept rising. It would level out somewhere around four hundred F, he knew. Anything more than that, and atmosphere would boil off into space. Satisfied he had acquired another fragment of potentially useful knowledge, he and his team members turned to leave.

A sound made them halt. It started as a low vibration in the soles of their boots, rising steadily until they could hear it clearly even within the sealed confines of the control room. Continuing to increase in intensity, it made the pilot think of a runaway drive on a long-range starship. The mercenaries stood as if frozen. Though there was no reason to think anything dangerous was passing above them, they eyed the ceiling instinctively. A sound as of a million hoofed animals stampeding in panic directly over their heads caused the pilot to flinch.

Toombs and the copilot thought to recheck the temperature readout. The number was an even three hundred F and still rising.

Raising her voice in order to make herself heard, the dazed copilot bawled aloud, "Jesus—what *is* that?"

No one answered her. Maybe, despite her effort, no one heard. Or maybe, despite their familiarity with the incredible winds driven by the pressure differential between the hot side and dark side, none of the guard techs wanted to take the time to look up from their instruments. Not until it had passed.

Though not nearly as frightening since it was diminished by distance and rock, the topside roaring could be heard down on the tiers as well. With the refresh completed, inmates knew they could safely emerge from their cells and hiding places. For a little while, at least, the atmosphere within the prison would be a tolerable mix of fresh air and human stench. Then the rising steam and sputtering sulfur vents would slowly corrupt it again, leaving it stinking and barely breathable until the next refresh—fifty-two hours hence.

Tracking Riddick, Kyra had followed his progress upward. Now as she approached she saw that he and the Guv were deep in discussion, with several other convicts paying close attention to what was being said. As was appropriate, she did not try to inject herself into the conversation; she merely halted off to one side, listened (which was permitted unless otherwise declared), and waited.

Taking note of her arrival, Riddick turned slightly. "When it happens, it'll happen fast. You can either stay here for the rest of your unnatural life, or be on my leg when I cut fence."

At his words, Kyra's expression turned hopeful—until she realized he had been speaking to the Guv. Or had he? Unsure whether to reflect optimism or despair, her expression went blank. Riddick did nothing to ease her concern.

One of the convicts grunted a common mantra. "Nobody outs from this place. Not alive. Never has happened, never will happen. Ain't no place to out, to."

Riddick let his gaze drift ceilingward. Toward the distant control room. "I ain't nobody." With that, he wandered off, tracked by a dozen intent, curious eyes. The Guv's were among them. His expression, Kyra decided, was full of uncertainty—and longing. It disgusted her. They didn't know Riddick, his lies, his phony promises, his falsely comforting words. They hadn't been abandoned by him.

"Go ahead," she snapped bitterly. "Listen to him. Eat it up. Fall for it. You won't be the first." Turning sharply, she stalked away.

XII

At first glance there appeared to be nothing at the nexus of all the chains. Links and barbs, hooks and bells, the elaborate metal conglomeration seemed to clank and jangle its way down the ceremonial steps of the Basilica without any visible driving force behind it. It was only on close inspection that trained eyes could make out a single figure secured in the middle. That figure appeared to fade in and out of reality, like an unstable vision induced by a hallucinogenic overdose.

Trailing metal, Aereon carefully made her way down the stairs in the company of an escort composed of Necromonger elite troops. Under their guidance she found herself steered toward a waiting warrior ship. She did not waste time and energy protesting her condition and treatment to those who obviously could not alter it.

Once secured in a room deep within the transport, her chains were removed. The interior was dimly lit, a condition favored by the Necromongers. As she began to come to grips with her new surroundings, a figure emerged from the darkness.

"Doesn't it strike you odd?" Dame Vaako offered conversationally as she approached. She was smiling pleasantly, as did many carnivores before beginning to feed.

Aereon did not bother to respond. More aware than the majority of their species of the steady passing of time, Elementals were not inclined to waste it on games.

Her silence did not trouble Dame Vaako, who halted nearby. "I tell you, it's quite interesting, some of the things that are happening. We do live in intriguing times. Here we have the current lord marshal engaged in the methodic slaughter and ruination of entire societies, the better to advance the faith. This demanding activity he directs without hesitation and with admirable thoroughness." Her eyes locked on those of the other woman.

"Yet he cannot bring himself to kill one stranded Elemental. Afflicted as I am with something of a curious nature, I find myself asking: why not?" This time, when no response was forthcoming, she seemed disappointed. Not that she had really expected a willing and forthright explanation. So she changed the subject, at least for now.

"You don't pray to our God. That is hardly a surprise. You pray to no God, I hear. That is not especially a surprise, either. My curiosity picking at me again, I suppose. What do you do instead? With what do you fill that void in human speculation?"

Aereon finally chose to respond. "Elementals—we calculate."

Dame Vaako struggled to repress a smile. "Oh, don't we all."

Grasping the irony, the other woman took a moment to clarify. "Please be certain you understand what I am saying. We calculate the odds of future scenarios. Different ways in which the universe might balance itself. We are doing this constantly. But we always do so with a neutral eye. Given our historical position, it would be wrong to involve ourselves in the day-to-day affairs of others. We believe in letting the rest of humankind work out its own intersocietal relationships." Her gaze met that of the much younger woman. "It would be immoral to impose ourselves and any opinions we might hold on other societies."

Dame Vaako could repress her rising amusement but not her deeper feelings. Sarcasm bubbled up within her like oil in a polluted spring.

"Spare me any lofty protestations of principled indifference. You have as much interest in what is going on in the civilized portions of the galaxy as the governing council on the most populated world or the members of a miners' cooperative on the most out-of-the-way moon. It is well-known that Elementals have their own agenda, their own design. Elementals don't believe in God because they hope to *be* God."

Their eyes locked. Neither blinked, neither looked away—but for a moment something new passed between them. Something kindred, perhaps, on a personal if not necessarily philosophical level.

It prompted Aereon's curious query. "And what of you, Dame Vaako? Companion to the noted military commander Vaako himself. What do you hope to be? What are your wishes for the future? Not as a member of Necromonger society, but as an individual? What, for example, do you hope to be when the current lord marshal is gone? For will that not affect you on a personal level, and also as a dutiful member of your social order? Do you not, despite your individual devotion to your cause, have desires that extend beyond it? It would be unnatural if you did not." Her expression shifted slightly. "You would not be human if you did not."

"Treasonous talk, Aereon. I like you already."

"Not treasonous for me," the Elemental replied. "I cannot speak treason against a society to which I do not belong. I am only making casual observations in response to your various inquiries."

Dame Vaako eyed her perceptively. "Calculating?"

Aereon did not exactly shrug. It was more a slight readjustment of her upper body. "As I have said, we are always calculating."

With a nod of acknowledgment, Dame Vaako turned to the pilot nearby. With a deepening hum, the transport rose from the ground. Conversation turned to the petty and inconsequential as Dame Vaako and her "guest" moved across the floor.

"This is all very interesting," she finally told the Elemental. "It is also a waste of time. There are many things I can spare, but time is not one of them. Not now. I look forward to pursuing our discussion of individual philosophies and personal motivations at some future date." Her voice darkened slightly. "I hope that will be possible. It would be regrettable if adverse circumstances were to intervene." She halted.

"As you may already have calculated," she continued, with just the right touch of mockery, "there are other, more important matters that require attention. Let us have first things first." Her words came faster now; clipped and demanding. "What of the individual known as Riddick? Where can he be found?"

Aereon did not hesitate. "In truth, I don't know where he went. We Elementals know many things, but we are not omniscient."

Dame Vaako stepped back. "In *truth,* I'm more interested in where he came from."

This time the Elemental hesitated. Dame Vaako responded, not with another query, but by operating a nearby control. A door opened beneath the other woman, forcing her to back up toward her host.

"Watch your step." Dame Vaako did not grin.

Beneath them, the devastated rooftops of the capital swam into view: ruined apartment complexes, individual residences, office buildings, commercial centers, government facilities, all reduced in perspective by the transport's slow ascent. The view was a reminder of, among other things, Necromonger prowess and power. Wind howled as the warmer air within the ship mixed with the cooler atmosphere outside. At a signal from Dame Vaako, the transport stopped its climb. It remained at the chosen altitude, hovering, as its operators waited for further instructions.

Dame Vaako eyed her guest, whose attention was directed downward. "In truth, still no recollection of the Riddick's origins?" Her voice turned coaxing. "No memory at all of his home world, his lineage, how and why he came to find himself on Helion Prime at this crucial time—or how we came to find him here?" She paused, allowing the Elemental a moment for reflection. Not only on the inquiry, but on their present relative position.

"Still nothing?" she finally pressed. "You say that your people are good at calculations. Do me a favor. Assuming your continued refusal to answer my questions, calculate the odds of your getting off this planet alive."

With a sharp gesture, she borrowed a long ceremonial blade from a watching soldier. After admiring the glint of the metal and the skill of the craftsman who had enhanced it, she promptly placed it across the width of Aereon's back. The Elemental's range of movement was now seriously restricted: razor-sharp edge behind and two-hundred meter drop in front.

"Done calculating?" she inquired politely. "Good." The long blade pressed a little more firmly against flesh and fabric. "Now cut those odds in half."

Though attentive, it was clear that the Elemental was not afraid. She proceeded to say as much. "Save your threats, Necromonger."

To Dame Vaako's shock, Aereon moved—straight

ahead and across the gaping portal in the floor. Once across the opening, she turned to regard her host. And smiled.

"I am quite happy to tell you for the asking. I only hesitated because my thoughts were momentarily directed elsewhere. Though I am at present your 'guest,' that does not mean you occupy all my thoughts." She paused a moment before continuing in a more declamatory tone, as if delivering a lecture whose importance she did not want to be misunderstood.

"It has to do with a fore-telling. A supposed prediction now more than thirty years old. As the tale tells it, a young soldier once consulted—call the person a 'seer,' of sorts. Or the individual in question might have been nothing more than a raving maniac imbued with a desire to instill uncertainty in a tormentor. There are many views on whether it is possible to predict the future. Or any future." She gathered herself.

"Regardless of how one views the scientific validity of such things, this person told the soldier that a child would be born on the planet Furya. A male child, who would someday cause the soldier's downfall."

When Dame Vaako had heard it all, she had heard enough. Ordering the transport to return to the Basilica, she remanded the Elemental to the respectful custody from which she had been borrowed, with a warning not to speak of the encounter to anyone (most especially the Lord Marshal). That accomplished, she then busied herself with a sufficiency of minor tasks to put off anyone who might have been assigned to keep tabs on her whereabouts.

It was later that evening when she made her way to a communications chamber. It boasted no advanced equipment, no glimmering electronics. There were only the appropriate decorations, dim lighting, and on the single slab before her, a lesser Quasi-Dead. By speaking to it, a Necromonger could speak through it, to another of its kind residing—elsewhere.

The receiving Quasi, to whom her words were relayed, was lying on a similar slab in a very dissimilar place—on board Vaako's frigate. For contact to be made it was only necessary for the Quasi whose abilities she was utilizing to "think" at its counterpart deep in space. Sharing similar minds, they shared a similar mental place—and time frame.

Wasting little time on pleasantries that did not extend beyond constructive flattery, it did not take her long to repeat the entire tale that had been told to her by the obliging Elemental. As she spoke, she could see the lips of the pale gray creature sprawled on the slab before her moving in responsive repetition.

". . . a downfall," she eventually finished, "that would result in the soldier's untimely death."

A response was forthcoming almost immediately. This time, when the mouth of the Quasi moved, she could hear the voice of her unimaginably distant companion.

"'Furya'?" Even across the parsecs, and even

though the words were being mouthed not by Vaako but by the communicator Quasi in front of her, she could make out the bemusement in her companion's voice. "I recall little mention of it. No reason to. A ruin of a world, with no remaining sentient life to speak of."

"For good reason," she told him through her Quasi. "The young soldier who participated in the attack that devastated Furya killed all the young males he could find, even personally strangling some with their birth-cords. An 'artful' fatal stroke, wouldn't you say?" In the absence of an immediate reply she could not resist adding, "Who do we know who favors the selected application of aesthetics to mass killing?"

The Quasi's lips moved hypnotically. "So this 'soldier,'" Vaako was saying to her from the depths of his distant ship, "the one who tried to pre-empt the prediction, would later become—"

"*That's* why he worries," she put in helpfully.

"Our lord marshal," Vaako continued. "And that would make the man-child—"

". . . whom he worries he overlooked killing, that child in the crib of whom this supposed seer spoke . . ."

"Our Riddick," Vaako concluded. "Do you believe any of this? Do you believe in prophecy? It is not science."

"I know," she told him, "but it doesn't matter what I believe. Or what you believe. It does not even matter if it is true prophecy or merely the ravings of an inspired lunatic." She smiled. It was a delicious smile. "What matters is that *he* believes it."

Another pause followed. Despite the immense distances involved and the lesser Quasi-Dead's ability to relay only words, she thought she could see her companion thinking.

"What is to be done?" Vaako asked finally.

Good. He was letting her take the lead. Also the leading risks, but that was fine with her. Given her current line of thought, she was in far more danger at that moment than he was on his ship in deep space.

"You do what your lord asks of you. Find and cleanse Riddick for him. In doing so, you prove your undying loyalty to him. Perhaps then, perhaps afterward . . ."

"He'll finally let down his guard," the Quasi whispered, repeating Vaako's words verbatim.

She straightened above the slab. As she did so, the Quasi's head lolled slowly to one side, the connection broken. "Until your return, my love," she murmured to the otherwise empty chamber. Then she bent low and, with the most extreme and grisly delicacy imaginable, lightly brushed her mouth across the gray lips of the unable to respond Quasi-Dead.

Later that night, she happened to pass the Lord Marshal and his retinue. They were deep in conversation, no doubt on some topic involving the continued pursuit of a war of occupation that had proven more troublesome than expected. The surviving forces of the Helion military were proving awkward in their obduracy. That was not her concern.

What did concern her was that as he passed by

seemingly without noticing her and she automatically dipped her head in deference, a second visage *did* turn to look in her direction. A wraithlike face of a sort possessed only by the most exalted and highly trained of her kind. The astral countenance regarded her coldly for a moment before vanishing inside the Lord Marshal's skull like a ghost returning to its coffin.

She did not shiver, but it was a chilling reminder of the Lord Marshal's vigilance and of the abilities that made him so powerful—and dangerous. He was not just one man.

He was one man—and something more.

On board the distant frigate, Vaako had terminated the connection at his own end, leaving the communicator Quasi to its chamber and to its rest. His thoughts were on the future. On its potential, that now as never before seemed as promising as it was confused. How fortunate he was to have a partner as devious and clever as she was beautiful and affectionate. No other commander could boast such a companion. Great things loomed on the horizon, he was sure, if only they chose the right route forward.

Lost in thought and much preoccupied by possibilities, he exited the chamber. As such, he did not notice the solitary figure that had stood concealed in shadows at its far end. Once the commander had departed, that figure stepped out of concealment and into the dim light. It eyed the recumbent, motionless figure of the Quasi for a long moment. Apparently reaching some silent, internal decision, it moved forward.

After a quick check to make certain there was no one to see him emerge, the Purifier walked out into the corridor and headed toward the front of the ship.

XIII

It was a green planet; shrouded in thick white cloud, lush with vegetation, fecund with life. It circled its unremarkable but benign star as it had for eons, out of the way and unnoticed, its distinctive denizens living out their lives in contentment and indifference to the rest of the universe.

And then, the hand came down.

A monstrous, slick-skinned apparition, it descended without warning, plunging through space, upper atmosphere, and clouds, to wreak a devastation that was as complete as it was merciless. Singly and in groups, young life-forms found themselves wrenched from their beds, their schools, their hiding places. Holding thousands at a time, the hand drew back, tiny children oozing from between its fingers. The latter moved, rubbing against each other, shaking off the small screaming shapes. Dropping them into the vastness of space where they were swallowed up by the unrelenting cold and dark and emptiness.

The hand vanished, to be replaced by a powerful,

advancing figure. It was a soldier, young and strong, perversely adorned with a helmet boasting three faces. But the single face within could not be seen.

A voice—not the soldier's—at once innocent and wise, young and mature, frightened and frightening, whispering of a near-forgotten moment. Whispering, wondering, uncertain.

"Are . . . you . . . familiar . . . to . . . me?"

The soldier said nothing. But an armored hand reached forward, fingers outstretched. . . .

Riddick shot up from where he had been sleeping. Senses fully alert, eyes wide, it took him only a second or two to thoroughly scan his surroundings. There was only rock and junk, the distant chatter of convicts and the rotten-egg stink of sulfur. That, and a memory that would not go away. Would not go away, he knew, until it had been understood.

Between culls and feeding, there wasn't much for a guard unlucky enough to be assigned to Crematoria to do. Either because it was too difficult, too boring, or too dangerous for humans to perform, automatics necessarily performed most of the routine maintenance. Though portions of the complex looked worn and battered, everything worked. It had to. On other worlds, in other similar facilities, if something broke down, it could wait until it was fixed. Wait to fix something on Crematoria, and there was a good chance people would die. This mattered to the staff, especially when they were at risk.

Presently, two of the guards were absorbed in a game of chess while others lazed at their stations, monitoring those functions on which machines were not qualified to render an opinion. The slam boss was there as well, busy working with a pad. One of the players moved a bishop. Utilizing shells designed to stop the biggest berserker of a convict in his tracks, the individual chess pieces maintained the size if not the exact shape of their ancient predecessors. The potentially explosive bishop gleamed as it was moved.

Toombs barely glanced in the direction of the game. Not that he disliked chess. He was an avid player, but with different pieces. One of those was the individual responsible for his trip to Crematoria. One by one, his crew filed in behind him.

Douruba greeted them effusively, his manner much more relaxed and open than previously. Toombs took it as a hopeful sign without being sucked in by it for a minute. He also noted that one of the guards had risen from his seat and was now moving in the direction of the office safe.

"Good news first?" the slam boss offered. He took the head mercenary's silence as an acknowledgment. "Talked things over with my comrades here." He indicated the other guards, none of whom bothered to look in the mercenaries' direction. "Since it was such a tough run for you, we've agreed it'd only be fair to split some of the aftermarket expenses. We'll cut you in for seven-hundred fifty K."

As he spoke, the guard who had moved to the safe had punched in the electronic combination and pulled back the door. Now he was taking out universal denomination money. No credit; real currency. Electronic credit transfers were all very well and good, but u.d. cash could not be monkeyed with, siphoned off, or put in some other fool's name at the touch of a button. Glancing around, Toombs noted the expressions on the faces of his surviving crew. Plainly, there was no need to put the offer to a vote.

They could be a little more circumspect about it, he thought. The sight of the money had transformed them from a bunch of hardened mercs into a pack of drooling puppies. Oh well—Douruba was right about one thing. It *had* been a difficult pickup. He had to admit he was as anxious as any of them to bid farewell to the pit-drop paradise vacation world of Crematoria—and find someplace suitably civilized and decadent to spend his share of the payoff.

There was apparently one more thing to deal with, however. He eyed the slam boss.

"What's the bad news? They closed the local whorehouse? I hear it was really hot."

The slam boss smiled appreciatively at the joke. By way of reply, he tossed a flexible hardcopy printout to the waiting mercs. It showed deep space. Squinting at it, Toombs and his colleagues saw nothing but star field.

"Look closer," the slam boss advised them. "Dead center."

Toombs did so. "Dark shape. Could be anything."

"Isn't anything," the slam boss assured him solemnly. "Our last resupply ship finished unloading here just before you showed. Its monitors caught that as it was system outbound. Means it must be fairly close in." Reaching out, he touched the dark shape. The image immediately enlarged within the printout, promptly resolving into the outline of a starship of unusual configuration.

Curious, one of the guards ambled over to have a look, cracking nuts between his teeth as he peered over Toombs's shoulder.

Ignoring the other man's uncomfortable proximity, the mercenary shrugged diffidently. "Huh. Never seen nuthin' like it."

Douruba's tone was guardedly neutral. "Almost looks like it could be a warship. But that's stupid, isn't it? What would a warship be doing in this system? What could it want here? There's nothing here but us."

Maybe it was the enlarged image in the printout. Maybe it was the slam boss's words. Or maybe a combination thereof. Whatever, something jogged the guard's memory. Munching a little more reflexively on his chosen snack of the moment, he backed away from Toombs.

"Didn't someone say you guys came here from Helion Prime?"

In the face of even a veiled accusation, Toombs always assumed a belligerent stance. "Yeah? So?"

The slam boss was studying the expression on the head mercenary's face intently. "Our cargo guy, he says he's checked and rechecked our deep-space monitors and that this thing"—he indicated the printout—"charts back to Helion Prime."

Reaching down, Toombs scratched his ass and said nothing. It was a visual indication of how relaxed he was, when he wasn't. A glance showed that the guard at the safe, detached from the conversation, was still pulling out bundles of u.d. certificates.

Meanwhile, Douruba wasn't finished. His tone was growing steadily less dispassionate. "You know, Anatoli's got a nose for trouble. And he thinks trouble follows you here."

It was hard for Toombs to concentrate on what the slam boss was saying while his attention was fixed on the piles of money that were rising outside the open safe. But enough of the other man's sentiment seeped through to suggest that, like a stripper's costume, things were starting to come apart. He hastened to reassure the slam boss.

"Look," he grumbled forcefully, "we dusted our tracks and made a clean exfil. I don't care what kind of tracking technology they had: there's no way we didn't lose them." He indicated the gap outside the access doors that opened onto the prison below. "There's *no way*. It doesn't matter if they're looking for something. This is my prisoner. Mine. Nobody else's. Possession is ten tenths of the law. And I think I want my money now."

Eyes widening slightly, Douruba took a step backward. "Them? So you stole a prisoner from *them*?"

For a simple pronoun, his final word packed an infinity of meanings, none of them favorable.

Toombs's crew might be newly assembled, but they weren't stiffs. It was the copilot who happened to notice that the chess-playing guards had called an end to their game and were removing the pieces from the board—and quietly slipping them into the weapons they had drawn from beneath the game table. Bishop's Knight to dead merc four. She considered mentioning this unique method of storage to Toombs, but decided there wasn't time. In the event serious discussion of the rules ensued, she intended to be the one to make the first move. She reached for her sidearm.

The explosive sounds that reverberated down the volcanic cone and off its tiered, cell-lined walls might have been celebratory, except that everyone within hearing range knew today was no holiday. Nor were the booming noises a day or two early. There were no holidays on Crematoria. The sounds of shooting and small explosives going off were accompanied by colorful flashes of light and the sporadic deeper boom as something seriously volatile was let loose. It could have passed for a showy fireworks display, except that no one was cheering.

Head back, interior lights reflected from his goggles, Riddick regarded the control room high above. Hanging halfway down the cone's throat, the chain attached to the service and supply winch jiggled and bounced with the occasional explosive reverberation.

Moments later, the lights in the control room died. Probably not the only thing to do so, he mused. Then a blast of actinic white light erupted that was bright enough to force him, even though protected by his goggles, to look away. Even so, he was able to catch a glimpse of a single figure as it dove through the overhead aperture and plunged downward. The explosion that followed close on his heels rocked the entire prison.

When Riddick looked back and the glare faded

from his goggles, he saw that the leaping figure had managed to grab onto the lower end of the winch chain. Fortunately for him, the winch had not been damaged in the last explosion. Unfortunately for him, Riddick recognized him immediately. It was Toombs.

Backing up, the big man readied himself. Putting one foot against a wall and using it like a sprinter's starting block, he pushed off hard, accelerating with every step. As a couple of other stupefied inmates looked on, he leaped to the railing and used it as a launching pad. The arc he described had been carefully judged. He had just enough room, built-up speed, and strength to cross the seemingly impossible gap and smack into the figure clinging desperately to the end of the chain. Somehow, Toombs absorbed the unexpected impact and managed to hold on. Arms straining to maintain his grip, he found himself penduluming back and forth with whoever had slammed into him. As soon as he was reasonably certain he wasn't going to fall, he brought his head around to get a look at the crazed fool who had almost knocked him from his perch.

And found himself virtually nose to nose with Riddick.

No gun. No backup. No heavily armed crew. No cuffs. All of which added up, in the sudden fit of near panic that threatened to eclipse Toombs's thoughts, to No Chance. For what seemed like an eternity, the two men hung there, swinging back and forth as the end of the chain slowly steadied. Just when the mercenary was convinced his former prisoner was going to start eating cereal out of his skull, Riddick spoke. His voice was unchanged, as if they were seated across from one another in a corner café. As if nothing had previously passed between them. As if what had passed had meant nothing then, and meant even less now.

"Shoulda taken the money."

Toombs would have gaped at him, or possibly even replied, except Riddick had started up the chain like a lemur and was using the mercenary's skull for a step-stone. The big man went up the links so fast Toombs didn't have time to reply even if he had been able to think of something to say. As soon as it sank in that he wasn't going to be kicked off, dismembered piecemeal, or have his medulla oblongata pulled out through his mouth, he started upward himself. His progress was notably slower than that of his predecessor.

The scene in the darkened control room resembled a party that had been crashed by Beelzebub and a few of his drinking buddies. The only light came from those few screens and readouts that hadn't been blasted to bits or forcibly deactivated. It was dim enough for Riddick to ungoggle, which he did gratefully. His too-constant companion, it was always a relief to be able to move around once in a while without it clinging to his face like some inescapable, symbiotic alien.

He had no trouble separating the bodies of the mercenaries from those of the guards, because he could not. They were indistinguishable from one another—those bits and pieces that still remained complete enough to be labeled as corpses. There were plenty of limbs that had been detached from torsos by the force of the explosion, as well as sundry body parts better left unexamined. One thing was immediately apparent: there was nothing left alive within the confines of the demolished control room.

Striding swiftly toward the door that led to the transport tunnel, he tried the lever. The outer doors groaned a protest, but parted. The inner barrier, however, remained stubbornly shut. On closer inspection, he was unable to tell if they had been incurably damaged by the explosion, or had been deliberately sabotaged. The distinction was irrelevant, he knew.

A tunnel monitor lay nearby, flickering feebly with lingering electronic life. Digging it out of the rubble, he brushed off the screen and studied the image. Though maddeningly inconsistent, it provided enough information to show that no one was going anywhere soon via the prison's internal transportation system. For one thing, the heavy travel sled had been blown clean off its tracks. As for the latter, they were in none too good a condition themselves. A quick glance was enough to tell him that fixing the system would require engineering staff, a full repair crew, heavy equipment, and worst of all, time. There was no sign of human life in the tunnel, either.

When no further detonations followed his ascent and he didn't come plunging back down through the access aperture with significant parts of his body missing, the convicts who had been waiting and watching below began to make their way upward in his wake. Kyra was the first one up, followed by the Guv and others. Toombs took the more direct route, tentatively hauling himself up the same service chain Riddick had utilized.

Most of them had found themselves in the control room at one time or another, usually to receive a declaration of punishment or reduction in privileges from the slam boss. Now the place was unrecognizable. Someone with more presence of mind than his dazed compatriots managed to reactivate the lights. Funny, that, the Guv mused. Usually, the problem on Crematoria was too much light.

A convict who'd accosted a prominent citizen on Veriel III and had suffered the misfortune of having to kill him when his prey had protested at the imposition gestured at the carnage as he came over.

"Mercenaries. Some guards here, too, but it can't be all of them. At least, I don't think so." He made a face. "I ain't about to count the total body parts and divide by the number of guards."

"Take a couple of the boys and pay the guard dorm a visit. Check their individual slots." The Guv nodded past the man. "Back in the living quarters. And be careful or you're liable to get yourselves shot on sight." He spat at the bloodstained floor. "Prison regs died along with everyone else in here."

A voice interrupted their exchange. "Guards ain't there."

Both convicts turned. The big man was holding a fleximage, a portion of which had been enlarged. It showed a dark outline, ominous and massive. While Riddick explained, the Guv and other convicts crowded around for a better look.

"Looks like the boss and the guards figured out Necromongers are coming."

"Necromongers?" someone asked.

Riddick glanced in the convict's direction. "The ones who've been taking out and shutting down worlds. Helion Prime was the most recent." When the questioner didn't react, the big man explained in terms a convict could understand. "Think thousands of mercs all dedicated to bringing you back dead or alive. Then forget the 'or alive.'" This time the man nodded comprehendingly.

"Looks like the back-up plan was to clean the bank, ghost the mercs, and break wide through the tube. Anybody comes here checking up afterwards would reasonably assume the mercs were responsible." He held up a shortshell launcher. Smoke still wafted from its barrel. "But one merc got off a shot with this party-crasher here and took out the sled." He smiled thinly. "Wish I coulda seen the looks on their faces when the guards found their getaway baby buggy all busted to hell.

"So they rigged the door so no one could follow, and took off on foot. And now they plan to jack that ship in the hangar and leave everyone else here to die."

More impressed than afraid, Toombs found himself gaping at his former prisoner. "How come you know all this shit? You wasn't even here."

Riddick favored the mercenary with a particularly disgusted look. "Cuz it was my plan."

In the tunnel, the slam boss and five remaining guards jogged methodically onward, their boots pounding rhythmically against the hard, compacted surface underfoot. Striking a rail, one man stumbled and, cursing, picked up the pace as he adjusted the gear that provided a flow of supplementary oxygen to his lungs. Douruba was having a harder time of it than his men. He was older, and not in as good a shape. A word to the overly energetic guard now leading the way slowed the younger man down.

"Stay together," he admonished them.

One of the other survivors frowned at his superior. "Why?" He glanced back in the direction of the prison. "Even if any of those half heads could figure out what happened, they can't follow us." He grinned as he ran. "Doors are jammed good. They can't get into the tunnel."

The slam boss nodded curtly. "You remember that last drop-off? The big man with the goggles? Keep moving. Stay together." Reaching up, he scratched his nose and lengthened his own stride, inspired—or maybe troubled—by his own words. "Damn supplementation units didn't provide nearly enough oxygen to complement an atmosphere that was largely nitrogen and argon," he muttered under his breath. He nudged the guide lever on his own unit to maximum flow.

Within the control room, exactly the kind of confusion and aimlessness that the slam boss had envisioned held sway. A few of the prisoners smashed and kicked anything intact they came across, futilely taking out years of anger and frustration on inanimate objects. Under the direction of the Guv, a semiorganized group was struggling to pry open the doors that led to the transport tunnel. Built to withstand everything from a major earth tremor to direct hits by heavy ordnance, the doors refused to cooperate. Nothing they found to attack the doors with was tougher than the doors themselves.

Kyra, meanwhile, was watching Riddick. The big man was seated in a chair, actively working a section of surviving instrumentation. She was pretty sure he wasn't dialing up the latest entertainment vid. That anything at all remained functional in the control room was something of a minor miracle in itself. That anything had survived that might prove useful was almost too much to hope for.

Something deep underfoot went ca-*thunk*. The floor trembled. Men raging at machines turned to look up from their festival of destruction. Those working on the tunnel doors halted their fruitless efforts to turn and stare.

The floor heaved. Not buckling, but rising. The small earthquake was machine generated. Ascending on its massive, solid screws, the battered control room began to drive toward the surface. Reluctantly at first, but with gathering efficiency, eased along by Riddick's demanding touch. As he worked the controls, Kyra walked over to stand next to him, her attention on his face. She nodded to herself.

"I know that look." He said nothing, busy at the instrumentation. "I don't like it. I don't like what it implies."

He spoke without looking up at her. "Plenty of choices. Don't have to follow."

"Yeah, right," she muttered. "Like I'm gonna stay here."

Between picking up what they could of the terse conversation and combining it with what Riddick was doing, even the slowest-witted prisoner soon had a pretty good idea of the big man's intention. Realization provoked disbelief, and debate.

"He's out of his mind," one man declared without hesitation. "Won't last five minutes out there."

His companion was staring out a port as the control room surfaced. It was still pitch-black outside—for a little while. "Five minutes?" He nodded at the vista of blackened, blasted lava; a twisted maze of extruded volcanic rock that could alternately trip, trap, or cut a man to shreds. "Sixty seconds in the sun will light you up like a match. You don't tan out there—you combust."

The prisoner behind him was nodding vigorously. "Traditional twenty-mile buffer zone. That's thirty klicks to the hangar. Then you got to find a way in—if you still got water in you."

"What is it?" another man was saying over and over. "What's he thinking?"

As he stared outside, the first convict was shaking his head: slowly and with conviction. "Thirty klicks. Over *that* terrain. Even if it was dead flat and covered in grass—"

"Don't talk about grass," another convict growled despondently.

"It'd still be a tough slog," the first man finished. "And me, I ain't no runner."

"Better alive in here than fried out there," someone else declaimed fervently.

Riddick was busy collecting guns from the floor, as indifferent to the discussion as he was to the identity of the weapons' former owners. Muscular arms almost full, he started to turn, hesitated, bent, and added a bag of nuts to the accumulated arsenal.

Trying to muster his own courage as much as that of his compatriots, the Guv gestured first at the blasted landscape outside, then at a surviving instrument. "Check out the chronograph. The terminator line's moving in the right direction—toward the hangar, more or less. We travel with it, stay behind the night and in front of the day. In the tolerable zone." Out of ideas, he turned to Riddick.

Black goggles surveyed the suddenly attentive convicts. "Gonna be one speed: mine. Anybody wants to tippy-toe their way is on their own. If you can't keep up, don't step up. You'll just die." He nodded toward the man who had indicated a preference for remaining behind. Clearly, his opinion was not an isolated one. "Dog that stays in its doghouse doesn't get many chances at freedom."

With that he started forward, brushing past Kyra. Her conflicted expression was almost as tormented as the terrain outside.

They had to blow a window. Designed to withstand the incredible extremes of temperature and the howling winds to which Crematoria was subjected, it could not simply be kicked out. Fortunately, one thing they now had plenty of was ammunition. Once some fringing, shattered shards of clinging acrylic was cleared, Riddick stepped through.

And out onto the surface of Crematoria.

No smooth-surfaced walkway or tunnel underfoot here. No comforting, protective walls. Nothing but black lava—mostly solidified ropy pahoehoe, with a sprinkling of dangerously sharp a'a.

Fuck geology, Riddick mused as he started forward without pausing. The bleak, blackened surface was something to be got over, to be crossed, to survive—not to be analyzed.

He was followed by three of the convicts; their mouths set, their expressions intense, their arms full of weaponry. Every man and woman dies someday, they all knew, and they were of a mind to do it fighting for their freedom rather than squatting in a hole in the ground waiting to be fed and toyed with like mice at the bottom of a well. If nothing else, they might get a chance to take one of their malevolent tormentors with them.

If they could catch up to the guards, or get to the hangar before them.

Another window got blown out. Kyra always did prefer to make her own way. Stepping through the new gap, she advanced to stand close to Riddick. As close as he ever let anyone, that is.

"I'm really not expecting this to work out, okay? Just looks like a cool way to check out." She offered up a wan smile. "I was getting kinda bored with the lifestyle, you know?"

"Just one rule this time." Digging through the gear he had scavenged, he tossed her an oxygen unit. "Stay out of the light."

She nodded knowingly. "Kinda reverses things, don't it?"

"Till I get my payday," voice interrupted.

It was Toombs. Weapon in hand, grinning unpleasantly, he stepped outside. A couple of the convicts thought about intervening, but hesitated. Whatever they might think of the big man, this was his business to settle, not theirs. And the mercenary had already demonstrated a disquieting ability not only to survive, but to thrive. Which was one way of saying he was a helluva quick shot.

"Technically speaking," the mercenary went on, losing the grin, "you're still my prisoner."

Riddick made no attempt to bring one of the guns he carried to bear. With black goggles between his eyes, and those of everyone around him, it was impossible to tell where they were focused. The same ambiguity did not apply to his words.

"Don't move."

Toombs took umbrage. Maybe the present situation wasn't quite what he would have preferred, but he was damned if he was going to put up with that kind of shit from a lousy prisoner.

"*Me* don't move? What is this, Reverso World? You're forgetting the totality of the reality, man. *You* don't move."

The big man didn't—but not because the mercenary had voiced an order. "Better adjust that attitude if you want to have a chance of getting out of this. And whatever you do, do *not* point that weapon at me."

Toombs's face twisted as if it had suddenly turned to putty. It might have been working toward another grin. No one would ever know, because as soon as the muzzle of the gun he was holding started to come up, something big, superfast, and nasty slammed into him fang first from behind.

Convicts blanched and backed away as the hellhound ripped into the mercenary. With the mad strength of the damned, Toombs somehow managed to wrench his gun around and fire. It blew a hole through his attacker, but by that time the beast was already crunching the mercenary's throat in its jaws. Man and monster died together, alien blood and human blood mixing indiscriminately on the black rock of a world foreign to both and beloved by neither.

In less than a minute, Toombs lay motionless, his life seeping out onto the rocks. Atop him, the hellhound was still breathing in short, shuddering gasps despite the gaping wound in its torso. Moving close, Riddick happened to notice the tag on the beast's ear. Number Five. Thrash. He bent over the dying animal.

Anxiously, the Guv was eyeing the predawn sky. Was the dark drape of the heavens a fragment brighter than just a few seconds ago? Or just a figment brighter? The distinction was crucial.

"Riddick," he muttered uneasily, "we'd better get moving."

Still staring down at the dying hellhound, the big man straightened. His words were directed to the animal before him, not the men beside him.

"I know how it feels."

Then he turned and, without a look back, started off into the rocks.

They ran as fast as they could, which is to say, as fast as the landscape would allow. There was no direct route straight through the congealed lava, no convenient path connecting the nerve center of the prison compound with the distant promise of the hangar. It had never occurred to the designers and the builders of the complex to construct such a route because it was impossible to envision anyone foolish enough to try and make use of it, even in an emergency. Anyone planning a jog across the open surface of Crematoria would have to be disturbed, deranged, mentally addled.

Or Riddick.

Being in prison often damages the mind but frequently improves the body. Diet may suck, but overeating is rarely a concern. So the fugitives stayed together pretty well as they made their way through the twisted, bizarre hoodoo towers and frozen cataracts of black stone. No one fell behind. No one dared to. It was unspoken but understood by all that if someone fell and twisted an ankle, or proved unable to maintain the pace, they were on their own. There would be no improvised stretchers, no willing carriers, to help them along. Even if any of the convicts were inclined to help a comrade in such a situation, everyone knew there would not be enough time. Better one should perish than two more trying to help him.

And all the while, they were being pursued. Not by something as mundane as guards or even hellhounds, but by a danger infinitely more threatening. Implacable, remorseless, and lethal. Dawn.

Hints of it began to show themselves back the way they had come; flecks of illumination, suggestions of sunshine. Innocent enough in themselves, but in reality the advance scouts of an approaching Hell. Survival depended on their remaining within the terminator as they ran on; within that tiny stripe of tolerability that divided Crematoria's fading, freezing night from its namesake approaching day. Meanwhile, the planet continued its slow but steady rotation, stalking them with a pursuing sun.

Mere thoughts of what was advancing steadily behind them were sufficient to keep them from freezing. That, and the heat of their own bodies as they burned calories to keep running. And always out in front, Riddick leading, searching, scanning with glittering eyes that could see better in the continuing dark than any instrument. Eyes that saw only the immediate future, backed by a mind sharply focused on the moment, and not the morrow.

While the dawn, normally a bringer of life but on Crematoria a burning, fiery angel of death, continued to gain on them.

The thing about the man leading them, was that nothing seemed to slow him down. If the fissure yawning ahead was too wide to jump, he angled left or right until it narrowed sufficiently. If the hill ahead was too steep or too slick with volcanic glass to climb, he would race around it. Where they might have stopped to argue and discuss, he just kept going. For men who had spent much of their lives leading others, it was a relief for a change to follow someone else. Especially someone who clearly knew what he was doing. They knew without having to discuss it what would happen if he did not. So they sucked oxygen and water from their respective suit units and sent to their legs the energy that normally would have been spent on complaining.

They had a bad moment when the big man seemed to have vanished into thin air. Anxiety rising, they searched their immediate surroundings in vain. There was no sight of him to right or left. As for straight ahead, that was blocked by an impossible rock face.

On top of which Riddick stood, waiting when he said he wouldn't wait. He continued to wait for them to scramble up to join him. No place to fall here, each of them knew. No time to slide back down and try again. No one looked downward, not because they feared the heights they were scaling, but because none of them wanted to see a place where they could never set foot again, and still live.

First one, then another, then Kyra and another, until almost all of them, panting hard, had joined the big man at the top. Slowed by his size, the Guv was last up, but he made it. As he did so, he shot a relieved look behind him. Something was tickling his shoulders, his upper spine, the back of his neck. Something persistent and creeping. It was the glow of the coming dawn. A rivulet of sweat coursed down his cheek.

He knew it would only be the first of many.

XIV

The escapees were not the only life-forms pantingly venting carbon dioxide into the thin atmosphere of Crematoria. Spread out within the transport tunnel, the fleeing guards were double-timing it up a rise, flanking the now useless sled rails. The ascent brought the tunnel, and those within, nearer to the actual surface.

It was the guard Anatoli who, after stepping around an unexpected headless body lying between the sled rails, noted the mole hole. Spaced along major and minor transport tunnels alike, capped with tough, heat-resistant alloy, these shafts allowed engineers and service techs to carry out the occasional quick and easy manual check of the terrain above the conduits. There was no reason to bother with one now, of course, but . . .

Anatoli hadn't survived as a prison guard for as long as he had without taking every precaution in his work, even when precaution seemed superfluous. Now he slowed slightly, frowning at the shaft. No real reason to bother with it, of course. No reason except that years of experience had told him that the best way to keep one's head on one's shoulders was to use it when everyone else was ignoring theirs. Besides, carrying out a quick check couldn't hurt anything, and those were the best, most reassuring kind to make.

"Boss," he muttered, nodding in the direction of the shaft. Wordless agreement passed between wary superior and valued subordinate. Douruba spoke curtly to the man on his right.

"Malak, grab a look. Check out the flowers."

The guard protested. "What the shit for? There's nothing up there. All the slugs are boxed up back in slam. Why waste the time? Because Anatoli says so?"

The slam boss was in no mood to argue. "Because his *nose* says so."

Grumbling under his breath, Malak turned to comply. Douruba ignored his muttered curses. In a job like this, in a place like this, a man needed to be able to let off steam. Let off steam on Crematoria, he thought. That was pretty funny. Nothing much funny had happened ever since that last fuckin' quick-tempered merc crew had arrived at his place with their one unsettling package.

Well, it would all work out. They had all the payoff money on hand and the mercs would get blamed for the destruction. The assorted powers that be who needed and funded a shit hole like Crematoria would bitch and moan about the cost of replacement. Then they'd sigh, suck it up, stick their constituents with some artfully hidden special tax, and come in and rebuild. He wouldn't be around to see it, though. He intended to take his share of the money and retire. To someplace cold. Where it snowed.

Still complaining, the guard at the bottom of the shaft activated the self-powered lift mechanism. There was a grinding sound as the metal cap elevated on screws that were miniatures of the ones that raised and lowered the slam control room. Punching through accumulated crust and dust, it hummed to a halt half a meter above the surface.

Resigned to the work, the muttering guard climbed up and cautiously positioned himself beneath the cap. From there he had a more or less 360-degree view of the surface terrain. A check of his chronometer showed that the sun was still below the horizon. If it wasn't, he wouldn't be up here. No sane person would.

But someone was.

His jaw dropped as he spied the moving shapes. Their movements too loosey-goosey for machines, they had to be human. While their sanity remained a matter for conjecture, there was no question that they were advancing, and advancing fast. They shouldn't be advancing anywhere, he knew. They should be dead.

That was a correctable anomaly. Bringing up his rifle, he started to level it with the intention of sighting in on the first figure. But just before he could lock on, the advancing column made a sharp turn and disappeared into a fissure. Had they seen him? That seemed impossible. Nobody could spot ground-level movement at such a distance. Or could they? Malak's thoughts turned, unwillingly, to a certain recently arrived inmate to whom Douruba had referred repeatedly.

"What the hell's going on up there?" came the impatient voice of the slam boss. Malak looked down.

"Better see for yourself, boss!"

In a moment, Douruba and Anatoli had made their way up to join the first man. Crowded together at the top of the molehole and at first seeing nothing in the still dim light, it took a moment for their eyes to focus and register on the figures that reemerged from the distant fissure, still moving forward but on a tack that kept them well out of range. Only one of them was readily recognizable, and the slam boss wished it wasn't.

"Riddick . . ."

"No way," mumbled Malak. "No way. He was down in the tiers when we broke out. How in the hell . . . ?"

"This *is* hell, remember?" snapped Douruba. He started hurriedly back down the shaft.

At the bottom, the new and unexpected development prompted a hasty conference. Various suggestions were mooted, some more hopeful than practical. Those Douruba ignored. If nothing else, he had always been a practical man.

"No chance do they get to the hangar first," Malak declared vehemently. "No chance."

"Nothin' but rock between here and there," another man put in. "They're in the crap zone. Black lava everywhere. They're toast." On Crematoria, such an assessment was not metaphorical.

"I dunno," the man standing next to him exclaimed. "That one guy, that Riddick—I don't like the idea of walkin' into the hangar with him maybe hangin' from the ceiling, waiting for us."

"And he's not alone," Anatoli pointed out. "Couldn't get a for-sure count, but maybe half a dozen total. All armed."

This revelation spurred more concern. When the uneasy chatter had died down, the slam boss stepped in. "All right. We make *sure* they don't get to the hangar first." His expression was hard. "We make sure they don't get to the hangar at all. Move out."

They did so, wordlessly and faster than before.

Up above, it was raining. On Crematoria, that meant ash: sometimes brown, occasionally white, but most often black. Where the crust was weak or thin and swirling magma came close to the surface, distant volcanoes and cinder cones erupted from the volatile ground, spewing hot tears of feathery-soft rock. Like black snow, it drifted down to layer the uncompromising ground with shards of shroud.

It also draped the fast-moving escapees in speckled cloaks. The freshly vented volcanic material was always hot. Fortunately, this particular ash fall was not searingly so. Under assault by falling ash and accumulated perspiration, the fugitives found themselves discarding bits and pieces of clothing as they ran. The ash clung to damp, sweaty skin, but it was still better than overheating inside attire that had not been intended for outside use. And there was at least one ancillary benefit: themselves covered in ash, the escapees blended in astonishingly well with their now ash-covered surroundings. Having unintentionally acquired the look of ancient tribal warriors, they ran on, following the big man in the lead.

Except he was no longer in the lead. Or at least, the Guv decided, squinting into the dense ash fall, he was no longer in view. He started to slow, only to be jostled from behind. Angry, he readied a choice couple of words for whoever had bumped into him. Unexpectedly, it was Kyra, the ferret of a girl no one had been able to get close to. Running steadily, smoothly alongside, she communicated without words. A nod forward, a quick shake of the head, and then a lengthening of stride as she moved into the lead. He understood her meaning perfectly. He just wasn't sure he accepted it.

But there was nothing else to do. Out here, on the surface of hell, he was no longer the Guv. He was just another batch of bound-together carbon molecules, another sack of animate water, waiting for the sun to come up and evaporate him. While it was not an end he looked forward to, it was an end he anticipated and was prepared to suffer. It was one he would probably meet, too. Unless the soft-spoken newcomer who had now vanished into the ash fall could pull off some kind of miracle. The Guv was not confident.

Miracles tended to elude convicts.

Directly ahead of them and still some distance away, the ground shuddered and cracked. Not from tectonic forces, but to allow for a thick cylinder of metal to rise above the surrounding stone and accumulating ash. It was the cap to a second molehole. As soon as open ports appeared below the cap, the lethal tube shape of an assault rifle eased forward out the opening.

The slam boss might move slow at times, the guard behind the weapon thought, but he knew his business. Estimating the best speed the escapees could make over the difficult, tricky terrain, he had chosen this shaft as the site for the ambush. Even so, the guard noted, they were almost too late. The fleeing convicts were really hoofing it. The key word, he knew, was "almost."

He saw them through the ashfall; not clearly, but well enough to count individual shapes. They were just silhouettes moving toward him, but that was enough. A hand whacked his lower leg and he looked down and whispered.

"We're just in time. They're right here. Three o'clock and moving fast."

"Tough bastards," another guard muttered from where he was squinched in below the first.

"Be dead bastards in a couple of minutes." The guard who had spotted the fugitives adjusted his electronic scope. Below him, his companions busied themselves chambering ammunition. A few bursts would be all it would take: death erupting unexpectedly from the ground.

The guard's view through the gun scope cleared as internal electronics resolved the view. He sighted in on the lead runner—and hesitated. Puzzlement was evident in his voice as he looked up and over the gun barrel.

"Hey. Where'd the big guy go?"

Standing atop the molehole lid, Riddick swung the metal spike around and down, its tip describing a perfect arc through the ash. Formerly an anchor loosely attached to the top of the molehole, it had been pressed into duty for which it had not been designed, but for which it proved more than sufficient. Proof of this arrived in the form of a loud crunching sound as it made direct contact with the startled guard's face. The face lost.

Finger convulsing on the trigger of his rifle, the already dead guard slipped backward. Stance lost, life lost, he tumbled down the molehole shaft like a ragdoll casually tossed aside by an uncaring child, bouncing and bumping off his stunned comrades who had clustered below. The single spontaneous shot from his weapon alerting the fugitives to the molehole's position, they unlimbered their own weapons and charged into the fray, firing at the pop-up target Riddick had already abandoned. After years of misery and abuse, the thrill of finally being able to strike back at their tormentors reinvigorated each and every one of them as effectively as a Spring shower.

Man-made chaos complemented the natural state of Crematoria's surface as the convicts attacked from several directions, careful to keep from spreading out too far lest they catch each other in a dangerous cross fire. Frozen lava provided plenty of cover that they used to good advantage, working their way ever closer to the molehole. Within, guards scrambled to bring their own weapons to bear. But they were constrained by their tight surroundings. With shells exploding on the ground and sending flesh-cutting splinters of rock flying through the port, and others exploding with ear-shattering force against the metal of the molehole itself, it was almost impossible to line up a decent shot.

Meanwhile, the convicts were closing in. As the guards went down the chute, the jubilant escapees crowded around and began emptying their weapons into the narrow shaft. For their part, the guards fired frantically upward, no longer even trying to take aim, just trying to hold off the rain of death that was being poured in on them from above.

Inside the molehole shaft there was no place to hide, no cover to be had. One guard went down, then another. Men kept firing, slamming into one another, bouncing off flesh and walls as they fought to get out of the shaft that had become a cylindrical metal coffin. When the last survivor, wide-eyed and frantic, finally spilled out of the bottom of the shaft like a panicked gerbil, the grim-faced boss slammed the control lever hard over.

Above, the molehole cap began to descend, ratcheting downward until it was once more level with the surface. Elated, the convicts stepped back to savor the small triumph over their despised tormentors. Only one did not. Unsatisfied, her face crazed with hatred, Kyra immediately attacked the edges of the cylinder with the barrel of her weapon.

"Gonna go down there," she was growling ferociously. "Find 'em. Just cut 'em up, gut 'em up, into little bite-size pieces. Wolf 'em down and shit them over the nearest cliff. C'mon, Riddick. Let's get nitty-gritty on their asses!" She looked up, frowned. "Riddick?"

There was no response—unless one counted the sight of a broad back and pistoning legs, moving fast and still picking up speed as they shrank steadily into the distance.

She wasn't sure if the adrenaline flowing through them after their triumph over the guards allowed them to catch up, or if he had subtlety slowed his pace. If the latter, he wouldn't have admitted to it. Irregardless, the escapees, now five, caught up to him atop an east-facing ridge. Between the ash and the creeping dawn that still thankfully lay behind them, the ambient temperature was well up above a hundred degrees Fahrenheit. Everyone was grateful for the fact that the ashfall had nearly ceased.

Drenched in sweat and wiping volcanic spew from her face, she drew alongside Riddick as they ran together along the ridge top. Having to reserve oxygen for breathing kept any conversation brief.

"Blasted the crap out of 'em." She chortled. "Been waiting a long time to do something like that." When he didn't reply, she added, "You?"

There was a pause as they pounded along side-by-side, the others keeping pace behind them, before he finally responded. "You even care if you get out of this alive?"

"Not really." She said it without emotion, as casually and indifferently as if contemplating the scenery. Together, they leaped off the last ledge and landed simultaneously on a lava bridge that spanned a significant cleft in the rocks.

"Well, maybe I do," he replied unexpectedly.

She eyed him uncertainly for a moment. There was more in that curt affirmation than a mere desire to stay alive. She did not expect it from him, and it kept her wondering and speculating on hidden meanings as she ran on.

Though the sulfur fissure through which they were taking a hoped-for shortcut was lined with a fortune in rare minerals, no one paused to do any informal collecting. There was no time, and money meant nothing now. Not out here, in the open. On the surface. Smooth and supportive underfoot, the fissure Riddick had found ran in exactly the direction they needed to take. With luck, it would dump them out only a short distance from the hangar site.

It dumped them out, all right, and at the expected location. There was only one problem. Their luck had run as dry as the volcanic surface underfoot.

"Oh no," the Guv was muttering. Stopped, staring, he just kept repeating it, over and over again. "No, no, no, no . . ."

There was something between them and the hangar site. Something none of them, knowing virtually nothing of the actual surface topography, could have foreseen. It was only a mountain. A small mountain, really. But still a mountain. Composed of melted and reformed sulphurous rock, it completely blocked the way forward. It was steep, and domineering, and immovable, and the Guv would have cried if he could have spared water for the tears.

"Shit," one of the other escapees snapped as he

lowered the weapon he was carrying. Not only his voice threatened to snap.

Knowing they were looking to him, Riddick could have consoled them with encouraging words. He might have strived to minimize the trial ahead. Instead, he did what he did best: spoke not a word, and kept moving forward. There was, after all, nothing else to do, and words would not get them over the obstacle a spiteful Nature had placed before them. Racing to the base of the mountain, he started climbing. No one hesitated to follow him. There was no going back now. There hadn't been for some time. Overhead, a brilliant razor's edge of light split the rapidly waning night sky.

The sun was coming up.

They scrambled and scraped their way upward, ignoring bloody fingers and frequent cuts, paying no attention to the increasingly lethal drop below them. If not directly helpful, Riddick was at least a target, a goal. Even vertically, he seemed to be making speed. They could not possibly catch up to him. They could not possibly fall too far behind. His receding form was encouragement enough.

With a shorter reach than the others, Kyra was beginning to struggle. Slipping once, she barely caught herself. If she let go, she'd fall all the way to the bottom: far enough now so that she would not have to worry about getting back up and trying again. Complicating matters, the increasing heat was making the rock itself almost too hot to touch.

Seeing her repeatedly flicking her hands to cool them for the next reach and grab, the Guv worked his way up alongside her. "Like this." He showed her his hands, both wrapped with belt leather. "Your belts, use your belts. Gun sling, anything."

Too tired to fire back one of her usual defiant responses, she just barked tiredly at him. "Go, go, go—I don't need your help. I'll make it."

He paused only briefly to favor her with a single lingering stare. Then he was moving again, size notwithstanding, passing her on the upward climb. He did not look back to see her cutting up her belt into pieces suitable for hand wrapping.

Above the others, Riddick caught a glimpse of what he had been hoping for. In lieu of the Promised Land, he would settle for the summit. With one powerful heave, he propelled himself to the top.

The view beyond was striking in its desolation. Distant volcanoes smoked on the horizon; rivers of congealed molten rock streaked a surface forever frozen in time; and, virtually at his feet, a rocky plateau sloped away into a great undulating valley of crazed volcanic glass. Rising from the center of the valley was a single stone steeple, a natural landmark that could not be missed even from atmosphere.

Below it, he knew, lay the hangar complex, and within that complex, the mercenary ship.

Sucking in each superheated breath as if it was his last, one of the convicts emerged on the crest beside him. As the man collapsed and lay fighting for air, Riddick turned to check behind him. The landscape was dominated by a towering volcano, but it wasn't geology that drew the big man's attention. It was the sliver of sunlight growing at its edge, a hidden solar assassin that was coming inexorably for them all. Reaching into a pocket, he drew out his black goggles and slipped them on. They might protect his vision, but they would do nothing to save his life.

Peering over, he scanned the cliff face on the backside of the mountain. Figures were evident, climbing toward him. He checked the sequin of sun once more. Not fast enough.

"Kyra!"

Looking up, she saw the familiar figure bent over the edge. "What?"

He had no time to go into details. Nor did he. The urgency was plain in his voice. "Get that ass moving! *Now*!"

It was enough. She knew he didn't raise his voice unless it was absolutely, positively, unavoidable. Which meant only one thing. She didn't need to look around to see the sun approaching behind her. She could feel it tickling her neck, feeling its way down her spine, considering how best to finish the puny sack of damp meat that was stuck to the rock wall like a paralyzed fly.

His words were all the jolt she needed. Finding a new gear, she threw everything she had into a last desperate acceleration, choosing speed over caution now. Anything to keep ascending, to keep moving upward. If she fell, she died. If the sun caught her out on the rock face, she died. The only way to survive was to make it to the top and to the other side. The shaded side.

Spidering to the top, the Guv reached the crest and, panting and wheezing, pulled himself up and over. As he rolled and sat up, the sky behind him exploded in whiteness sharp and hard as a diamond as Crematoria's sun finally appeared.

Where she clung to the face of the cliff, sunlight smashed into Kyra with almost physical force, drawing a gasp that mixed fear and desperation. A nearby crevice offered the only hope, the only respite. The only shade. She threw herself into it. Nearby, the only other convict still on the sunward side of the mountain found another cleft and did likewise. Up above, Riddick, the Guv, and the other remaining survivor of the breakout had already ducked down into the still tolerable shade zone provided by the backside of the mountain. Rocky outcroppings provided additional cover. Cover that would last only until the sun rose above the mountaintop.

From below, a still strong but increasingly plaintive voice cried, *"Riddick?"*

"Yeah," he responded, not moving from behind his chosen rock.

There was a brief pause, then, "'Know what I said about not caring if I lived or died?"

"Yeah." As always, there was no change in the big man's tone, nothing to indicate what he might be thinking.

"'Knew I was kiddin', right?"

By now her voice had faded, not in intensity, but in maturity: a change in age forced by a change in surroundings. She sounded like the kid he had once known, a little girl named Jack. He said nothing—but his attention shifted to a coil of cable that was secured at the Guv's belt.

Noticing the direction of his stare, the Guv felt compelled to remind the big man of his own words. "One speed. That's what you said. That's what we agreed to." Riddick didn't reply. His gaze traveled from the cable coil to the crest of the mountain. But he was thinking.

Meanwhile, the third member of the little band who had managed to make it to the top finally gave in to burning curiosity and peered guardedly around the edge of his protective outcropping. He didn't say anything, but his eyes went wide and his jaws parted. It wasn't necessary to give words to what he was seeing. There were no words, anyway.

Generated by the abrupt change and huge rise in temperature as the sun ascended above this part of the world, a visible thermal front had appeared. Caught between the lingering cold of the night side and the soaring temperature of Crematoria's morning, the resultant pressure differential spawned a solid line of superheated wind which, when combined with the thermal front, came thundering across the landscape from north to south, riding the front line of the terminator. The ground quaked as the wind and heat front passed over it, shattering loose scree and sending ash and gravel flying. Safe in their subterranean prison tiers, the Guv and the convicts had heard it, could time chronometers by it, every fifty-two hours. But in those depths it was muffled by solid rock and hushed by distance. Out here, on the surface, the tsunami of wind and heat had nothing to mute the roar of its relentless advance.

And it was driving pitilessly straight toward the mountain.

Kyra heard it first. Then, peering out from the depths of her protective crevice, she saw it. All thoughts of stoicism fled, all pretext at toughness and indifference falling away like so much desiccated, disintegrating tissue, she screamed.

"RIDDICK!"

Peering out from his own shelter, the Guv stared at the approaching wave in fascination. Over the years he'd heard it hundreds of times and had tried to visualize it, with little success.

"Jesus Christ," he murmured to no one in particular. "So *that's* what it looks like." Nearby, the other convict who had managed to make it to the top was also staring, mesmerized and mumbling to himself.

"Temperature differential, pressure differential; wind and heat from the north pole to the south. Meeting the advancing terminator every new day. Round and round she goes, and where she hits, everything blows. . . ."

He looked around sharply. Riddick was close by, still hugging the shade. The big man was even more commanding than usual, and there was unusual intensity in his voice.

"Gimme cable, shirt, your water—all of it. Then get the hell gone. Go. *Move.*"

They didn't argue with him. First, because it would not have done any good. Second, because they owed him for having brought them this far. And lastly, because they could tell from his tone and see from his expression that if they did not give him what he needed, he would take it anyway. Neither man tried to argue. There was no time here, now, in this place, to piss away on internal dissention. They turned over the goods, not knowing what he wanted them for and not asking. Not asking, because he might decide to ask them to join him in whatever crazy move he was contemplating.

As soon as the last of the gear had been handed over, both men started down the backside of the mountain. The temperature continued to rise, but they still had plenty of shade. For how much longer, it was impossible to predict. The stone tower, with its promise of man-made shelter and a ship beneath, was all the incentive they needed to send them all but bounding over the treacherous rocks.

Behind and above them now, Riddick moved fast but methodically. First he donned the Guv's commodious overshirt, tugging the ends of the sleeves as far down as he could, covering as much exposed skin as possible. Then he fashioned loops at both ends of the cable. One went around an upthrust rock; a solid stone protrusion, a finger of mountain that would not break off no matter what kind of crazy pressure he chose to apply to it. The other, larger loop went around his waist.

In his mind, he'd already run the necessary calculations. As always in such situations, there were factors he could not account for, could not wholly quantify. That was physics for you: always throwing some shit in your face whenever you thought you had everything worked out. He took a long drink of the accumulated water, then dumped the rest of it over him, carefully saturating as much clothing as possible. Moving as fast as he could to minimize evaporation time, he gripped the cable not far above where it looped around his waist, took a running jump, and threw himself toward the sun. Out in front of him, the sound of the approaching thermal wind front had risen to explosive proportions.

His kick-off carried him far to one side. Reaching the apex of his leap, Riddick-become-pendulum started dropping and swinging back. As he did so, he turned in mid-air and freed one hand, hanging onto the cable with the other, black goggles flashing, flashing, as they fought off the hungry sunlight.

Below, the heated wind front had reached the base of the mountain and was screaming upward. Just three people were there to see it, hypnotized and terrified at once by the line of implacable force that was rising toward their inadequate hiding places. Mouth agape, Kyra could only stare at the monster that was climbing toward her. Riddick could have studied it, too. But he was busy.

Then she was airborne, soaring sideways, having been plucked out of her crevice as neatly as a raptor chick by its mother. Her slim form was locked in Riddick's arm and shielded by his body. As the pendulum effect began to slow, the big man made contact with the cliff face. His feet slamming against the rock, he began running—sideways, perpendicular to the precipice, regaining speed. It was a crazy, impossible sprint, racing against gravity and common sense. But Riddick was an impossible man. As to his sanity, there were those who might have debated it. But not to his face.

Witnessing the implausible rescue, the unfortunate convict who had trapped himself in another fissure on the rock face moved when he should have waited, hoping the big man would come back for him. He should have summoned what courage remained to him and tried the rock, tried to climb. Instead, the only move he made was to peer tentatively out from his hiding place. Out and down, at the ascending thermal wind. He was able to gape at it for several seconds before it met his face. And took it off.

Pounding, digging forcefully against the cliff, Riddick's legs provided just enough additional thrust to carry him and his burden back up to the top of the mountain. Almost before they lost the last of their forward momentum, he had dropped her and was disengaging himself from the cable. All the banshees of hell were howling in his ears when he threw himself down and forward.

Just in time for the leading edge of the thermal front to reach the crest of the mountain and blast over it.

Rolling hard, he and Kyra tumbled downslope, farther into the shade and safety of the back of the mountain. When they both finally came to a stop, scratched and dirty, she was the first one to sit up. That in itself being unusual, she quickly saw the reason why.

Steam was pouring off Riddick as he rose, staggering slightly. He had been exposed for less than a minute—but it had been a minute in the devil's own sauna. Black ash that had adhered to his skin in places had actually helped to protect him. As for those areas not protected by ash or clothing, boots or goggles, it was fortunate his ancestry was not exclusively Caucasoid. There was just enough melanin in his skin to have saved him from a serious, if widely scattered, burn. He gave silent thanks to favorable genetics.

Nearby, Kyra was staring at him. A look passed between them. Then she shrugged, *Hey, I woulda made it,* and without another word, started down.

XV

It had been a long time since the Guv had done any running, and it was finally starting to take its toll. Not that what he and his companion were doing at the moment could exactly be called running. It was more akin to slipping, sliding, stumbling, and praying you didn't fall flat on your ass and, worse, break something you might need later. Like a femur.

The ground underfoot was as broken and nasty as a slam guard's heart. Barefoot, their feet would have been cut to shreds in minutes by the planes and blades of volcanic glass. Here and there the two men encountered shallow depressions in which falling ash had accumulated and compacted. Grateful for these softer patches, they tried to move along them, hopscotching their way steadily forward.

Though they'd made pretty good time since abandoning the top of the mountain that now loomed behind them, they were starting to run out of gas. Impetus to keep going came from the knowledge that though they were still in shade, it wouldn't be long before the steadily rising sun put in its inevitable soul-sucking appearance above the ragged peak. Thought of what would happen to them when that happened was enough to keep legs moving and brains focused.

Looking up, the Guv saw something that provided yet another shot of the adrenaline he thought had all been used up. The stone pillar that marked the location of the underground hangar was just ahead, jutting above the last rise. The entrance to the hangar itself couldn't be more than five hundred meters off.

"Almost there," he gasped, lips cracked from the heat and lack of water.

"Almost," the other convict wheezed. "One more hill. Just one more fucking hill."

Practically on hands and knees, the two men started up the final rise, slipping and scrabbling on the maddeningly slick, glassy surface. The crest was ten meters away. Then seven. Then three . . .

Something grabbed the Guv's ankle.

Shocked, stunned, he whipped around and looked down, mixed exclamation and curse rising in his throat. At the sight of who was holding him, he stifled the incipient shout aborning.

"Dead mouth," Riddick said warningly.

He did not have to put finger to lips. The words were enough. Laying flat against the surface of the rise, the Guv fought to still his breathing. Nearby, his companion was panting hard. Making absolutely no noise, Riddick slid up alongside the other man and placed a hand over his mouth to muffle the labored breathing. Taking the hint, the convict nodded tersely and strove for absolute silence.

At first there was nothing, the thermal wind having moved on past the far sides of the valley, its perpetual thunder a distant memory now. Then a hint of something. Something new and not natural. A low, ominous thrumming.

Motioning for the Guv and the other convict to stay where they were, Riddick snaked his way to the top of the rise. Unable to restrain her curiosity, or to sit still, Kyra wormed up beside him. What she saw took away what little breath she still had.

They were not alone.

Engines humming, an imposing black warship hovered over the landing strip that had been hewn from Crematoria's surface. Below and nearby gleamed the hangar doors, still in shade. They were shut tight. In front of them, foot soldiers in battle gear busied themselves like so many black ants; checking, inspecting, appraising, searching. Pulling on their leashes, lensing Necros were actively scanning every meter of building and ground. In the midst of them and clearly in charge was a figure Riddick recognized from his holiday on Helion Prime: the Necromonger commander called Vaako.

Next to him, Kyra queried in the softest whisper possible, "And those would be . . . ?"

"Necromongers," Riddick told her.

She turned back to the view below. "So that's what they look like. Creepy bastards, aren't they?"

"That's the idea," he rumbled quietly.

She made a face. "Shit. I *hate* not being the bad guys."

In the midst of the inspection, one of the lensors suddenly turned away from the ground it had been scrutinizing, its head angling toward a nearby rise. It stood like that for a moment. Not entirely human, not wholly machine, indicator lights on its head and sides winking to show that it was alive. Or more properly, functioning. Then it signaled. In response, several soldiers stopped what they were doing and trotted off in the direction of the indicated slope, weapons held at the ready.

It was not good. The escapees now found themselves caught between the advancing and wary Necromonger troops and the rising sun behind. If they went forward, without cover, the soldiers would mow them down in seconds. If they tried to retreat and find a place to hide, the ascending sun would soon poach them just as effectively.

Kyra saw it and lay figuring the odds. So did the Guv and his companion, who had crawled up alongside her. At least if they all charged together, they might catch a soldier or two mentally napping. The trick would be to take down the squad advancing toward them and get close in to the hangar before other troops realized what was happening and could bring heavy weapons to bear. She licked her lips. Not because they were dry, but in anticipation. If there was anything she hated, it was sitting and waiting. Once you let the other guy take the initiative, you've lost half the battle already.

"Figure one minute to get inside that hangar." She glanced back over her shoulder. The soldiers might change course, but the sun would not. "We gonna do this or not?"

Lying on the ground, it was immediately apparent what Riddick was going to do. It was plain to see: it just didn't make any sense. To all intents and purposes, he was relaxing, popping nuts from a bag he carried into his mouth.

"Wait."

The convict flattened out on already too-hot volcanic rock alongside the Guv hissed at him. "What am I waitin' for? To turn into freakin' charcoal?"

Riddick glanced in his direction, not raising his voice. Hardly ever raising his voice. "Just wait."

Kyra glared at the convict. Frustrated and frightened, the man looked to the Guv for direction. The Guv said nothing; just kissed his battered, scarred wedding ring for whatever luck it might hold, and—waited. There was nothing else to do. They would all hang together or, as the ancient saying went, they would surely hang separately.

There was a faraway look in his eyes, and when he spoke it was as if he was trying to speed his words, at least, on their way to someplace off this world. Someplace better.

"Her name was Ellen," he murmured reminiscently, his tone haunted. "I never really forgot. And we lived on Helion Prime."

Riddick nodded once, understanding. He usually did understand: he just rarely found any reason to show that he did.

On the other side of the rise, the squad of soldiers had begun moving upslope in the direction indicated by the suspicious lensor. A noise made them halt, and turn. Behind them, the hangar doors were rumbling open. Anticipating that others of their number had made it inside and were operating the relevant instrumentation, they paused only out of curiosity. In a moment, they would resume their climb.

Except that the figures who appeared in the open portal wore no body armor, wore nothing common to Necromonger society, wore no insignia of any rank. In fact, the only thing they wore besides strange uniforms were expressions of utter bewilderment. In this they were matched by more than one of the now flabbergasted soldiers.

Then someone let off a shot, and looks of confusion were obscured by the sound and fury of concentrated gunfire.

On the other side of the rise, Riddick finished the last of the nuts, cast a thoughtful glance in the direction of the rising sun, matched the number of shots fired to the number of seconds expired, and finally turned, unlimbering his own weapons as he did so.

"*Now* we get nitty-gritty," he said to Kyra. He might also have winked, but if so, it was hidden by those omnipresent goggles. Leading his army of three, he started over the top of the rise.

Recently trapped between the advancing soldiers and the rising sun, the escaped convicts now closed a trap of their own, catching the startled Necromongers between a screaming charge from the far side of the rise and the concentrated firepower that was being unleashed on the squad by the sharp-shooting slam guards. While the soldiers were more heavily armed, their body armor restricted their movements, and the guards had the advantage of good cover inside the hangar.

None of which mattered to Riddick, who advanced as methodically as a tank on rails; shooting and slashing, cutting down anything that got in his way as he made a straight line for the hangar. Eyes blazing with glee at again being granted an opportunity to hit out at something, anything, Kyra buzzed around him like a frigate around a dreadnought, putting down anything in armor that threatened the big man's progress. Those soldiers who did not go down immediately before that relentless double assault were picked off by the Guv and his buddy, bringing up the rear. Given the lethal efficiency being displayed by the big man and small woman, their workload was relatively light.

In such close quarters, the heavy rifles carried by the Necromongers were of little use. By the time they realized it and started going for sidearms and ceremonial blades, it was inevitably too late.

Floating around the perimeter of the intense hand-to-hand firefight, Vaako bided his time. Ignoring everything else, focusing his attention, he kept his gaze trained on the big man in the center of the clash. Take out the command and control center of the enemy, he knew, and opposition would collapse. That was as true of small-scale combat as it was for operations involving entire fleets.

He was not the only one whose attention was devoted to Riddick's steady advance. On the far side of the runway, a singular figure had appeared. Robes of office hanging limp around him in the rising heat, the Purifier tracked the big man's advance toward the hangar. His gaze was steady, his thoughts aligned. He knew what he must do. But everything depended on the outcome of the battle he was observing. Different consequences, he knew, generated different reactions.

Their attention concentrated on the source of the heaviest gunfire, reinforcements had allowed the soldiers to push the guards deeper and deeper into the hangar. One by one the guards went down; cursing their awful luck, lamenting a wondrous opportunity lost, and more or less wondering what the hell had gone wrong. Too busy shooting and reloading, none of them had time to lament what their bizarre assailants were doing on an out-of-the-way, godawful sump pit of a world like Crematoria, or what kind of ultimate objective was important enough to have brought them there. Had there been time to talk, they might even have cooperated, might have struck a deal with the remorseless men in armor who were shooting them down. But that's what happens when weapons go off before mouths. Bullets are not susceptible to reason, and it's hard to make one's arguments heard above the sound of gunfire.

As Riddick well knew.

Then only the slam boss himself was left. Trapped inside the hangar, all of his men dead, he took a last sorrowful look at the case containing the currency that was intended to pay off arriving mercenaries. Better it had been packed with explosives. For a moment, he thought of wrenching it open and flinging its contents at the troops who were closing in around him. Then he realized it might as well be full of colored paper. You could reason with cops, for example—but not with fanatics.

What the hell. Sometimes, no matter how hard you tried, things just didn't fucking work out.

Gun blazing, he burst from his hiding place, yelling defiance as he made a break straight for the merc ship. Unfortunately, there were far too many soldiers in his way. He went down, riddled and dead, his thoughts still on what he might have done with the stolen money. As a last dying dream, it wasn't bad.

And all the while as the battle raged, albeit reduced in intensity due to the continuous shrinkage in the number of combatants, Crematoria's sun continued its inexorable rise.

Led by Riddick, Kyra and the Guv reached the near edge of the runway. Amazed that they had actually made it this far, the Guv offered an evaluation that emerged as a war cry.

"We might goddamn well do this!"

To an outsider, it looked as if they actually might. But an outsider would probably not have seen Vaako, who had positioned himself advantageously to unleash a personal withering crossfire on the three survivors. Sighting in carefully on Riddick, he fired his weapon.

In the split second between the time the commander's finger tightened on the trigger of his rifle and the burst he let loose crossed the intervening space, Riddick moved. Just missing, the powerful blast from the heavy weapon slammed into the runway and blew him right off his feet, sending him tumbling hard to the ground. Seeing the fugitives go down, a pair of pursuing soldiers accelerated, closing for the kill.

Only to be intercepted by Kyra, howling defiance. Harried by the ferocious little harridan, they were forced to postpone the coup de grace to deal with her first. Letting them think they were forcing her backward, she continued to fend them off, leading them in the opposite direction, away from the two men lying on the ground—one dead, the other dazed.

There was another, however, who was not distracted. Rising and racing forward, Vaako rapidly closed the distance between himself and the big man. He could feel his quarry's neck beneath his fingers, could anticipate the cracking of bones, could. . . .

Something slammed into him hard from behind. Surprised, he fought and rolled. The man who had knocked him down was nothing more than a convict, a lesser specimen of the human species. His expression as he fought with the Necromonger commander was an odd mix of resignation and determination, with just an inexplicable hint of amusement—as if death had been his companion for so long he had come to regard it as a companion and not an enemy.

Worn out from the debilitating run across the unsparing surface of Crematoria, exhausted by the exertions that had been demanded of his body, the Guv was no match for the energetic and rested Vaako. Finally lifting the other man over his head, the Commander brought him down in a move that was as simple as it was fatal, breaking his adversary's spine. It had been an interruption, a divertissement—nothing more. Pivoting away from the motionless body, he turned once more toward his principal quarry.

He arrived as Riddick, tired and bruised, the wind knocked out of him, was still struggling to get to his knees. Nodding slowly to himself, knowing it was over now, Vaako advanced the rest of the way at leisure.

"So you *can* kneel. Not that it matters. You were given the choice, between *the* Way, and *this* way." Drawing his sidearm, he stood over the wounded creature and unhurriedly raised the muzzle toward the big man's head.

He was going to die, Riddick knew. It didn't trouble him. He had been expecting to die ever since he had been a child. Everything he had done since then, every effort he had expended, had been a rear-guard effort to postpone that inevitability. Now that it was at an end, he had no regrets. He had done all that he could do. All that any one man could do. He ought to be resigned, to let it come. To welcome an end to all the running, and fighting, and killing. There was only one problem.

He was still mad.

In his madness, time and space itself seemed to distort. The movements of the man standing before him, the man who had come to kill him, appeared to slow.

The terrain around him warped, twisted. Instead of bare rock, there was forest. Instead of a heat-sink of a sky, clear blue and white clouds.

He knew he was losing consciousness when a figure stepped *through* his nascent assassin.

It was a figure he had seen before, in a dream. Or had it been a dream? The voice was the same as well; familiar, soothing, somehow reassuring.

"Remember what they did . . . ," it was saying.

Time frozen, space constrained, she knelt beside him. As on the merc ship, a hand reached out toward him. But unlike then, this time there was contact. Something passed between them. Memories. Emotions. And—a certain energy.

"And remember your primitive side. It's always been there."

Time and space collapsed back to normalcy. The woman was gone. The man who had killed the Guv was still there.

Vaako saw what Riddick, inundated by the surge of something far stranger and more powerful than mere adrenaline, could not. It was fury of a unique kind made real, made visible. Expanding from somewhere deep within the man kneeling before him, it expanded as it rushed to the limits of the big man's body, reaching every extremity, coursing down arms, legs, fingers, up his neck, into his skull. Blood began to trickle from Riddick's ears. Blood under pressure. Rising pressure.

Staring, not comprehending. The gun in Vaako's hand fell to his side as he began to backpedal, his pace increasing with every step.

Something burst forth from the kneeling man. Too intent on finding cover, any kind of cover, Vaako didn't see it. Neither did the Necromonger soldiers it flattened, each and every one unlucky enough to be standing within the radius of that expanding, palpable fury when it finally unleashed. Only one escaped the devastating effects of the silent discharge.

Standing nearby, the Purifier found himself rocked. Mentally as well as physically, but far more so the first. He was not knocked down, he was not shattered. But inside, something was blown away.

The singular detonation had caught and flattened the two soldiers who had been pursuing Kyra, but not her. Fortuitously, she had been retreating behind the runway berm in an attempt to lure them close enough for her blades to reach. When she finally rolled forward for a better look, she was startled to see both of them lying prone, dead on the runway. The smooth, flat approach to the hangar was littered with Necromonger corpses. A few were moving, but feebly, as if the life-force itself had been blasted out of them. At the epicenter of the eerie silence, one unarmored body lay motionless. Even at a distance, it was instantly recognizable.

Rising, she stared at the unmoving form. It continued to lie dormant. Maybe if she gazed at it long enough and hard enough, she thought, it would get up, move, at least twitch. But the intensity of her stare had no effect on the familiar shape. It just lay there, seemingly as dead as the scattered bodies surrounding it.

"Riddick?" she mumbled.

Another figure was moving. Staggering, stumbling, mind and body both dazed by something he did not understand but in nowise dead, Vaako struggled to his feet. Gathering himself, he also focused his attention on the motionless, goggled, apparently unbreathing form. As his mind cleared, he bent to pick up a dropped blade and started forward. From what he could see, whatever had detonated had killed the man Riddick as surely as it had flattened everyone around him. But good soldier that he was, Vaako wanted to make sure, needed to make sure. And no one was going to stop him. No one.

The sun flared over the top of the nearby mountain.

Most of the runway suddenly bleached out, as if every drop of color had abruptly been washed from the hard surface. Kyra dove for safety behind the nearest rocks while Vaako and those soldiers who had survived the mysterious blast effect fled toward their ship's landing zone. There were some things not even the implacable servants of Necropolis could face.

Out on the runway, the uninhibited sun struck the unmoving bodies. Several of them began to smolder. Riddick remained where he had fallen.

"You bastard," Kyra found herself muttering silently. "You son of a bitch. It's not supposed to end like this. What the hell am I supposed to do now? What do you expect me to do? Get up, get up!"

A quick glance, stolen from the unrelenting sunlight, showed the big man still lying in the center of the field of Necromonger corpses. It had not moved.

But in the rapidly shrinking shadows, others did: soldiers and support personnel, lensors and officers, retreating rapidly in the direction of their hovering frigate.

In most things, she told the truth. In most things. But when it came to not caring about dying she was, as she had just recently told Riddick, a terrible liar. In some ways, the choice she made now was an easy one. When one hope is gone, most people naturally gravitate to the next. Abandoning her hiding place, that the still rising sun would find all too soon, she rose to her feet and ran—toward the potential safe haven that was the Necromonger ship.

Within the rapidly intensifying hell that was the runway now exposed to the full glare of Crematoria's sun, nothing moved except waves of rising heat and the beginnings of combustion from several of the prone human shapes. But within the shadows of the abandoned hangar, something did. Advancing deliberately out into the searing light, a human shape wound its way through the scattered bodies. The expensive and technically advanced cloak and hood of office it wore fended off the lethal effects of the naked sun for a little while. Long enough, anyway, for the figure to find what it was looking for, hook the motionless body under both arms, and drag the second man back into the still barely tolerable shade of the hangar. With the doors standing open, powerful internal cooling units struggled desperately to maintain the hangar temperature within habitable human limits.

Letting the body he had scavenged fall limp to the hangar floor, the Purifier pushed back the hood of his cloak, slightly burning his fingers in the process. The fabric was remarkably resilient, but if he had been forced to hike another twenty meters or so out in the sunlight, it, too, would have started to burn.

Speaking of burns, the exposed flesh of the man he had dragged off the runway was already showing signs of blistering in places. Only the dark goggles he wore had prevented his eyes from boiling away. The all-purpose hygienic spray the Purifier pulled from a pouch concealed within his raiment and proceeded to apply to these surfaces was normally used in Necromonger purification ceremonies to heal damaged faces before their soul-abandoned bodies were consigned permanently to oblivion. Now it worked its restorative epidermal magic on the man he had pulled out of the lethal sunlight.

The shock of instant healing combined with lingering pain to snap Riddick back to consciousness. He sat up with a suddenness that would have startled anyone other than the Purifier. But he was not looking at his rescuer, or thinking about him.

Something had happened out on the runway, in that instant frozen in time when Riddick had finally run out of strength, resources, and ideas. It had happened when the Necromonger commander had stood over him, gun in hand, muzzle aimed at his head. He could not put a name to it, did not know how he had done whatever it was that he had done. Only that it was as much a part of him, of his mental and physical makeup, as the fingers on his hands and the implants in his eyes. The experience had defined him in ways he had not imagined, and now it enabled him to better define himself.

"I'm Furyan," he declared, his tone a mixture of assurance and wonder. Then he turned slightly to study the scene outside the hangar.

The thermal wind had reached the runway and passed on, tossing dead soldiers about like broken dolls. Those who still lay within view were beginning to steam as the water that composed most of their bodies boiled away. Muscles shrank inside armor and desiccated skin contracted to shrink-wrap the underlying bones. The goggles that had saved his eyes from the ravening sun scanned back and forth across the runway, nearby rocks, the protective berms that flanked the pavement. All the bodies he saw wore Necromonger gear of one kind or another. Of one small, lithe, unarmored woman there was no sign.

Moments later the sky was filled with a deep thrumming like a snoring whale. Slowly, majestically, the Necromonger warship hove into view. Riddick and the Purifier ducked farther back into the shelter of the hangar, watching. The frigate circled once overhead. No destructive fire poured from its powerful weapons systems. There was no need. Nature herself had already covered the hangar area with a different kind of fire. Accelerating slowly, the great ship angled upward and away in the direction of the planetary darkside.

Focused as always on the problem at hand,

Riddick started for the mercenary ship that beckoned from its nearby parking slot. While his mind was nearly up to speed, his body wasn't. Still reeling from the aftereffects of lying exposed to Crematoria's sun for just a few minutes, he staggered.

Recover, he told himself. *Balance, surroundings, direction. Then move.*

Immersed in thoughts of the absent Kyra, he had nearly forgotten about the man who had saved him. As he stood gathering himself, he saw that the Purifier was busy at a task that made no sense. Wordlessly, efficiently, the man was removing all the trappings of his high office; rings, insignia, helmet, and more. Standing there regaining his strength, Riddick could only speculate on the reasons behind the enigmatic divestiture.

Seeing the big man gazing intently at him, the Purifier spoke while continuing to shed the elegant accouterments that defined his status. "You're not just a Furyan, Riddick. You're an alpha Furyan." He nodded in the direction of the steaming bodies outside. "In the event anyone doubted it, there lies the tangible proof, laid out for all to see." Clad now only in simple underlying clothing devoid of any evidence of his eminence, he came toward the staring big man.

"I'm supposed to deliver a message to you if Vaako failed to kill you," he said, in the manner of one relaying something of solemn importance. "It is a message from Lord Marshal himself. If you live, you are warned to stay away from Helion—and to stay away from him." Dangling from the fingers of his right hand as he drew nearer was the spectral dagger that had once protruded trophy-like from the back of the slayer Irgun, and which Riddick had drawn and used to kill its former owner. Its presence in the Purifier's hand did not escape the big man's notice.

"But Vaako will most likely report you dead. Certainly you appeared to be so. Unable to explain what happened on the runway, he will neglect to expound upon it. I do not think the Lord Marshal will press him on the details, so grateful will he be to hear of your passing. And Vaako will be convincing, since he will be speaking the truth as he saw it." He was very close now to the man he had saved, the dagger glinting in the shadow of his side.

Two more steps, and Riddick had him by the throat. It was a restraining grip, not a killing one. But with a slight tensing of muscles, it could easily be transformed from one into the other.

Reaching down slowly, making no sudden moves, his eyes on the lenses of those black goggles, the Purifier used his free hand to pull his shirt wide and expose his bare chest. On it was a mark; unmistakable in its design, unyielding in its import. A handprint. The mark of Furya, on the chest of a Necromonger. Riddick could only stare.

"We all began as something else," the Purifier was saying gently. "All Necromongers begin as something else. Given the choice to live anew or die as we were, most accepted the offer and opportunity. I was confused, unsure, and translated that into eagerness to adapt myself. I've done unbelievable things in the name of a faith that wasn't my own. The ability of the individual human being to adjust morality and beliefs to changing circumstances is depressingly common."

Riddick nodded tersely. He still maintained his grip, but loosely. "I've seen it. Too often."

"My alternative was to bend to the Necromonger way, or to die," the Purifier continued. "Not much of a choice. If Vaako reports you dead, you have a better choice—and that's a powerful thing."

His fingers opened, and the unearthly blade dropped to the ground. As Riddick's clutching fingers relaxed, the Purifier stepped out of the big man's grasp and around him, heading for the open hangar portal. Riddick watched him go, saying nothing, making no move either physically or verbally to intercept the man who had saved his life. It was what he wanted, or he wouldn't be doing it. Atonement, perhaps. A solitary expression of regret. Or maybe the man who had been Furyan and had become the Purifier was simply tired.

Stepping out into the ferocious glare of direct sunlight, he soon started to smoke. Flames, small at first, then curling larger, began to erupt from his head, his arms, and all other exposed skin. As he walked, he talked, conversing with himself as he had been and as he was now.

The last words Riddick heard him speak were, "If only I could still feel the pain. . . ." Then he crumbled to his knees, and the flames and sunshine consumed him utterly: by his own hand, the Purifier had been purified.

Riddick watched him burn until white bone began to show. Then he bent and picked up the dagger. It was cold in his fingers, maybe as cold as the Under-Verse itself. Turning, he started silently toward the merc ship.

XVI

From space, Helion Prime looked no different. Clouds continued to form and scatter, waves continued to break on its shores, flora still reached for the sun while native fauna crept through the depths of its forests. Only in the cities and the places altered by man was change noticeable. Here and there fighting still raged as remnant government forces continued to contest the uncompromising Necromonger onslaught. But with the major centers of population now brought under control, it was only a matter of time before the last pockets of resistance were subdued and the planet added to the growing list of those that had been brought under the sway of Necropolis.

Within the Basilica, it was a time of celebration. In keeping with Necromonger tradition, there were no flaring banners, no blaring bands. Like everything else in Necromonger society, salutation was a matter of solemnity.

Vaako stood tall as the new cloak of rank was

draped across his shoulders and new ceremonial armor was fitted to his existing undergarments. Burnished and glowing, it confirmed his promotion to the rank of commander general. Arrayed around him were his fellow commanders, their envy kept under control as strict as their posture. Standing nearby was a singular female figure. To look at her, one might have thought it was Dame Vaako who was receiving the honors and not the commander himself. In a sense, it was.

The Lord Marshal beamed with satisfaction as he spoke to the newly anointed commander general. "I may have lost a Purifier, but I gain a First among commanders. The one is as valuable as the other, and the other can be replaced. It's overdue, isn't it, that we acknowledge your many accomplishments in the service of the Faith, your steady ethic, and above all, your unflinching loyalty." He smiled, and for once, it seemed to be an honest smile.

"I know how you felt about this expedition. That you believed it to be unnecessary and a waste of time. But you went, and carried out the task that was assigned to you. For this as much as for the success you achieved you are to be commended."

Aware of all the eyes that were on him, Vaako stiffened. "Obedience without question. That is our way."

The Lord Marshal nodded approvingly. "Well done, Vaako. This is a day of days, to be remembered by all who have witnessed it. Again, my congratulations."

With that, he turned and departed, leaving Vaako

to be congratulated—sometimes honestly, sometimes grudgingly—by his fellow commanders. One by one, they filed past to pay their respects.

"First and always, Vaako . . . Whatever He ordains is so . . . Death in due time come to us all. . . ."

When the last of the senior officers had left the room, only two remained—and of them, only Vaako seemed unimpressed by his own success.

Sensing his disenchantment, his companion strove to buoy his spirits. As always, Dame Vaako spoke as eloquently with her body and her eyes as she did with her voice.

"Try to look more pleased, Vaako," she admonished. "You are promoted to commander general. No higher rank can be achieved short of Lord Marshal. What more could you desire from this episode, that began with such disagreement? You've laid to rest both his enemy *and* his suspicions." She put a hand on his arm. "By so doing, you've acquired something more precious than mere rank. You've gained freedom." Now she leaned closer and her voice fell to a whisper. "The freedom to move—in whatever direction you choose."

Vaako only half heard her. Perfectionist to a fault, rather than enjoying his moment of triumph, he was still obsessing over what he had *not* done. Of course the breeder Riddick was dead. Vaako had left him dead following the peculiar and still unexplained incident that had also killed a number of his troops. Even if some small flicker of life had remained in the man, a few moments exposed to the raw sunshine of Crematoria would have been more than enough to reduce to ashes anything that remained. There was no reason to be second-guessing his actions. He'd been forced to move, and move fast, to save his own life and that of his surviving soldiers from the full force of the rising sun. It would not do for them to perish before due time.

Still . . .

"Should've brought back the head."

Dame Vaako sighed wearily. No matter how hard she tried to bolster this man, it seemed he would be forever reconsidering his labors. She resigned herself to having to, once more, reassure him.

"You told me everything that transpired. I see no reason for your anxiety. You saw him go down. You saw him unbreathing. You saw him dead on the ground. You may not be able to explain everything that happened, but that does not matter. All that matters is the result, not the mechanism by which it was achieved. What is important is that he is dead, not how it came to pass."

Vaako was shaking his head in remembered bewilderment, refusing to be so easily reassured. "I don't like what I can't understand." He turned to her. "This Riddick, he was no common breeder. Something happened out there the like of which I have never encountered before, nor heard reported. As he himself went down, he dropped twenty of my team without raising a finger. No weapons, no gas; nothing. One moment they were advancing on him, and the next . . ." His voice trailed off, unable to find words to explain what he had seen.

Entirely prosaic, Dame Vaako shrugged off his

confusion. "All mysteries are not miracles. Not even in this religion. I was not there, but I am sure there is a perfectly sound scientific explanation for what you witnessed. Provide the details to our analysts, and I have no doubt that they will supply one that satisfies even you, my worrying love."

When he still did not appear convinced, she struggled to contain her frustration. "Come, come, Vaako; this doubt does not become the fleet's newest commander general. You say that you saw him die, and left him dead. That is what matters. If you say *you're* certain about it, then it *is* certain. And we've already said it, haven't we?"

He nodded slowly, taking the full import of her words. "That we have."

"And who would dare to contradict the word of a commander general recently anointed by Lord Marshal himself?" She turned coquettish, seeking to draw him away from depressing thoughts and back to the more festive present. "Now you must come with me, so that I can bestow upon you a promotion of my own devising." Slipping her arm into his and smiling suggestively, she led him away from the chamber and toward their private quarters.

The special bonds were forged of much more than mere metal. Designed to hold a being who had the unnerving ability to move through the air without seeming to set foot to ground, they had been built to restrain anything short of sheer aether.

Certainly they seemed to be doing an efficient job

of holding in one place the Elemental known as Aereon. Like overlapping spiderwebs, the overkill of restraints kept her unceremoniously staked to the floor. Despite this, her bearing was of one patiently waiting for something rather than that of an individual in fear for her life.

She didn't even bother to turn when the door to the holding room opened. She knew who it was. The man's aura preceded him, poisoning the air ahead of his advance.

The Lord Marshal stopped directly in front of her. She could have turned away, but chose not to. She could have protested her treatment, but chose not to. Aereon was the very embodiment of the patience for which the Elementals were famed.

Unlike her, her visitor, however, was far less inclined to waste time in idle contemplation of his immediate surroundings.

"Tell me the report is true. Vaako was very confident. That is not the same thing as being utterly positive. Tell me the Furyan is gone and I can close this campaign without hearing his bootsteps."

"Let me see." Just the faintest hint of mockery tinged her response. "If he is dead, I sense I'm not far from the same fate, being of no further use to you. So, as a matter of self-preservation, shouldn't I tell you that Riddick is still alive?"

Elementals and their elliptical responses were a pain to all who were forced to endure them, he thought. "Don't try me, Aereon. I can plow you under with the rest of Helion Prime. Push me the wrong way and I'll bury you so deep your precious air will never reach you."

"Dear me," she replied, her tone unchanged. "Then I'd best mind what I say, hadn't I?" The mocking tone vanished and she became quite serious. "No one really knows the future. What people call clairvoyance is in reality nothing more than acute intuitive insight. Or a lucky guess. It is certainly not the infallible talent some claim. Inerrancy, Lord Marshal, is a fallacy to which only fools aspire."

If she was speaking of those claiming to be clairvoyants, then she was answering his question. If she was using the subject under discussion to deliver a veiled warning, he ought to have her killed for insolence. Since he couldn't be sure of either, he forbore from ordering the latter.

He tried another tack. "Very well. If you cannot foresee what is to come, and insist no one else can, either, then tell me the odds that Vaako met with success. That I'll now be the one to carry my people across the Threshold and into the UnderVerse where they can begin True Life." He smiled unpleasantly. "Surely you can do that for me, Aereon. Since, as you say, you people are always calculating. Tell me what I want to hear—and maybe I'll save your home world. For last."

Somewhat to his surprise, she didn't hesitate. Nor did she attempt to dance around his query any longer. Eyeing him without flinching, or even without rancor, she murmured, "The odds are good."

"'The odds are good,'" he repeated irritably. "The odds are good—for what?"

"That you'll reach the UnderVerse soon."

He nodded understandingly and, apparently satisfied, turned to leave. He was partway down the access corridor when the alternate import of her response struck him. Turning, he glanced back the way he had come. Nothing was drifting down the corridor toward him, and the shadowed alcoves of the walkway remained devoid of flickering, dancing shapes. Only the shadows mocked him. Since he could not order their arrest and execution, he had no choice but to continue on, more unnerved than he would have cared to admit.

Having no equal, he was forced to debate with himself what to do. Helion Prime had not yet been completely subjugated. But it was badly weakened, and unlikely to offer serious resistance if attacked afresh. Vaako had been so certain, but still, still . . .

Standing at the railing allowed him a sweeping view over Necropolis. Now he turned abruptly, so abruptly that his move startled the officer standing behind him.

"Ascension protocol. Now. Relay the order throughout the fleet and to all ground units."

Caught off guard by both the speed of the Lord Marshal's turn and the nature of his request, the officer blinked uncertainly. "We still have numbers out there, Lord Marshal. Sweep teams, recon ships, mop-up squads that—"

Another man might have yelled in the officer's face. Lord Marshal's astral self snapped out furiously, slamming the unlucky officer across the room and into a wall, smashing his bones. The hesitant officer crumpled wordlessly to the floor, a broken heap. Without so much as a murmur of regret, the Necromonger's supreme commander growled at the next officer in rank.

"Get my armada off the ground."

The officer did not need to be told twice, nor did he think to question the inexplicable command. He had already seen what happened to someone who did. Indicating acquiescence, he took steps to issue the necessary orders.

Across the surface of Helion Prime, warships began to withdraw from sites they had been patrolling. Ongoing attacks were halted as vessel after vessel lifted and turned toward the rendezvous point near the capital. Foot soldiers raced for transports' loading bays. Too dazed to celebrate, and worried that what they were witnessing might be nothing more than an elaborate feint, Helion's surviving defenders were hesitant to emerge from their remaining redoubts. But their instruments marked the departure of both Necromonger ground troops and ships and their gathering in the skies above the capital. Was another massive demonstration of power to be forthcoming, or was something afoot that not even the most eclectic strategist could visualize?

In the ravaged capital itself, Necromonger officers and nobles congregated on the Basilica steps to observe the gathering of forces. While none knew the reason for the contraction, all had confidence in the decision-making ability of the Lord Marshal and his staff. Preparing some devastating surprise for the remaining stubborn resistance, no doubt. That was the general consensus.

Dame Vaako watched as columns of troops filed past the onlookers and into the Basilica itself. The flurry of activity was as puzzling as it had been unpredictable. Why were their forces withdrawing from the objective, when the final conquest of all Helion Prime loomed so near? Had the Helions unearthed some previously unsuspected deadly weapon, or been promised allies from out system? If so, she'd heard nothing of either, and there was little that escaped her notice.

So little that, as the Basilica steps themselves began to retract, her eye was caught by a profile. One profile in a sea of profiles, all rendered vague and distorted by helmets and visors.

She could have sounded a general alarm. But if she was wrong, and her admittedly slight suspicion was proven false, under the circumstances she could be charged with the serious offense of interfering with a mass evacuation. There were those within Necromonger society who would be more than happy to attend the punishment hearing that would follow. Before she said or did anything, she had to be certain that what she had glimpsed was more than just a disturbing memory impinging on a field of faces.

Forsaking her place, she drew her robes about her and hurried into the ship, moving fast as she labored to catch up to the officer she had seen. Unwilling to call for assistance until she knew for sure whether she was hallucinating or not, she was forced to push her way through the sea of soldiers and personnel that packed the Basilica's main entrance. Where was he? In the ocean of armor, it was almost impossible to distinguish one soldier from another. But she persevered, wanting to be sure, *needing* to be sure—that she was wrong.

Then a set of inner doors began to close, separating soldiers from the rest of the vessel as they continued toward their quarters. Officer after officer turned in her direction as dim internal illumination took over from external sunshine.

Just before the inner doors shut tight, the pupils of one officer glinted with a singular flash.

Too stunned by the news to pace, object, or do more than gape uncomprehendingly at his companion, Vaako could only blurt, "You mean, 'on Helion'?"

A handsome fool was still a fool, she told herself heatedly, but this man was the best she could do. Berating him aloud would only be counterproductive. In the scheme of things, there was no alternative to the newly promoted commander general. She had too much invested in him to alienate him now.

They had been handed a shock. Well, she had dealt with difficult, unforeseen circumstances before. Many who had underestimated her resourcefulness and resolve had preceded her to the Threshold—prematurely. She was not about to let one man, whatever his abilities, send her on that untimely journey now.

"I mean on this very ship," she snapped. "Right here, in the sanctuary of the Basilica itself."

Though he had never had reason to doubt her before, Vaako found it hard to believe. Difficult enough to imagine anyone surviving direct exposure to the sun of Crematoria. To expect him to believe that Riddick had not only survived, but made it back to Helion Prime and onto the Basilica, was almost too much to envision. Yet no matter how strongly or sensibly he objected, she continued to insist that she had seen him here.

Presented with a seeming impossibility, he sought other explanations. "Could you be wrong? Could your mind just be fabricating what we fear? We have been under considerable stress lately; stress caused both by professional demands and personal expectations." He moved closer to her, searching her face, meeting her gaze. *"Could you be wrong?"*

She saw that he did not want to accept an unpleasant reality. Well, he'd better find a way to accept it, and fast. Whatever Riddick had in mind, she doubted the breeder would wait long before putting it in play. They needed to be ready. For whatever might come.

"Not so wrong as when you left him alive," she chided her companion. She knew that, had she been on Crematoria, that oversight would not have occurred. Her thoughts swirled as she tried to anticipate possible eventualities. "It's twice a mistake. Not only your failure to make certain of his passing, but now we have to live with your report that the expedition was a success." She was pacing fiercely now, a panther barely caged, muttering to herself as much as to him. “How do we salvage this . . . how . . . ?”

Vaako chose that moment to reveal that they were not thinking along similar lines. “The Lord Marshal,” he exclaimed with a start. “He’s got to be warned. Even if it turns out that you were mistaken, it’s a risk that cannot be ignored.” He turned and started for the door.

She did not move to intercept him. Nor did she raise her voice or sputter curses. Her tone was perfectly steady. “You will never see UnderVerse. He’ll kill us both before due time. And it won’t matter whether Riddick is here or not. I’ve seen how he acts when the breeder is discussed. Just the possibility that you might have failed will be enough to set him off. Is that what you want?”

Vaako halted, confusion and uncertainty writ plain on his face. “Then—what do we do?”

“It is truly the wise one who can turn seeming adversity into advantage.” She moved closer, her voice at once conspiratorial and ferocious. “This Riddick is persistent beyond reason. I say give him his chance. You saw what he did when confronted by the Quasi-Dead. No one in my experience or I daresay in yours has shown such resolve, such resilience. Such skill. If he is half of what Lord Marshal fears, then perhaps he can at least wound him.” Her gaze met that of her companion, bold and unwavering.

“It may be enough. If hurt, he will hesitate. When he hesitates, that is when you must act.”

Vaako balked. What she was saying, this woman to whom he had hitched his life, went against every teaching he had absorbed since becoming a soldier. "Just to take his place? I am made commander general. Is that not enough? Must I do this just to keep what I kill?"

"It is the Necromonger way. No lord marshal reigns forever." She all but spat the words. "This one's time for replacement is overdue. You will be doing him a favor. Send him on his way to UnderVerse. Advance him to his due time."

Torn between desire for her and loyalty to his superior, between his own dreams and the faith to which he had pledged himself, he looked away and gave voice to the emotions that were churning inside him.

"It is not enough."

She contained her exasperation. Where would this man be without her to motivate him? On the battlefield he reigned supreme: none could touch him for bravery or skill. But when thrust into the maze of politics and court intrigue, he was like a lost child. It fell to her to lead him.

"Then if you will not do it for yourself, and you will not do it for me, do it for the faith."

That brought a reaction. The intended one. Having struck the right nerve, she continued without pause.

"He fears this Riddick. If he shows fear, he demonstrates weakness. Weakness can be treated and cured within the junior ranks, and tolerated among the senior staff, but a lord marshal who exhibits weakness proves himself unworthy of that office. That is *not* the Necromonger way." Sidling close, she placed a hand on his chest, ran it slowly up and down.

"You know that what I speak is the truth. Sending you all the way to a distant system, in the midst of war, to find and kill one man. Does that demonstrate the kind of nerve that is needed to lead our people? At the time, you questioned the decision. Why can you not now see the need to question the man behind the decision? How can someone so fearful of one individual be deemed fit to continue defending the cause?" She stepped back.

"You *must* act. There *is* no one else. No one with your ability to seize the moment. No one with your skill to carry out the sentence. What we do now, we do not for ourselves, but for all who subscribe to the Necromonger way of life. And of death. Besides," she added, "you will only be sending him onward to the place where we all wish to go. That should be considered a boon, not a punishment."

"What," he wondered, slowly warming to the idea in spite of himself, "if it is not his due time?"

"The Lord Marshal? It is always his due time. He only needs someone to give him a helping hand to the Threshold. You will be doing him, as well as our people, a great favor."

He was coming around, she saw. He always did. It was only a matter of time, of placing the right words in his ear and sometimes hands in the right places. The best blade, she knew, was a sword that was malleable in the hands of the one who wielded it.

"To protect the Faith . . . ," he was murmuring, his eyes now focused on something distant.

"To protect the Faith," she echoed impatiently. Get on with it, man! But she saw that he still needed further reassurance. "This can still be a day of days, as the Lord Marshal declared. But the timing must be flawless." Without a hint of cynicism she added, "The Lord Marshal may not entirely approve of the generous gesture you are going to make on his behalf."

One more time, he met her eyes. Were they really going to do this? Once committed, he knew, he would have no chance to back out. There would be no turning back. Explanations after the fact were unlikely to be accepted.

Unaware of the complex machinations being plotted by others, Riddick strode purposefully down the corridor. Having traded battle armor for the stolen lightweight dress cloak and attire of an off-duty officer, he advanced without being questioned by the occasional guard or preoccupied passerby. Everyone was too intent on discussing the preeminent issue of the moment to notice him anyway, as soldiers and support personnel alike tried to come up with a reason why the armada should be ordered off the surface of Helion Prime before that stubbornly resistant world had been fully subdued. Such an action was unprecedented. Some even, in carefully guarded whispers and dark corners, were bold enough to voice concern about the current Lord Marshal's resolve.

Though he made his way forward with care for the

position of his cloak, Riddick could not prevent it from billowing slightly open as he mechanically saluted representatives of the lower ranks. At such times, anyone with a sharp eye and an inclination to peer beneath might have noticed that underneath his cloak of rank the big man's vest was decorated not with symbols of accomplishment or medals of valor, but with blades. Lots of blades, among which was the unusual dagger that had once adorned the right deltoid muscle of a now dead soldier named Irgun. Primitive weapons, knives. But they wouldn't jam on you, they emitted no telltale radiation, they were silent, they contained no electronics that could be jammed by a routine room-spanning security field, and they did their job just as effectively as any shell or beam weapon.

He stiffened slightly as he saw the two figures coming toward him. No one had questioned or challenged him until now, but—one of the figures was a lensor. Keeping his eyes straight and striving to appear preoccupied, he kept on. Like everyone else he had encountered in the Basilica, the pair walked right past him.

Right past him, and then the lensor turned. And issued an alert.

"You, sir—a moment, if you please," the soldier with it exclaimed. Not too loudly, for which Riddick was grateful.

Turning, he waited while they approached. "Something wrong, soldier?"

The younger man hesitated, glanced at the lensor,

received information, and gathered courage. "Nothing really, sir. Might I speak with you a moment?"

How to play this? the big man thought rapidly. At the moment, the corridor was not crowded, but neither was it deserted. Taking another step forward, he lowered his voice.

"Sure. But I'm not really supposed to be off duty right now." Turning to his right, he gestured toward a dark side alcove. "Over there, okay?"

The soldier nodded knowingly. Together, he and his lensor accompanied Riddick into the recess. Once inside, Riddick reached beneath his cloak and pulled out his identification. Two of them.

No one else confronted him as he emerged from the now silent alcove, resumed his march down the corridor, and disappeared around a corner.

The view of Helion's capital as seen through the large, floor-mounted port continued to expand as the Basilica gained altitude. Very soon now, every ship would be in position. There was nothing left to do but issue the necessary commands. Obliged by the need to preserve the lives of as many potential converts as possible, he had already put this off too long.

"Final protocol," the Lord Marshal told the officer responsible for following through. "It is time to deliver a lasting lesson and simultaneously put an end to this obstinacy on the part of a few reluctant locals. With one blow, we will crush any remaining will to resist." He turned back to the port. "Execute on my order." Interesting he mused, how certain words could have such significant double meanings. "Execute," for example.

Wordlessly, the officer made the necessary preparations. Among them was the appearance at his station of a control whose appearance was as much ceremonial as functional: a small replica of the great conquest icon itself.

Far below, the surviving citizens of the capital crept from their hiding places to gaze skyward in wonder at the impressive gathering of invading ships. One such house had suffered comparatively little damage. Its patriarch was dead. Unable without his help to reach the evacuation vessel that had been designated for them, mother and daughter had returned home. As one of the warrior ships thrummed malevolently low overhead, Lajjun clutched Ziza even tighter to her breast.

One by one, their massive engines combining to generate a deep-throated mechanical drone that drowned out every other sound, warships were gathering around the conquest icon, almost as if they were on parade. But their assembling had nothing to do with pageantry, and everything to do with death.

Like a broken piece of machinery, the dead lensor was dumped at the Lord Marshal's feet. Ordinarily, it would not have been brought directly to his attention. Especially not now, when an event of considerable significance was about to transpire. But someone had already reviewed the lensor's recording pack and deemed the information contained therein of sufficient importance that it should be viewed immediately by the highest authority.

To preserve the privacy of the transmission, an umbilical was jacked into an appropriate port in the lensor's back and the other end into a console. The use of a cord was testament to the sensitivity of the information about to be displayed: any over-the-air transmission was susceptible to interception.

As the technician adjusted the flow, a wall screen displayed the lensor's final recordings. A Necromonger handler was shown walking down a corridor in the company of a subofficer, both of them with their backs to the lensor. Entering a darkened alcove, they turned to face one another. Seeing the face of the subofficer in profile, the Lord Marshal sucked in his breath imperceptibly.

There was a brief exchange of questions. Then the scene turned chaotic as Riddick, in the guise of a Necromonger subofficer, attacked in a blur of motion. The screen went dark, as had the lensor.

The Lord Marshal ripped the umbilical out of its socket. "Commander Toal . . ."

Toal was already at his leader's side, anticipating. "Don't worry, Lord Marshal. He won't escape twice." He gestured freely. "This time, there's no place for him to go. If he seeks to flee again via one of the landing support struts, this time my men will be there to help him step outside." His expression was mirthless. "It will be a longer step, this time."

Whirling, Toal mobilized his subordinates. Shouts and orders were exchanged. The commander known as Scalp-Taker began relaying instructions to the subofficers in charge of the Elites.

Indifferent to the rising frenzy of preparation, the

Lord Marshal stood staring at the connection cord he still held in his hand. Then, very deliberately, he wound it securely around his palm, the action coming naturally to him, as if he had done something very similar once before.

If Riddick was half the trouble he appeared to be, it would take time to hunt him down. Meanwhile, there remained the little matter of a stern lesson to be delivered to the intractable population of Helion Prime. Idly, he moved to the balcony that overlooked the reaches of Necropolis. A mass of new converts, drawn from the world below, was shuffling across the floor on their way to the First Stage of Education. The sight was pleasing and relaxed him a little. But it did not change his mind.

Protocol needed to be followed.

Behind him, the officer in charge of lesson deliverance methodically opened the three heads of the fateful icon control. Visible via the floor port, on monitors throughout the Basilica and the rest of the armada, and from the surface of Helion itself, the three heads atop the conquest icon that impaled the surface of the planet began to bow. A gigantic maw appeared between them, its dark interior now open to the sky. From within, something belched skyward. A swirling, rotating mass of multicolored energy, in appearance and shape it was not unlike the gravitational weapons that had been used against massed Helion foot soldiers and their reinforced installations. There was only one significant difference.

This one was much, *much* bigger.

Rising like a ring of flashing, lightning-imbued

cloud, it expanded in diameter until its outermost fringes shadowed the farthest reaches of the capital. It hung there; ominous, growling, alight with foreboding. Waiting for a command.

The command to deliver a lesson.

XVII

Under Toal's personal direction, a special squad of soldiers and lensors rushed through the most significant portions of the Basilica, all senses on high alert, searching for one subofficer who shouldn't be there. Among the militarily sensitive sites they scanned and cleared was the dark grotto of the Quasi-Dead. Finding it empty, as expected, the search team moved on.

In doing so, the otherwise alert commander just missed seeing one Quasi sliding out of its protective hollow. There was nothing unusual about this. When they were not in full sleep, curious Quasis sometimes moved about on their own. What was unusual was the presence on the Quasi's torso of a live person. One hand covered the Quasi's mouth while the other gripped the dagger that was plunged into the creature's heart, visible indication that one Quasi-Dead had recently and unwillingly been promoted to Full Dead. Whether out of ignorance of what had taken place or out of fear of knowing that it had, the remaining Quasis remained completely silent.

Slipping down from the dead thing's body, Riddick advanced soundlessly until he came to a door panel that allowed him to see into the throne room. Standing before that imposing seat and tantalizingly near was the Lord Marshal, speaking to an important new convert. Both his back and the rear of the throne faced the wall where Riddick hid.

Silently, the big man calculated. Angle, distance, time required. There was the small matter of some ceremonial guards located between him and his objective. He moved.

The pair of Elites stationed inside the doors that separated the throne room from the sacred grotto of the Quasi-Dead heard the peculiar metal scraping sound at the same time. When it continued, they exchanged a glance and turned to peer through the decorative ports set into the ceremonial doorway.

A sound came from two blades being scraped together. Not that they really needed the additional sharpening, but Riddick needed the attracting noise. Corkscrewing up and around as he sensed the presence of the two Elites on the other side of the doorway, he buried both blades in their curious faces and in the same motion threw his weight against the doors. He did not so much enter as explode into the throne room.

He'd run through it all in his mind before he'd taken a single step. Dispose of the two guards—done. One quick-step and leap over the back of the throne—done. The inimitable dagger he had pulled from the back of the murderer Irgun in his hand, bringing it down and forward toward. . . .

The Lord Marshal—who spun, caught the dagger hand, countered, and slammed Riddick halfway across the floor. The speed and strength the big man encountered were unprecedented in his experience. He had been ready for a possible defense, but nothing like this. It was almost as if he was fighting two men simultaneously.

Which, in a sense, he was—except that one of them was not exactly a man.

Gathering himself quickly, Riddick sprang to his feet and readied himself for another charge. Recovering from the shock of his appearance, flanking Elites surged forward to intervene, to interpose themselves between the attacker and the esteemed Lord Marshal. As much to Riddick's surprise as to their own, that worthy swept out a commanding hand as he stepped forward away from the throne.

"Stay!"

A trick, Riddick thought. His attention was everywhere—watching, waiting, expecting an assault to drop from the ceiling or rise from the floor. What he did not expect, what no one in the room who was privy to the drama being played out before them expected, was for the Lord Marshal to approach not his assailant, but a simple convert.

Roughly pulling the figure up off its knees, he ripped back the convert's cowl to reveal the face beneath. For an instant, Riddick refused to believe. Reality, unfortunately, is cold, remorseless, and will not be denied.

Kyra.

On the balcony above arrived two figures with more than the usual interest in the clash taking place below. Having received word of the confrontation that was happening in the throne room, Vaako and his companion had rushed there just in time to see Toal's men and Scalp-Taker's Elites encircling Riddick. Not being present when the Lord Marshal had given the order for his troops to stay their hand, the commander general and his consort struggled to interpret the scene before them.

Breathing hard, Riddick was aware of the soldiers all around him. Any chance of escape was now blocked. He didn't care. All that mattered was the tall man in the black armor standing before him. After that small business was resolved, he would deal with whatever else might come. Or so he tried to convince himself. Unfortunately, a new element had been added into the mix. He fought not to look at her.

Satisfied with the effect his revelation had produced, the Lord Marshal determined to use it to his best advantage. That would lie not in killing this intruder, which he was now confident he could do, but in winning him over to the Faith. That which does not defeat us makes us stronger, he knew. As true for a cause as for an individual. This audacious breeder would make a fine replacement for Irgun.

"If you fall here, now," he boomed, "you'll never rise. You'll be as the rest of the unconverted: nothing more than food for worms. But if you choose another way," and he glanced down at Kyra, "if you choose the *Necromonger* way, you'll die in due time—only to rise again in the UnderVerse. Rise afresh to a new beginning, and a new life."

Controlling his breathing, Riddick stared at the Lord Marshal. "I've made my choice."

"This life is nothing. A spark in time. The Under-Verse is everything." Glancing down at the woman kneeling at his feet, he said commandingly, "Go to him. Save him."

As she approached, Riddick noticed that even her walk was different. Instead of the bold, confident stride he knew from memory, she came toward him with steps that were measured and hesitant. His augmented gaze roved over her, taking in the paled flesh, the downcast eyes, the freshly applied purification marks that scarred both sides of her neck. She had been altered, and not just physically. It was Kyra—and yet it wasn't.

Seeing the uncertainty in his expression, she struggled for an explanation. Even her voice was subdued, beaten down by hopelessness and circumstance. "It hurt at first. It hurt a lot. They want to be sure of you. But after a while, pain goes away just like they said it would." She mustered a wan, humorless smile. "I've had so much pain, Riddick. I didn't want any more. They promised to make it go away, and they did."

His expression didn't change an iota. "Did they? What else did they make go away, Kyra? I don't wanna know what you had to do. I don't need to know what you had to do. What I do need to know is, where you comin' down?" His eyes bored deep into her own. "That's all I wanna hear."

Her gaze rose, and he saw that she'd hardly heard what he'd said. She was in another place now, and it was one where he knew he would never go.

"Then there was—a moment," she was saying, as if trying to recount the details of a dream. "A moment where I think I saw it. Saw this new 'verse through His eyes." She glanced in the direction of the Lord Marshal, who stood stolid and approving, saying nothing, but watching, watching. She turned back to the man standing motionless before her. "It sounds beautiful, Riddick. A place to really start over in. A place without—pain."

He swallowed what he really wanted to say, said quietly instead, "Which side, Kyra?"

From across the floor that separated them, that was at once smaller than the throne room and larger than space, the Lord Marshal paraphrased. "Which side, Riddick?"

Kyra looked up at him. "I thought you were dead. I thought. . ." With that, she shuffled away, leaving him to his fate. Leaving him to his decision. He shut his eyes, but it did not shut out the pain.

"Convert now, or fall forever," the Lord Marshal challenged the intruder, seizing on the other's obvious hesitation.

The play was almost over, and the Lord Marshal knew the ending as well as he did its heroes and the villains. If the breeder would only make the right choice, there would be none of the latter and he would be welcomed into the fold. It was what the Lord Marshal expected. It was the logical, right thing to do.

It was, however, not the Riddick thing to do.

Moving so fast his action was literally a blur, the big man drew the Irgun dagger, spun, and flung it so hard and fast at the Lord Marshal that it was impossible for any human to avoid.

The Lord Marshal, though, was no longer wholly human. Nor were his reactions.

Reaching up, an armored hand deflected the blade. Or did it? A collective gasp of disbelief filled the throne room as the defender of the Faith dropped to his knees.

On the balcony above, Vaako immediately grabbed one of the ancient, ceremonial poleaxes that formed a fence of blades behind him and started forward—only to be stopped by his companion.

"Wait, wait." Dame Vaako's attention was torn between her consort and what was happening on the floor below. "Too quick, it was too quick. A Half Dead doesn't die so easily. You don't take down a lord marshal with a knife throw."

Truly, the resources of the Half Dead are astounding to see. Turning slowly, as if from a punch that could not put him down, the Lord Marshal once again faced his assailant. Blood trickled down his cheek. He had deflected the blade just in time, and it had only grazed his face.

One hand dabbing at the cut, he contemplated the red stain quietly. "A long time since I've seen my own blood. Maybe too long. One can become too comfortable. Success breeds confidence. Too much success breeds overconfidence. I should thank you for reawakening that within me that made me what I am."

With one sweeping gesture he motioned everyone back; Elites, regular guards, onlookers—everyone. He would confront his own demons now. Both of him.

His astral self exploded forward, raging across the hall at the one who had dared to deny the offer of conversion, and who had drawn the Lord Marshal's blood. When his physical body caught up, the two combined to strike.

The blow went right through Riddick's defenses, slamming him backward into a pillar hard enough to dent it. As he slid to the deck, dazed, a new figure materialized high above. Unnoticed and unobserved, but intensely interested in the proceedings, Aereon watched from her hiding place.

Unaffected by the impact, the Lord Marshal gathered himself for another assault. This would be as profound a lesson as the coming destruction of the capital below, he had decided. Let everyone see and understand what it meant to be the Lord Marshal, who could command forces not only of this world but of the other. Let them see, and remember.

Unsteadily, Riddick struggled back to his feet. Pulling another blade, he made a sudden and unexpectedly forceful lunge straight at his adversary.

Or rather, where his adversary had been. As his physical self stayed clear of the fighting, almost a contemptuous observer, the Lord Marshal's astral self blurred around Riddick, hammering on him from behind, below, above. Riddick fought back, as he'd always fought back, but every time he struck, his blade cleaved only empty air.

The beating went on until even the big man could no longer stand. Unable to absorb one more unblockable blow, he finally went down. Only then did the physical lord marshal move forward, astral hands exposed and extended, reaching for the man now prone on the ground. The ethereal claws reached down, digging into the thick body, until they found the soul they were hunting for and started to pull, to extract . . .

Howling in pain and outrage, Riddick somehow found the strength to kick free, jump back, and stand once more on his feet: battered, wounded, but still defiant. As he did so, his essence snapped back into place. This was one soul that would not be so easily extracted from its owner.

Muttering at his failure, the Lord Marshal saw that, lesson or no lesson, this was one foe he was going to have to full-kill first. Projecting, his astral self flew into one of the two giant statues that guarded the entrance to Necropolis and cracked off an oversized spike. Clutching now a weapon that was not only deadly but was rich with mythological import, the wraithlike shape again launched itself at Riddick.

Who dodged at the last possible instant. Striking the floor, the spike shattered in half, only for the broken end to be picked up by the Lord Marshal's physical self and thrust toward Riddick. Preoccupied with his adversary's constantly harrying astral counterpart, the big man found himself driven back all the way to the throne area. A blow to the head finally dropped him. He lay there, stunned.

It was time. Stepping over to an Elite guard, the Lord Marshal took possession of the man's staff. Returning to his fallen adversary, he slipped the staff beneath him and seemingly with little effort flipped him into a standing position. With a simple twist of both hands, and before Riddick could fall back to the floor, the Lord Marshal positioned the staff firmly against the big man's neck and began to apply pressure. Slowly but irresisitibly, so that this troublesome interloper would have time to feel death coming for him. Through his manner of dying, the breeder's passing would serve as a reminder as well as a lesson.

Something was happening. A glow, lights, strengthening not within the prone figure's clothing but from within the body itself. The Lord Marshal hesitated, uncertain, staring. The singular internal lights began to flicker.

And then—they went out. Faded away, along with the rest of the big man's strength. Smiling viciously to himself, the Lord Marshal prepared to coil a length of cable around the breeder's neck. Both his physical and astral self were completely focused on the task at hand. On finishing it.

"They'll write poetry about this moment. A paean to the present Lord Marshal."

His jaws parted and his mouth opened preparatory to letting out a cry of triumph. What emerged instead was a gasp, accompanied by a wide-eyed look of surprise and shock. His astral face spun around, seeking the source of the interruption. Of the surprise. Of the spike that had been plunged deeply into the back of his physical being.

A young woman stared back at him, her gaze no longer distant.

With waning strength, both the physical and astral Lord Marshal lashed out simultaneously. The blow sent Kyra flying across the room to smash into the protruding spikes of a decorative column. They bit—deeply. Her eyes widened as she slipped off the spikes and fell to the floor. They stayed that way, open and staring, even when she stopped moving. She did not move again.

On the balcony above, Dame Vaako had taken it all in. Waiting, waiting for just the right moment. Waiting to be sure.

"Now!" she yelled at her consort. "Kill the beast while it's wounded! *Now.*"

Ceremonial poleax in hand, Vaako leaped from the balustrade, landed on the floor below, and raced toward the throne.

Wallowing in agony, unable to pull the deeply set spike from his back with either physical or astral hand, the Lord Marshal saw his commander general rushing toward him. Hope surged above the pain.

"Vaako . . . help me. . . ."

Halting, heart racing, Vaako stood above the older man, staring. Then he raised the ancient but still serviceable weapon. Its blade edge, beautifully and reverently maintained, glinted in the somber light of Necropolis.

The Lord Marshal's expression changed from one of expectation to one of complete disbelief.

"Vaako?"

Taking aim at the neck of the man lying prone before him, the commander general's fingers clenched convulsively on the staff of the weapon he held. At the same time, the Lord Marshal's astral body surged clear, away from any possible death blow. Separated, it could rejoin and rejuvenate its physical self even after a seemingly fatal strike. Then appropriate chastisement could be meted out to the traitor, after which . . .

Riddick was there, standing over the astral form. A minor inconvenience, that turbulent part of the Lord Marshal knew. No ordinary weapon could harm an astral body.

Only too late did it realize that the dagger that swept down in a sweeping arc was the one that had been pulled from the back of Irgun the Strange.

Instinctively, the Lord Marshal's physical self snapped away from Vaako's blow. The downward slicing blade sent sparks flying as it struck the floor, leaving a gouge behind it. The Lord Marshal's physical body then automatically rejoined his astral self, despite a cry from the latter.

And at that precise moment of physical and astral convergence, Riddick finished his swing, sinking the supernal blade clutched tightly in his fist up to its hilt in the Lord Marshal's conjoined skull. Mouth gaping, instantly now made Full Dead, the Lord Marshal fell forward to the floor. As he did so, the blade that had been sunk into his brain broke with an audible snap.

From above, realizing what had happened, realizing how in the blink of an eye it had all gone completely, utterly, terribly wrong, Dame Vaako screamed as if she had been stabbed herself.

"Nooooo!"

And further back, and higher up still, a certain inquisitive Elemental noted the unexpected outcome and did not quite chuckle to herself.

"Now what would be the odds of that . . . ," she murmured, though none were present to overhear.

On the scarred surface of the planet below, the citizens of Helion Prime stared up at their tormented sky. It was as if a strange calm had suddenly settled over the world. The vast, intimidating torus of energy that had appeared above their capital city had begun to evaporate, as if it held bound within it nothing more threatening than water vapor. The mouth of the conquest icon was closing, and the ships that had assembled around it breaking formation, rising toward outer atmosphere, and dispersing.

Ziza looked up at her mother, who glanced down and smiled reassuringly before looking skyward one more time. One last time, perhaps. As for the little girl she held tightly to her, Ziza was thinking of a man. Gone now, her father. Or just possibly, she was thinking of someone else.

Within the throne room of Necropolis, no one moved. Time itself seemed suspended. Never one to stand still for Time or anything else, Riddick pivoted away from the Full-Dead body of the Lord Marshal and stalked over to where Kyra lay fallen, eyes wide and open, staring at a place where, hopefully, there was no pain.

Exhausted, disgusted, empty, he ignored the hundreds of intent eyes that were fastened on him and following his every move. Nearby, Vaako, realizing what had happened, realizing what it *meant,* let the ancient poleax he still held fall to the ground. In the silence, its metallic clattering was the only noise.

Moving to distance himself from Kyra's body, Riddick slumped into the first seat that presented itself, which happened to be the throne. Of Necropolis.

Gradually he became aware of more than eyes upon him. In seconds, his drawn expression changed from one of bitter anguish and resignation to utter astonishment at the sight before him.

Everyone in the Necropolis—every man and woman, young and old, experienced and new—was kneeling. Kneeling before the new Lord Marshal. Which was when it struck him. Something he had heard several times before. Something he had believed, had known, would only apply to others. Fate, it seemed, had one more surprise in store. One more great, cosmic joke.

"You keep what you kill . . . ," he murmured under his breath.

EPILOGUE

All he wanted was to be left alone. That's all he'd ever wanted. But there were forces at work that would not leave him to himself. He had never backed away from a challenge in his life. When men refused to leave him be, he had dealt with them. When governments had refused to leave him be, he had dealt with them. Now the universe, it seemed, refused to leave him be.

Very well. He would deal with the universe.

He became aware that a senior Necromonger officer was hovering nearby, apparently waiting for something. When he turned to the man, the armored commander took one more step forward.

"Your orders, Lord Marshal."

Lord Marshal. Nothing about the sound of it rang true. But he had to do something. He had to respond. What could he do? Was there anything, anything left, that he *wanted* to do? Roused from his introspection by need and circumstance, the somber man on the throne finally said evenly, "To the Threshold."

The commander was clearly taken aback. "The *Threshold,* Lord Marshal? But the people are not prepared. They have not been properly purified and do not know the Way. They have . . ."

Black goggles turned to him. "Are you questioning my order?"

"No, Lord Marshal, it is only that—" Breaking off, the bewildered officer dipped his head slightly and started to turn away, mentally preparing himself to pass along the extraordinary command.

"One more thing," the brooding man on the throne added, halting the officer in mid-stride. "Don't call me Lord Marshal.

"My name is Riddick."

APPENDIX
Historians' Note on Pre-Necroism

Let it be noted that our grasp of pre-Necroism history is still incomplete, some of the early firsthand accounts of this epoch having been lost in the course of the conflicts of the Fourth Regime. Blessedly, other accounts remain in our possession. Yet ever since pyro-encoding became the accepted norm for documentation, our ability to interpret such writings has been compromised. We are hard at work on these documents. When deciphered, doubtless they will yield more information about the glorious and ever-expanding Necromonger Empire.

Truly it is important work. The sixth Lord Marshal has ordained that, when our work here is done and the known 'verse is properly cleansed, a great monument will be erected at the shoals of the Threshold. This monument will be inscribed with all our known history. It will serve as a dire warning for any other race that may cross over from some as-yet undiscovered 'verse, to turn them back forever.

—Cevris, Historian Principal
212 A.D.C.

Austeres and the Outcasting of Covu

Genetically at least, we can chart our beginnings to a modest group known as the Brotherhood of Austeres. Devout themselves, they believed that all other known religions were too iconic, their histories too soaked in blood, their teachings too dogmatic and without room for personal expression. The Austeres were monotheistic and isolationist. They sought distance from the other worlds of man that they found so corrupting. Though they numbered only in the thousands, the Austeres were strong in their belief that theirs would prove to be the one true faith.

Traveling long in ships with conventional drives, they lost many of their numbers to the rigors of the journey. But ultimately, the Austeres made planetfall and colonized a world they named Asylum.

Quickly, dissension arose. Covu, an important scientist-philosopher, began teaching the then radical belief that there might be more than one God—indeed, that there might be as many Gods as there were "universes."

One must remember that the Monoverse theory held great sway at the time. One God seemed ample for the job of overseeing one 'verse, large though it must have seemed.

Covu decried monotheism as an unnecessary vestige of Jesusism. He believed that it should be shed with other Christian trappings already left behind by the Austeres. For this stance, Covu was persecuted by the Austeres. When he declined to recant his positions, deemed heretical, the Austeres tortured Covu day and night, and the abuse was so relentless that Covu lost the ability to feel pain.

Soon the Austeres turned their ire on Covu's family, torturing and killing them. Covu would have died at the hands of the Austeres, too, had it not been for the few followers—Covulytes—who had been drawn to his teachings and who helped Covu to escape.

Outcast, Covu wandered space with the corpses of his wife and children. How long he journeyed is unclear, but eventually Covu made a discovery of unimaginable import: a rift in known space that constituted a crossover to another 'verse.

It was the Threshold itself!

The Covulytes were afraid to approach this strange and turbulent corner of uncharted space. Only Covu pushed ahead, perhaps driven by the need to lay his family to rest in a place that would remain undisturbed by the Austeres.

Only minutes later, Covu returned—yet he seemed years older. Too, he seemed stronger, more resolute in his words and ways. Speaking to his astounded followers, Covu claimed his family was no longer dead, that they had risen and walked again in the 'verse on the far side of the Threshold, a glorious place he called "UnderVerse."

Imbued with an almost magical new strength, Covu took righteous retribution on the Austeres who had cast him out. He fought and killed their commanders, claiming their heads as he did so. Looking into their newly dead eyes, he was overheard to whisper, "You keep what you kill."

In victory, Covu assumed the new office of "lord marshal," the one rank that cannot be superceded. After forcing them to bow before him, Covu reorganized the last living Austeres into a more regimented—though still pre-military—society. So different was this society that it begged for a new name and a new place of worship.

Covu termed this new ideological order "Necroism." As a powerful testament to it, Necropolis—our most hallowed hall—was erected on the tallest mountain of Asylum.

The First Regime: Covu the Transcended

Covu had seen, firsthand, the beauty that is the UnderVerse.

So compelling was the sight that he taught that all life elsewhere was "a spontaneous outbreak," an "unguided mistake" that needed correction. The Natural State was death and what came afterward. Covu and all Necromongers were also part of this "grand error," but having seen the truth, they were duty bound to remain alive until the known 'verse was swept clean of all human life.

Some years later, Covu chose a successor. It was Oltovm the Builder, the officer who had laid the first and last stone of Necropolis. Oltovm set out with Covu to return to the Threshold. It was an arduous journey, months long. Some in their company wondered aloud if Covu had ever seen the Threshold at all, and they started to doubt his word.

But then it was found! Oltovm describes the Threshold as "Surrounded by great tidal forces of space, treacherous to navigate near, yes, but exotically beautiful, hinting at the dark wonders that lurk beyond."

Days were spent waiting for the tidal forces to ease, and then finally the Threshold opened! Covu ordered all Necromongers except Oltovm to turn their backs as approach was made, and that forever established how a Necromonger vessel nears the open Threshold: aftward first. Indeed, no living Necromonger except a Lord Marshal may cast his eyes upon the UnderVerse.

On the Threshold the two men stood—the once and future lord marshals—both now gazing into the beautiful strangeness of UnderVerse. What words passed between them was never recorded. But while Oltovm held his place, Covu strode on into the UnderVerse and was never seen again.

The Second Regime: Oltovm the Builder

Intent on never losing his way to this remarkable place, Oltovm erected hidden navigational markers that would lead him back. Never again would anyone doubt its existence! Once the way was charted, Oltovm initiated the construction of a portal around the Threshold—forces that could resist the vortices of space and force open the Threshold on demand.

A trusted officer was tasked with guarding the Threshold against marauding races. His name was never recorded, so he is simply referred to herein as the Guardian of the UnderVerse. Said to be nearly three meters tall, the Guardian and his legion of faithful will repel any non-Necromonger who may make unauthorized approach to this most holy of places. During those times when the Threshold is opened to admit a Lord Marshal on pilgrimage, the Guardian and his warriors must turn their backs so as not to gaze upon the UnderVerse.

Early in the Second Regime there arose a controversy. How can procreation be tolerated in a faith devoted to non-life? The solution was to ban all breeding (though of course not the sex act itself). This prohibition led to the inevitable conclusion that the Faith would die out in one generation's time unless new converts could be found.

The Faith was still great, but distances of space were greater. More ships with improved drives were needed. Now, Oltovm was no longer a young man, and the construction of the Threshold portal had occupied many of his years. Still, he became devoted to the idea of gifting Necromongers with the greatest armada ever seen.

The manpower needs were tremendous. The task of meeting that need fell to a fiery young commander full of the Faith, named Baylock. An ardent student of the teachings of Covu, Baylock was admired even if some of his actions drew criticism. Among other things, he used unconventional means to subjugate all the races of Boroneau V. Strong backs and new resources were needed to build the armada, and Baylock delivered them at whip's end.

Oltovm never saw First Ascension, the day the new Necromonger armada rose from Asylum. Instead, he chose his successor and then chose ritualistic suicide at the edge of the Threshold. Oltovm had told others it was "due time" for his death, and it is he who is now credited with this important distinction of Necroism. Even while we covet death, there is a right and proper moment for any death. Unless a Necromonger dies in "due time," he will be prohibited from entering the UnderVerse.

The Third Regime: Naphemil the Navigator

Naphemil had risen fast in the military ranks, a young cartographer who helped lay the foundations for what we now call, simply, the Campaign: the plan to rid the known 'verse of all human life. Oltovm chose wisely when he named Naphemil as the leader of this epoch of Necroism.

Rather than leave Necropolis behind on Asylum, Naphemil ordered the structure unearthed and entombed in a far larger ship, the Basilica. The first Necromonger church would travel with the armada through space, into which it ventured on Ascension Day.

In the short years of the Third Regime, Necromonger society did well at spreading the word of

Covu, gathering converts by the thousands. The swell of new blood brought refinements in the conversion process. It was no longer enough to bow before the Lord Marshal and take an oath of fidelity. True purification was necessary.

The pain-deadening act we know today is a faint echo of Covu's experience at the hands of the Austeres. Just as he was tortured to the point of non-feeling, new converts are put through a process that demonstrates how one kind of pain can deaden others; how pain can actually bring spiritual bliss. The office of "Purifier Principal" was created to oversee new conversions.

Despite these gains, the Necromonger faith began bleeding off numbers, as infighting among officers and natural attrition outpaced conversions. After the enormous expenditure of resource that marked the Second Regime, it seemed the faith was floundering.

Some Necromongers began to see Naphemil as more planner than leader, more strategist than warrior. He was, as Oltovm concluded, a good choice for the ascension period of Necromonger history—but that period was now challenged by new realities.

Naphemil was killed in a dispute with then-commander Baylock, and this unapologetic murder marked the first time that a lord marshal had been dethroned by violence. Debate raged as to whether Baylock was entitled to the post of lord marshal. Ultimately, the teachings of Covu prevailed, as Baylock defended his act with Covu's own words: "You keep what you kill." Baylock ascended to the throne of Necropolis, and all Necromongers knelt before him. The society now knew two kinds of succession: appointment and murder.

The Fourth Regime: Baylock the Brutal

Baylock was the last lord marshal born to Necroism, and the first of the modern lord marshals. During his regime, planetary subjugation became the norm. The plan that had served him well on Boroneau V was applied to new worlds on a grand scale.

Baylock also taught that it was not enough to gain converts. Those who refused conversion should be ground to dust. Once again he relied for justification of his actions on the words of Covu, who said to the last of the Austeres, "Convert, or fall forever."

By all accounts, Baylock's regime would have met with unparalleled success had he not encountered the dread Carthodox. This was another militarized faith, monotheistic and procreative but potent nonetheless. The Carthodox, too, were seeking converts in the planetary system Neibaum, and when paths crossed, the worlds of Neibaum became the holy battlefield.

An interesting though probably irrelevant footnote to the history of this particular conflict: there are suggestions—oral history only—that the Elemental race was advising the Carthodox in the course of this war. But many doubt this, citing the traditional neutrality of all Elementals.

The Carthodox had strange new weaponry, some of it superior to the corresponding Necromonger armament. Losses among the supporters of the Faith grew catastrophic. Officers complained that communications were not sufficiently secure, allowing the Carthodox to know their moves in advance.

Baylock's commanders advised retreat from the Neibaum system. If they could only swell the ranks by converting worlds beyond, they could return to fight the Carthodox anew, refreshed and strengthened. But Baylock the Brutal would have none of it.

"They may count God on their side, but we count many Gods," Baylock is said to have bellowed. "It begins and ends in this system."

Kryll was a technical officer in charge of an emerging order within the Necromonger movement. He called it the Order of the Quasi-Dead.

The "Quasies" (as they are now known) began as monk-like ascetics who voluntarily deprived themselves of virtually all nourishment. Their goal was to slow down bodily function to the point where their existence walked the cusp between life and death. They are fragile yet powerful beings, as all bodily resources are devoted to mental pursuits.

After years of overseeing the growth of this order, Kryll came forward to offer Baylock and the military the use of Quasi-Deads as telepathic conduits. Once the advantages promised by such a system were recognized, the offer was quickly accepted. A network of Quasi-Deads was hastened into service, with at least one installed on every command ship, a practice followed to this day. The Quasis enjoyed quick success. At last, here was the incorruptible line of communication the military had been seeking! The impact of the Quasis began to be felt on the battlefield, as their point-to-point communications could not be intercepted by the Carthodox, who had no equivalent resource. They were helping to turn the tide of war when something extraordinary occurred.

Baylock died in a landing accident on Neibaum Prime.

Questions outnumbered answers. Who was now in charge? Would the commanders appoint a lord marshal from among their own ranks? Or would they fall to fighting one another even as they did battle with the Carthodox?

The corpse of Baylock was dispatched to the Threshold. There, the Guardian floated the corpse in an open ark and sailed it into the UnderVerse. As the corpse vanished, the Guardian—as he later swore before a congress of commanders—heard Baylock stir and speak. And with his final words, Baylock named a successor.

The Fifth Regime: Kryll

The Carthodox were overcome. Their false icons were burned or otherwise laid aside, their numbers purified and absorbed. Though it had been predicted that the Carthodox, being pious themselves, would never convert to Necroism, most Carthodox did so with surprising readiness. Some would later become respected Necromonger warriors, and many other documents chronicle their stories.

Perhaps as an act of gratitude, Kryll overruled the Necromonger prohibition on the raising of personal icons to erect a mountainous statue of Baylock the Brutal. It was left behind on the cratered remains of Neibaum Prime, a reminder of the battles that Baylock prosecuted there. This was the first of the great planetary icons which would, in the next regime, take on greater import. Moreover, Kryll ordered statuary to grace the ancient interior of Necropolis, including images of all the lord marshals, past and present.

Ever mindful of challenges from within the Faith, Kryll refined his Quasi-Deads, creating the Order of the Greater Quasi-Deads. This group was comprised of five highly evolved—toward death—individuals who could probe the minds of any individual. So powerful were they that, when grouped together, they could hemorrhage the brain of a resistant subject.

Today, the "Greater Quasies" serve at the pleasure of the reigning lord marshal, while the "Lesser Quasies" fill both military and private deep-space communication needs.

The Carthodox weaponry, so formidable, was fitted on Necromonger warships, making the armada stronger than ever. Necroism, a movement that had already absorbed two other faiths, was poised to spread to new worlds with new speed. . . .

Kryll's time ended unexpectedly. With no verbal announcement, he committed ritualistic suicide. Thankfully, a pyro-doc was found near his corpse by a trusted officer, Zhylaw, and this succession document averted the rancorous in-fighting that marked the transition between the Fourth and Fifth Regimes.

The Sixth Regime: Zhylaw the Last

The succession document named Zhylaw as the next lord marshal—as an historian, it is not my duty to report rumor. But since, in this case, rumor led to tribunal, it should be mentioned that a public debate ensued, some suggesting that Zhylaw was somehow complicit in the passing of Kryll. Zhylaw was promptly exonerated, and the perpetuators of these spiteful stories were hunted out and killed before due time. In an attempt to protect his reputation for the ages, Zhylaw had the succession document naming him lord marshal stored in our most secure vaults, under the tightest of guard. There it will remain, protected for all posterity.

As a young warrior Zhylaw distinguished himself in forward operations, a branch of the armada that forays to unexplored worlds. Normally these teams conduct simple mapping and targeting missions, but Zhylaw—with a fleet of fast frigates at his disposal—redefined its role. He attacked and removed nascent colonies of man wherever he found them, before they could grow to military significance.

Zhylaw believed in killing his enemies young. His actions won the praise of his superiors—including Lord Marshal Kryll, who came to think of Zhylaw as a brilliant if wayward son.

As we are living, it is too early to write the true

history of this regime. But as the Campaign grows and the worlds of man dwindle, there is a swelling belief that Zhylaw will be the last lord marshal—the one who will lead all Necromongers through the Threshold and into the glory that is the UnderVerse.